# PEGASUS SOULED

# PEGASUS SOULED
## DRAGON OF SHADOW AND AIR BOOK NINE

### JESS MOUNTIFIELD

DISRUPTIVE IMAGINATION

THE PEGASUS SOULED TEAM

**Thanks to our JIT Team:**

Deb Mader
Diane L. Smith
Dave Hicks

*If We've missed anyone, please let us know!*

**Editor**
SkyHunter Editing Team

This book is a work of fiction. All of the characters, organizations, and events portrayed in this novel are either products of the author's imagination or are used fictitiously. Sometimes both.

Copyright © 2021 Jess Mountifield

LMBPN Publishing supports the right to free expression and the value of copyright. The purpose of copyright is to encourage writers and artists to produce the creative works that enrich our culture.

The distribution of this book without permission is a theft of the author's intellectual property. If you would like permission to use material from the book (other than for review purposes), please contact support@lmbpn.com. Thank you for your support of the author's rights.

LMBPN Publishing
PMB 196, 2540 South Maryland Pkwy
Las Vegas, NV 89109

Version 1.00 October 2021
eBook ISBN: 978-1-68500-496-5
Print ISBN: 978-1-68500-497-2

*Dedication:*

*To everyone who has tried so hard and not quite succeeded. Sometimes it isn't your fault. Sometimes you did everything right. Pick yourself back up again, because there's always another way.*

## CHAPTER ONE

As I studied the main photo in the pile of documents I had been given, my stomach churned. This proved there was a large set of tablets like the one the US military had found, which I'd had to destroy once it was stolen.

I had no idea if the US government was angry with me for that. I hadn't asked. I'd been too focused on everything that had followed. I'd thwarted the plans of the Mexican elven cult and made it very hard for them to get a portal open. It wasn't a full halt to their plans, but it was enough to make them hate me.

Of course, I wasn't happy with myself either. I'd killed an elf the last time I was there. A young air elf who could have done so much more with her life had she not been intent on opening a portal to the elven homeworld where a great evil was trapped.

Zephyr, Sen, and Roth assured me I hadn't been to blame. That I had simply prevented the portal from opening, and she had put herself in danger, knowing that she could be torn apart by the pillars protecting it. I knew how it felt to fight those pillars. I had an idea of how painful her last moments had been. I didn't wish that on anyone.

Zephyr nuzzled into me in dragon form, sensing my emotions and no doubt hearing a lot of my thoughts. I'd never been very good at keeping them out of his head.

*We should go to Minsheng with this*, Zephyr said a moment later. *Tell him everything.*

*And the Sanctuary*, I replied. *They'll want to know of the threat that more of these things represents.*

*It will also do you good to talk about this man connected to your birth and what he means in terms of finding your parents.*

I sighed and nodded. Zephyr was right. We'd gone north and into Canada a couple of days earlier to find a man in a photo. A man a private investigator had linked to the day I'd been dropped off in a wooden box at the doorstep of the police station. My adopted parents had managed to get me that much. I'd hit a dead end.

A very strange dead end.

The guy's house had been deserted with evidence of a struggle but no death, and an array of photos and information about the portals, pillars, and stone tablets that made many elven abilities easier. It appeared he had been researching the very artifacts I was encountering. He'd located a cache of tablets.

I had so many more questions, but I also needed to protect this world from Cherisse and her cult. That meant I had to find this cache, if it existed, and make sure it didn't fall into their hands. Although I'd managed to stop Cherisse once from opening the portal, she'd only had one tablet and one set of elves strong enough to break the pillars.

If she got her hands on several of the strange, rune-covered stone tablets, she'd have more than enough that she could take her pick of the elves and still get the job done. In the meantime, she needed me. Or more precisely, Zephyr.

Sighing once more, I got up from my perch on the roof of the warehouse building and made my way inside. We'd not been back from Canada for long but we hadn't let anyone know yet, wanting to make sure I had everything straight before I talked to anyone.

Minsheng didn't take long to notice us, having been in his room, not far from the entrance at the top of the building. He beamed as he saw us.

"Good weekend?" he asked, referring to our cover story for going. That we finally wanted to attempt traveling and have a long weekend away together.

"Interesting weekend. As long as everyone here was fine while we were gone, we need to have a chat about what happened."

Minsheng raised his eyebrows as I motioned for him to follow me. There was no way I wanted everyone in the building to know about this yet. Not only was it worrying, but I still wasn't sure how we'd gotten to this point. Something about it was off. As if gods I had no idea of were controlling me. Or as if fate would keep leading me the way I was going.

"I found these," I said, showing him the photos, maps, and other documents without any other ceremony as soon as we were alone.

Minsheng's eyes went wide but he didn't reply, scanning the information instead.

"You didn't go north to have a holiday with your mythicals, did you?" Minsheng asked.

It took all my control not to laugh as I shook my head. I'd handed him evidence of a big problem, and he was more interested in my deception and why than how much danger we might be in. It was the perfect reaction, and I shrugged.

"I didn't go because I knew this would be there," I said a moment later. "I didn't expect it, and I am as surprised as you are."

"Then why did you go?" Minsheng asked. "What were you looking for when you found this?"

After exhaling and sitting down on the end of the bed, I told Minsheng everything. About the envelope, photo, and the hope I'd get answers of a different kind, not more riddles and problems I had to worry about.

Minsheng did as he always did. He listened without judgment, with the skill of a patient man who knew the person in front of him needed empathy more than anything else. When I was done, I felt a lot better. My hands were steady for the first time in several days, and I understood more about the sad weight that had settled over my heart at coming back without any answers.

"It appears as if your quest for answers and what must be done to protect this planet are linking up in ways that are bound to challenge anyone's sense of self. I wish I could untangle them for you," Minsheng said. "But I have a feeling that many events in your life have been linked. I'll do everything I can to help you find answers."

"Thank you," I said as the first tears threatened to fall.

Holding them inside, I pulled up a photo again.

"This cache looks pretty large. I think we're going to need to find it. But I don't know what any of this other information means. The addresses and information on its rumored whereabouts are half there at best."

"Are you willing to trust the organization?" Minsheng asked a moment later.

I lifted an eyebrow as I nodded, wondering if I should be shaking my head instead. So far, they'd had their moments where they had smothered me and made me follow their rules and regulations, but they'd also come through for me at several key points. They had also paid for almost everything I'd ever wanted to do.

If Minsheng thought they could help, I was inclined to trust them once more.

"Just make sure the necessary people get to see this," I said as I handed it over to Minsheng.

The organization as a whole might have been awesome, but I also knew they couldn't be sure everyone within their fold was trustworthy. Chris, a part-gnome who had saved my life on more than one occasion and had my back in battle more times than I could count, had turned out to be a member of the cult wanting to open the portals.

I still remembered the moment I'd found out. How it had felt to know someone I trusted entirely had betrayed us. A conversation with him had shown it for what it was—a misguided sense of doing what was best. Chris had meant no harm by it. He had genuinely been helping me. He'd cared about me enough to keep me alive.

The problem was, Chris also wanted to let an evil far greater than any elf alive had faced onto the Earth. There was no doubt about the evil being alive in my mind.

Minsheng took copies of everything I'd given him. We took another copy, and I shoved it into my go-bag. We tucked the originals into a secret compartment in our room, something I'd created while playing with my abilities.

Although I could use the communication stone and tell the Sanctuary what they needed to know via Ronan, the centaur on the Sanctuary's council, I hadn't been to see them in a while, and I had some questions for the fire and water masters.

*We should eat first*, Zephyr said.

I thought of pizza and grinned. It was our usual, and I knew it would brighten our mood. There had been a distinct lack of pizza on our trip.

Within minutes we were in the kitchen surrounded by our friends and thoughts of danger and what might come next momentarily gone from our heads.

It was the balm we needed to rest. Minsheng came in toward the end and joined us. When no one else was looking, he gave me a small nod. A subtle hint that the organization was looking into the info we'd found.

After the meal ended and everyone returned to their lives, it was time to make our way to the Sanctuary.

*Before we go, I've got a small confession to make*, Zephyr said.

He sounded so serious that I stopped to look at him. *What's wrong?*

*I lost the game.*

I groaned, ready to blast whoever had told him about the game off their feet with air, but Sen and Roth began laughing. Within seconds, I was chuckling too.

Reaching out for Zephyr as I calmed, I leaned into him, my hands moving over his smooth scales and marveling at the feel of them. He was exactly what I needed in my life.

Without any more hesitation, I grabbed my away bag and let Daisy know I'd be back as soon as I could. Thankfully she didn't ask for an explanation, and I figured Minsheng would tell her what was going on if he needed to.

Within minutes we were in the sky, Sen and Roth rising along behind Zephyr and me. Instead of using my abilities to help myself fly, I hunkered down low on Zephyr's back and helped Roth keep up, extending the slipstream around Zephyr to include the winged water horse and bring us along together.

It was how we'd flown for the entire journey north and back. Now we weren't trying to preserve our strength, frightened of being attacked at every turn, we could use magic to help us fly. That said, at some point, I would see everyone in the cult again. There was no way Cherisse was about to give up; it wouldn't be long before they came after us again.

We couldn't live in fear, though. It was clear they were still licking their wounds. We had several contacts in the US intelligence agencies, thanks to our high security clearance and the need to make sure the Texas portal stayed safe.

Cherisse and her elves were still holed up in their mountain. We'd know the second they weren't any longer.

Although the flight to the Sanctuary was enjoyable, part of me realized we'd made it many times now, our bodies flying the route automatically while we talked or gazed at the horizon.

Eventually, the Sanctuary came into view and we spotted Ronan and Ruehnar. I waved to them as they looked up and was relieved to see the smiles that greeted us. I still remembered the first time I'd come to the Sanctuary looking for safety. Ronan's face had been the first one I'd seen and he'd welcomed me.

Of course, that first visit hadn't been easygoing. I'd been pursued by agents and the council had all but asked me to leave again.

This time, however, they could have no reason to send me away. Although I had a feeling I wouldn't be staying long and I'd be asked to help find out where these tablets were and stop them from falling into the hands of the cult.

As we landed, more of the mythicals in the Sanctuary came over, smiles on everyone's faces. I greeted them all, using their names and hugging or bowing where appropriate.

"Do we need to convene the council?" Ronan asked when the conversation quietened.

I sighed, wishing the answer to that question wasn't always yes, and then nodded.

"It's okay. You keep us safe and bring us news we would struggle to get in time. The council has long known to listen to anything you bring us with respect and appreciation," the large centaur said before bowing.

I bowed back, gratitude making it hard for me to know what else to do. It was a relief to know I wasn't thought of as a constant bearer of bad news.

After sending Roth and Sen to the guest house we used,

Zephyr and I walked through the streets and followed Ronan to the council chambers.

Since we'd last been here, there were changes. The buildings were more defensible, and there were newer ones made from the same rock of the mountain. No doubt it had been built and modified to help the elves here defend against the attack from the cult a couple of weeks earlier.

It wasn't the first time I was grateful we'd succeeded, and there had been no fatalities.

On the way to the council chambers, I also noticed that elves were missing from their usual posts. They were the elves at the portal site in Texas, and it showed the Sanctuary was still working with the US government to protect it. Something I was very grateful for.

The council was present by the time Ronan, Zephyr, and I joined them. There was also food laid out for us.

"We were about to begin a session," Sierrathen said as she motioned for Zephyr and me to sit near her.

I ate as I passed around the documents I'd found, knowing I'd probably hijacked whatever they'd intended to discuss but wanting to get on with it.

Although most of the council focused on the tablets and what they might be able to do, the fairy Martyl was more interested in some of the other notes.

"It says here something about a location the Sanctuary was close to once. At least, I believe so. I don't know if the tablets would have been there then..." His eyes looked off somewhere as he searched his memories.

I waited to see if he offered me anything else, but it was all he said until he passed the piece of paper on. Not long later, I had it back in a pile in front of me.

"What do you plan to do?" Vestan asked, the male elf looking my way.

"I think I need to find them and, if I can, bring them here," I replied, not sure I had much of a plan beyond that.

"You don't want to destroy them?" Sierrathen asked.

I blinked, unable to reply, shocked I wasn't being told what to do but asked and respected about what I thought was best. It was novel, and I wasn't sure how to handle it.

"If there's no other way to stop them from being used to open the portals, I will destroy them," I said after a moment of thought. "We can study them. If we learn something that perhaps the elves have forgotten, and makes our lives better, then I will try to preserve that."

This seemed to satisfy the council, and we parted ways to let them get to their regular business.

I leaned into Zephyr as we walked to the guest house, my mind still unsettled. We had found something unexpected, and I had no idea what to do with it. Most oddly, no one was trying to dictate our actions going forward. I was free to decide for myself.

CHAPTER TWO

As Zephyr flew down to the Texas portal site, I tried to look more awake. After spending the night at the Sanctuary, Minsheng had mentioned that the major we often liaised with at the portal had called us. Although I wasn't surprised that they wanted to know what was going on and if they should be aware of anything, I had been surprised by the request they'd made for me to do some training.

I'd trained at the site before. That part wasn't new, but the rest was. Someone was coming to the site who needed to be impressed by the sounds of things. Although that hadn't been said officially.

*If it's my best guess, someone in the military above those in command here,* Zephyr said as I slid off his back and landed beside him.

*And with a high level of security clearance,* I replied, looking around for whoever might give me an indication where we were needed. Before I could do anything more than use my abilities to help the dust settle that Roth kicked up on landing, the major appeared. He grinned as he came striding over to me.

"Aella. Thank you for coming." When he reached me, he opened his arms to pull me into a hug.

I hesitated, not used to affection from him, but he kept pulling and gave me little choice.

"I've got a problem I was hoping you'd help with," he whispered. "I need to show someone what the elves are capable of."

I lifted my eyebrows and formed the first of the questions flying through my mind, but none of them came out. What on earth was he talking about?

The question didn't remain unanswered for long. A general appeared, coming out of the main building, an aide at his side who I had seen rush in when Zephyr and I were several hundred yards up.

I smiled and went to greet him though I didn't have a clue who this was.

"Major, explain," the man said, barely looking at me before he glared at the dragon hulking nearby.

Not hiding our confusion, Zephyr and I looked at each other.

"Aella, here, and her mythicals, Zephyr, Roth, and Sen, are the ones the colonel and I have been telling you about. They train the elves here and provide consultancy and information on what's happening in the elven community."

The major's words came out too bright and cheery. As if he was trying too hard to make a good impression and be upbeat about everything. If it had any impact on the general, I couldn't tell.

"We're busy right now," the general said, looking me up

and down as if I were something a coyote had dragged in from the desert. "Perhaps you could come tomorrow and book your training sessions with the colonel in the future. I want to be able to pre-approve them."

Again, I wasn't sure exactly what to say, but I lifted an eyebrow.

*Now would be a really good time to be calm*, Zephyr said. *But I don't like this guy, and I have a feeling if I'm the one to show him we don't like being talked to that way, he'll keep doing it to you.*

*Are you advocating that I have a pissing match with this guy?*

*Maybe.*

*What makes this any different from the contest I had with the major?*

*You need not threaten his life directly. Show off. A lot.*

I frowned, feeling the general's eyes on me.

"You do speak English, don't you?" the older, very trim man asked a moment later.

"Yes. I was trying to decide if I should dignify your previous sentence with a response. I'm here to train and protect the portal, as are the elves here. I was invited by the President to make sure this portal doesn't get opened or attacked in a way that can't be defended."

"So I've heard, but everyone here is under my command now. If I require your assistance, I'm sure I can request it. Of course, if taking orders from a superior is something you're not used to, I can have the President recommend your help be redirected elsewhere. I have a phone line directly to him. I'm sure it won't take long to sort out."

I took a deep breath at the general's words, seeing the

implied threat and his confidence in it and not sure what to make of it. Part of me wanted to tell him to go ahead and call the President, but I didn't know if that was the wisest thing to do. I wasn't sure that the President would back me up, and I had a feeling that if he did, it wasn't going to gain the general's respect.

Zephyr snorted, making it clear he thought little of the general's words and dragging the man's attention to him.

"Are you familiar with the cult that wants the portals open?" Zephyr asked, projecting his voice louder and with a deeper tone than normal.

The major jumped, but the general merely stared. It was clear no one was going to answer Zephyr, so he tilted his head to one side while I watched and waited, pretty sure my bonded dragon had thought of something.

"They've attacked this place several times and come close to opening the portal. Often only a few of them at once. Aella here has witnessed what they're capable of. And she's the only elf I know who is powerful enough to hold off the forces they command alone. She's been training for it for many years. And she trains the elves here to help make sure this portal is safe."

"You've said a lot of this. It doesn't change the fact that I am in charge here—"

"No, I don't think you understand." Zephyr lifted higher, shaking his large wings out. "Aella. I want you to attack the base. Try to get to the portal so you could turn it on if you wanted to. Use whatever forces you think the cult would."

I merely blinked, having never been given an order by the large creature. Normally I had the final say and he deferred to me. I got the impression that trusting him was a good idea.

Quickly I swept most of the soldiers I could see off their feet, banging heads together accidentally and knocking them out with dart guns as Sen rushed to my side to help with the fight.

The general flinched a couple of times as he looked around, but then he looked at me. I smiled as I continued to take control of the elements, enjoying the havoc I could cause.

It didn't take long for someone to sound the attack alarm, and the general finally snapped out of his panic.

"Stop this at once. You cannot be allowed to do this. I will consider it a hostile attack. I will command my men to use lethal force." The general's face grew redder as he spoke.

I looked at Zephyr, not sure if I should listen or not.

"Keep on," his booming voice commanded, firm.

*There will be bullets*, I said.

*I won't let any hit you, but be careful.*

Not intending to argue with Zephyr, I nodded and pushed the general, careful not to hurt him. The major stepped out of my way, and I strode toward the main building as people responded to the alarm.

It felt strange to see both elves and soldiers rushing to their posts to find me as the threat, Zephyr doing as he said and flying up and over, his tail coming across to block an attack as the general pulled out a pistol and fired. The bullets bounded off Zephyr's scales, but everyone else hesitated, especially the elves who also responded.

"Training," I yelled. "Stop me claiming the portal. Don't hold back."

This seemed to snap most of them out of their confusion, and I felt elves trying to challenge me for control of the elements. Feeling water in a nearby tank, I directed Roth to start using it as I kept walking, keeping my grip but nothing else for now.

As I neared a group of soldiers about to fire weapons for the first time, I shook the ground beneath their feet, and their bullets went wide. At the same time, I used the air to create a wall around Sen and me as she bounded onto my shoulder, her dart gun in hand.

*Zephyr, breath*, I said as I pulled the door to the building open, yanking it out of the hand of a soldier trying to hide behind it for cover.

The large dragon landed again as he obliged me, exhaling into the main part of the building. As he did, I felt a blast of air hit my barrier, and it wobbled me before I managed to reach out with my mind and hit the elf who'd done it with a stream of water from Roth. I felt myself relax as I did so, aware these were friends but grateful they were beginning to go all out too.

Zephyr blocked more bullets from my right as a group of soldiers got to their feet, and I directed more of the gas inside the building. I had no idea how many had gas masks or if they were nearby, but I had to make headway. I'd started the battle out in the middle of a training ground. I was vulnerable and out in the open instead of having fought a route in.

Thankfully Roth and Sen were good at keeping the worst of the bullets from coming my way, each of them firing water, ice, or trank darts at the soldiers and elves who appeared to be most threatening behind and beside us.

I blocked another challenge to my abilities, feeling rather than seeing a strong elf inside the building. I was hoping it was Emily. The water elf was one of the few on the base who could present a significant challenge to me.

Whoever it was, however, they didn't come running, and I was left to wonder. More soldiers appeared, all of them firing, their faces unfamiliar. As the general barked orders behind me, I reached toward the plant life and found something that would grow swiftly enough to wrap him and cover his mouth.

I barely looked as Zephyr pounced on another two soldiers. I used my air abilities to pull guns out of the hands of the soldiers to my right, where he couldn't defend me.

At the same time, I was almost knocked off my feet again, and Sen wobbled on my shoulder. Roth came to our rescue, blasting an elf I'd missed with water. As another barrage of bullets came toward me, I flew into the air, still trying to get inside the main building but aware I needed to buy time for Zephyr's breath weapon to seep through the interior.

I dodged and wove as more soldiers joined the battle. One by one, I continued to disarm them, taking away the most lethal of the weapons turned on me.

After piling them on the roof, out of reach of anyone, and making sure that the general's weapon was obviously among them, I did one last sweep with the earth, knocking everyone outside off their feet and then sucking them into the sand-like rock a little. It mostly pinned them there, although it wouldn't hold them for long.

With that finally done, I blasted air into the portal building, clearing Zephyr's gas out. I didn't have a gas mask with me, and despite my elven abilities, I was as susceptible to being knocked out and paralyzed as everyone else was when breathing it.

As soon as it was clear again, I strode inside, Sen still on my shoulder but low on darts. Roth trotted along behind. Zephyr could fit inside, but he opted to hold our rear for a while and ensure the soldiers and elves on the outside couldn't get in.

I wondered if there was anyone left standing inside at all, but then I felt it—the subtle movement of someone in the air ahead and around the corner.

Trying to work out where they were, I rippled the floor and wobbled them. It seemed to work; I heard an *oof* as someone fell over.

I grinned as I moved forward, blasting more air in from the open door to keep the air fresh and make sure no one could rush me. They tried, more soldiers and elves defending the portal room, but I kept going, knocking them back with air.

A couple more times I was challenged or blasted, and I could feel Seth trying to set fires, but Roth was using the water he'd stored to douse them, and Zephyr stomped out a few.

Behind me, I could hear a commotion as some of the elves managed to free themselves. The general could finally yell and give orders again.

*I'll hold them off*, Zephyr said. *You three secure the portal room. Then we'll have made our point.*

I wasn't going to argue, but the elves had regrouped, and I was tired. It wasn't going to be easy for me to take the portal room. Everything depended on me doing so, though.

The pressure almost got to me, but Emily managed to get to her feet and focus. She could overwhelm Roth, so I reached for the water near him and helped him harness it and keep it from her.

At the same time, I reached for the air and earth and tried to rock Emily around again. She managed to hold steady, another air elf appearing to help her. The challenge was an interesting one, but it made me pleased too. The training was paying off, and this shouldn't be easy for me.

That said, I needed to get past them before Zephyr was overwhelmed.

Going out and hoping they could keep safe, I fought their control and watched them rock as if they had mentally been whipped. Feeling guilty, I blasted them off their feet, cushioning them before they slammed into the wall. There I bent a door to hold them until Sen could hit both with her darts.

Once they were unconscious, I went toward the portal room since there were more elves in there. I felt for them in the air before I could see them, then I took control of the earth and dropped each into a small pit.

Although some of them could easily get out, it meant I could quickly redirect darts and focus on disarming the remaining soldiers.

Zephyr stepped away from the door outside in time to

let the general and the major through with the few remaining soldiers who weren't out cold. As they did, I leaned against the barrier and smiled.

"So. If I did this with my mythicals and not one of you could stop me, do you think everyone here needs more training or not?" I asked. The general's mouth fell open, and he shuffled forward.

"How?" he asked.

"Because she's Henera," Zephyr said, lifting his head and puffing out his chest. "The most powerful elf on the planet. Admittedly, there are elves who come close to her level, at least in a single element, but you're looking at the elf who you want to make sure is on your team."

I didn't say anything as the general looked between Zephyr and me. It was clear he had a lot to process, and I didn't want to make it any harder on him.

"I had no idea you could do so much. It looked to be...parlor tricks."

"No tricks," I said as I helped Seth to his feet. "Raw power, and there's a cult full of elves who are going to be here soon."

"Then we had best make sure we can defend against them."

The general came forward and offered to shake my hand. With a great deal of relief, I accepted.

## CHAPTER THREE

Exhausted, I flopped down to eat in the canteen. I was still at the portal site the following day, putting the elves through their paces. They were improving, and keeping them learning and fighting to improve was having the same effect on me. I was having to grow and push myself to handle more of them at once.

It was good. It gave me confidence that we could face whatever came. We needed that.

We ate quickly, but we also ate a lot more than most and that meant we were sitting there long enough that others around us came and went. On top of winning the general over the previous day, our little demonstration of power had generated a fair bit of conversation, and there was no shortage of it at the dining tables.

Although the general had been magnanimous in front of the others and had been man enough to publicly admit he'd underestimated us, I still got the impression that I wasn't welcome and I was upsetting his meticulous routines. Part of me didn't care.

It was far more important that I made sure the portal was protected and everyone around it knew what could hit them than it was that I kept everyone happy with my decisions and training processes.

That said, I was eager to finally have a patch of time where I got along well with the person I had to work with. Sometimes I was fortunate enough to, but other times I was at loggerheads with those around me.

I had almost finished eating, feeling a lot better for the rest, when my communication stone lit up and I felt the familiar tug of being called to Ronan and the dark room.

"Hi," I said as soon as I had finished making my way to the small room on base assigned to Zephyr and me. I didn't want to enter a trance with him while there were lots of onlookers.

Ronan stood before me, his face calm, as if he'd been waiting a while, but didn't mind doing so if necessary.

"What's wrong?" I asked when he still didn't send anything.

"Nothing major," the large centaur replied.

I lifted my eyebrows, confused by the words.

"Minsheng is here. Talking to the elven masters about many things that could help us. While here, he received a communication that he wished to be sent to you securely."

I understood Ronan's hesitance. He was being used as a glorified messenger, and it wasn't a role he was particularly comfortable with. Frowning, I motioned for him to keep on.

"The organization has looked into the information on the documents you provided. They have found that it points to one of two locations."

"I can work with that," I replied, grateful.

"Hopefully, the Sanctuary can also help. Martyl believes that the second location is more likely. It is near where the Sanctuary was a long time ago. He is the eldest mythical on the council, and I believe he has remembered something useful." At this, Ronan raised his head higher, and his chest swelled.

"Then I am once again grateful to have the Sanctuary in my life. I will start there and hope I am the first to arrive. Thank you, Ronan. You continue to be both an ally and a friend who is not easily discovered elsewhere. Please accept my gratitude and pass it to Martyl. I have every hope that we'll save these tablets, and I'll be able to safely bring them to you."

Ronan bowed, letting me know that whatever had upset him didn't come from me, and I returned the gesture. I respected him, but I could do no more than say so and hope that it was enough.

I was soon back in the small room in the barracks with Zephyr beside me. The dragon had been part of the communication, his mind traveling with mine to somewhere else entirely, but he'd chosen not to speak.

*It seems the politics in the Sanctuary gets to everyone at times. I imagine he feels very tied into his duty and doing everything a very set way*, Zephyr said, making it clear that he had picked up on the same moment of awkwardness as I had.

*The Sanctuary has kept a lot of mythicals safe for a long time. We're adjusting to what's happening now. Humans used to be the threat, and now they're not. And they're even allies on occasions. On top of that, a dormant, long-forgotten cult of elves is attacking us.*

*And yet, we still hold firm and will continue to do so. None of us are perfect, but we'll do what we need to.*

*Exactly*, I replied, relieved I had Zephyr to converse with.

We lapsed into silence as I thought about the task ahead of us. We would need others to help us if our knowledge was correct. If nothing else, there were too many tablets for us to transport alone. I didn't like the thought of heading into danger without some backup from other powerful elves and allies. Who knew what would be waiting for us.

I needed more information. And I needed a lot of it.

Getting my laptop, I made sure I had everything I could find out about the place, and then I prepared to leave. If we were going to plan what to do to get these tablets safe, we needed to go to the Sanctuary.

Once my away bag was packed again, I considered the general and how I could let him know that I might need some of his elves, and I was leaving not that long after I'd arrived.

It wasn't going to be easy, but it was necessary.

Thankfully, the general seemed to be in a good mood when I found his office, and he welcomed me and my mythicals inside with something akin to a smile.

"I saw your training earlier," he said before I could begin saying anything. "I must say I'm very impressed."

I thanked him but didn't want to get derailed.

"I'm going to have to fly to the Sanctuary and gather some allies. We've received intel on something that the elves used to be able to use. Something that would be bad in the wrong hands." I paused to study the general's reaction to my words, but he seemed calm and understanding so far, his head nodding in the right places.

"We want to make sure it's safe, and we might run into some trouble," Zephyr said aloud, his deep rumble making the general jump.

This made the older man frown, but he sat and studied us.

"Can you tell me what it is you're going after?" he asked a moment later.

"It's a cache of old elven objects," I replied. "But we don't know how they work exactly or what they do. We do know that someone is very interested in them and not in a good way."

"Then do what you need to but don't take anyone we ought to be keeping here."

I blinked, surprised by the statement and the trust that went with it. I'd expected to be told I had to be far more careful. Or that I couldn't take anyone at all.

"I'd like Seth and Emily, but I can probably leave everyone else here," I replied after a moment.

They were two of the most powerful elves there, but they were also the two who best complimented my strengths.

"A couple of soldiers and a land vehicle that can off-road would be useful if you can spare it, but I don't know who would be best for that, and I don't know if you can part with some men or not without needing authority from higher up."

The general put down his pen and sat back. Again I expected him to say no, but instead, he looked thoughtful and then reached for a piece of paper that had a roster on it.

"There's a guard team you could take. I won't need them again for a few days, and I believe they've been stationed here for long enough they'll be more familiar with you."

As he pointed at two names on the roster, I couldn't help but grin. Rick and Frank were two soldiers I'd become familiar with. I'd been on a tour of the portal site with them the first time I'd been here, and we'd fought in a battle side by side.

If I was going to bring anyone with me, they were a good choice.

"Get the major to assign you a vehicle and sign off on the paperwork for the pair. But I expect them to be taken care of and for you to bring them back in one piece."

I gave the general my reassurances that I would treat the soldiers with the same respect and care that I did anyone who walked into danger with me. I would ensure nothing was asked of them that I wouldn't be willing to do, and I would do my best to see that no harm came to them.

It was all that needed to be said, and I found the major more accommodating when it came to an appropriate off-road-ready vehicle.

Within half an hour, we were heading to the Sanctuary, Zephyr flying alone above us while I rested my abilities, Roth rested his wings, and we waited for the miles to pass by.

I kept an air bubble around the vehicle, in case, but it was something light, more to give me a warning if anything came our way than a direct safety net.

While Frank drove, Seth, Emily, and Rick sat together in the back. I was sitting in the front with Frank, making sure I could see the sky and get out of the vehicle swiftly if we were attacked. It was a fun way to travel, and it was quickly clear that Seth and Emily knew the two soldiers in the vehicle with us better than I'd realized.

They talked of kids and anniversaries. Of a birthday rescued by a suggestion Seth had made for a present and all sorts of other information I barely noticed, my mind preoccupied.

Somewhere out there was a man who knew more about my parents. But finding him was proving hard. And I had no other leads than these tablets.

More than grateful for the organization and the Sanctuary combined, their support something I couldn't do without, I focused on the positive. I wasn't out of options yet, though I was confused.

We arrived at the Sanctuary several hours later, my body weary. The greeting from Ronan made the trip worth it. His face was full of relief, and he'd been busy while we traveled. Minsheng was with him, a bag packed and weapons galore. With him was Erlan with his fire salamander Newton and an air elf I had trained with in the past, a quick young woman I adored.

I smiled and hugged them before petting Newton. He changed color until he was deep purple and nuzzled into my fingers with each stroke. Although he had grown since I last saw him, he still fit on Erlan's shoulder. I was once again grateful. I might have rescued the small creature a long time ago, but he'd brought another elf into my life when they'd bonded.

Motioning for the others to get into the truck, I turned to Ronan.

"Thank you, my friend," I said as I bowed low.

Instead of returning the gesture and stepping into the Sanctuary boundaries, however, Ronan strode toward the truck. It was then I noticed that he also bore a pack—a leather satchel I'd seen in the past.

"You're joining us?" I asked as I walked beside him.

"Forgive me. Yes, I'd like to. This is your mission, however. I would request your permission to do so. It means a lot to me to be able to protect the Sanctuary, and I believe this is one of the best ways I can do that."

I nodded without hesitation. Ronan was someone I was never going to say no to when it came to having an ally in battle. He'd proved himself many times, and he took his role as head of security for the Sanctuary very seriously. Both of us felt the loss of the centaur who had held the role previously.

It didn't take long to get Ronan settled, the truck wonderfully versatile for something designed for humans.

Once again, Zephyr took to the air. Minsheng acted as our navigator. This time I sat at the back of the group and watched. I had several powerful elves with me, plus my Shishou, the best mythical in the Sanctuary, and a couple of human soldiers who also had my back. I couldn't have headed out with a better team.

Sen and Roth enjoyed the extra fuss and attention, the myconid bounding about with Newton and generally getting up to mischief and helping people stay amused while we traveled.

We had a serious amount of miles to cover, heading east

again and farther north. The place we wanted was near the Canadian border. Somewhere not too far from the house I'd found the information in.

After stopping several times for toilet breaks, food, and to let the two soldiers swap driving duties, we were finally getting close as night fell.

I wanted to keep going without stopping, eager to get there and find my answers, but I kept the thought to myself, Zephyr reminding me that we needed to rest and eat to keep our strength up.

Several times I used my powers to help him, knowing this was hardest on him. He was flying through the day for hours and not complaining.

*I was designed to do this*, he reminded me when I asked him if he was okay for the fifth time.

*And I apparently was intended to control the elements like no one before me. It doesn't mean I don't get tired and need to stop now and then.*

*Fair point. But I'm truly fine. I might ache tomorrow, but I can glide easily enough, and you keep helping without thinking about it.*

I paused, having not realized what I was doing. I had taken control of the air around him and had improved his slipstream as I did while riding him. I was also giving him lift with a gentle blast under his wings now and then.

*It's becoming entirely second nature to use your powers. You've clearly got the strength now to keep up low-level activities with it all day. Just as you breathe all day.*

Zephyr was right, and I drew some comfort from it. Perhaps I'd finally gotten to the point where my air ability was always going to be there.

Either way, I was relieved as the truck turned off the road and down a small dirt track that had seen better days. We were bumped and jostled as the soldier gripped the steering wheel and did his best to navigate around the worst of it.

"Almost there," Minsheng called, making sure everyone knew that it was about to be game time.

## CHAPTER FOUR

The last few miles had rattled my bones and left me feeling tired despite how little I'd been using my abilities all day. Off-road wasn't as much fun as it looked.

As we approached a large, old, warehouse-looking building beside a lake, Zephyr flew lower to do a reconnaissance scout for us.

I was the first to get out, powering into the air out of the back of the truck in case danger came at us. The whole place was deathly quiet, not even the sound of birds in the air. Something was wrong. We might have been able to scare birds away, but there should have been some there unless something else had been making lots of noise here.

*Or something worse*, my mind offered me.

I shuddered as Zephyr flew in lower circles and I made my way toward the building.

It didn't take long before Zephyr and I spotted that one of the side doors had a broken lock on it, the wooden plank raised a fraction compared to the rest of the building.

If it had been the only sign that something wasn't right, or the building had been old and unused looking, I might not have worried about it.

As it was, an open, broken door partway into an abandoned warehouse out in the middle of nowhere and no wildlife had me spooked.

Turning slow circles, I tried to figure out who or what had been here and if they were still a threat. At first, I didn't see much of anything except the door, but then I noticed some faint footprints near a side door, this one shut. I also noticed that as I turned and waited and watched, some of the birds returned.

Whatever had spooked them, it had been recent. Was it us? I had no way of knowing for sure.

Landing again, I put my finger to my lips as Minsheng also got out of the truck. He was silent. Everyone else had the sense to pick up on the body language and make sure they were quiet.

Rick switched the ignition off, and everyone got out.

*Still no movement?* I asked Zephyr once everyone had a weapon ready and was spreading out in case there was trouble.

*No. But I think something is down there in that building... I can feel it.*

I reached forward with my powers, wondering what he meant. Roth and Sen came to my side, the large pegasus unfurling his wings and Sen jumping onto my shoulder.

It didn't take long for me to feel the control of another elf on the air inside the building. But there was something else, something far stranger. Almost as if it was sucking the power out of me, I could feel a strange tugging sensation.

While I stood there, trying to work out what to do with this information, it grew fainter although originating from the same point. I had no idea what was going on, but I didn't like it.

"There are elves inside," I whispered loud enough that Minsheng could hear me. I watched as the message rippled outward and everyone went on alert.

I didn't hesitate and started moving forward. If there was an air elf inside who was half as powerful as I was, they would be picking up my mind reaching around their control and know someone was here, even if they didn't know what I was capable of.

That meant I didn't have the luxury of surprise. Not against mythicals like me.

Moving to the side door, I crept my control even closer inside to work out how many I was up against, but someone didn't like me prying. I was soon aware of an area of air that was closed off to me and housing other elves. I could feel the control, someone strong simply holding on to the air and blocking my mind.

Not sure how many were inside and with no way to confirm anything without being extremely aggressive, I walked closer, masking the sound of my moving body and that of those with me. I brought Erlan with me and sent Seth with the other elves toward another door. The soldiers also followed me and my mythicals, leaving Minsheng and Ronan to go with the other group.

It wasn't a perfectly split group of us. I was the most powerful with the most bonded mythicals, but it was the best we could do in terms of the raw power of the few people going in.

When we were feet from the side door, it burst open, and a flashlight shone on my face. After moving around in the dark for several minutes, my eyes had adjusted, and the bright gleam made me squint and struggle to respond.

Reaching for the air around me with my mind, I used that to see, detecting the presence of ten strong elves and more behind. There were a lot of them, and it made me wonder if we had any chance of beating them.

Not knowing what else to do, I blasted them off their feet with the air I had control of. It worked, some of them going sprawling, but several more stayed steady, something or someone keeping them that way. The four who hadn't rocked were carrying a large crate between them.

Pretty sure the tablets were in the crate since I was feeling the strange sensation and desire to be close to them as well as the usual range of emotions I always had when I was fighting other elves, I lunged forward to get the crate off them. I hit them again, but an air blast smacked hard into my side, not only knocking me off my feet but sending me flying into the air, my side aching from the impact.

I managed to stop myself from hitting the ground hard and damaging the other side of me, but I was left stunned. Whoever had hit me, they were one powerful air elemental. Not only had I not felt their approaching control, but they'd blasted through the barrier I had around me at every waking moment.

*Are you okay?* Zephyr asked before swooping down low and exhaling a cloud of his gas across the path of the running elves.

*Yes. Just a wounded ego.*

I quickly took control of more air and rushed into position to stop the elves before they could skirt Zephyr's gas cloud. The air elf from the Sanctuary was taking control of it as I would have, the elf having run through the warehouse.

Taking a deep breath, I focused on the four elves and the large crate they carried between them. It was heavy, but the tablets were inside, and I didn't want to break them.

Any attacks were going to have to be careful. I thought of how I'd killed the elf in Mexico, stopping where I was. I'd not been careful enough then, acting in the heat of battle and getting it wrong.

*Aella, do something*, Zephyr's words sounded, snapping me out of the hesitant trance I'd fallen into.

I refocused my control, but all I could think of doing was trying to blast the crate upward with air, to yank it out of the hands of the elves. It worked, the crate wobbling, but it was heavy, and I'd been too light with my attack. One elf's grip was loosened enough. Thankfully Emily appeared at my side and, working with Roth, she hurled water at the distracted elf.

They were knocked away, and I found myself having to concentrate to keep the crate in the air, but the other three elves continued to try to haul it away.

I put pressure on it, trying to keep it where it was, but another elf chose that moment to hit me with a blast of some air while another rocked the ground beneath my feet. I lost control and the crate should have fallen, no longer supported by me as I wobbled over. It didn't, however, someone else's control keeping it from dropping.

By the time I was on my feet again, the crate was farther away, and Zephyr's vapor cloud had been torn into multiple wisps. Zephyr was on the ground, trying to block the escape, but the crate was floating, held by two elves, the rest fighting in a circle around it, blasting air, fire, water, and plant life or sound around them and at anyone who came too close.

I reached for control of the air underneath the tablets but met with the strong air elf in command. It took me time to push at it, probing. It didn't feel like the control of any of the other elves in the cult, but something different, someone with more power and more nuance.

Still, I managed to work out how to get through eventually, but the crate was farther away by then, and I had Zephyr, Roth, and Sen working as hard as they could to defend me and the other elves.

Before my eyes, more cult members rushed out of the nearby trees, several of them elves I recognized from the first few times I was attacked by the cult. Powerful water and air elementals.

*Shitsticks.*

*We can't win this,* Zephyr said. *There are too many of them. But I might be able to help more in human form.*

*No. This isn't the time to let more of the enemy see you. You're right. We can't win this. We got here too late, and they have the advantage. They're trying to run.*

Growling my anger, I threw everything I could at the elves that had appeared and blasted them off their feet. At the same time, I pushed everything else I had into taking control of the crate. As the air became mine, I focused on the crate.

*Defend me*, I said to Zephyr, feeling the dragon fly overhead.

*Always.*

He landed at my side as Roth and Sen came to me and helped block the air and water sent my way. I took control of the earth below my feet and the plants, instinctively growing them around me. Then I concentrated on using the air and water around to bring the crate to me.

At first, the elves holding on didn't seem to know how to respond, and they were dragged backward with the crate. I could feel the extra effort of having to bring them along, but it grew worse as they got their footing and actively resisted.

While they were making my task harder, the rest of the elves either came close to help them or attack me. Zephyr blocked an air blast while Roth took on more water before spouting it at an elf near the crate. While this was happening, I felt the powerful air elf try to take control.

For now, I held on, and the crate came toward me. But it was painfully slow, and I had no idea how long I could keep control and resistance when I had so much pressure on me and against my control.

I moved it faster, but the extra air needed to do so made my head hurt. I wasn't going to be able to keep it up.

*I should take human form*, Zephyr said.

*No. Then you couldn't block the elements. You're large enough to shield me almost entirely*, I replied, my thoughts stilted and struggling against the barrage.

When four more elves came out of the trees and started moving the elements, it was too much. They were fresh, and they punished the group defending me. At the same time, my control of the plants around me was challenged. It was one of my weaker elements, so I struggled to hold on.

Finally, I had to give way and let go of the air around the crate, my head pounding alarmingly. At the same time, a blast hit Emily so hard she was knocked off her feet and smacked her head against the side of the warehouse with a sickening crack.

I rushed to her side, no one else being able to move with the barrage of attacks being directed at us.

The young elf let me help her up, her eyes appearing to swim in her head as she wobbled. It was too much.

"Fall into the warehouse," I said, not sure what else we could do at this point.

The elves, centaur, and humans looked to me as if I'd grown four heads, but they did as suggested, and as a group, we retreated inside. The fight went out of the cult and they focused on the crate again, picking it up manually and carrying it away between the elves.

Once I was inside the building, I took control of the air again and pulled the crate down and away, but this newcomer was controlling it once more, and I couldn't fight them and resist.

Sinking into a sitting position and feeling defeated, I let go of the elements, preserving what was left of my energy to keep my bond with my mythicals open.

I tried to think through what I had to do next, but I simply felt exhausted. This wasn't how anything like this was supposed to go. I was supposed to have more than enough power alone. But it was clear that I didn't. I could still be overwhelmed with numbers. Especially if I was bombarded with elves who had been training their whole lives and had some serious skills.

Sen hugged me as Roth walked and leaned his head down. I stroked the pegasus absentmindedly, wondering if I'd ever get used to how he felt. Something both water and fluid, yet firm and strong.

"We're going to need to follow them," Minsheng said. "We can't let them get away from us."

"I know, but we don't have someone who can track them and I'm out of other ideas," I replied, barely able to keep my anger inside.

I exhaled, aware I shouldn't be taking my temper out on everyone else. I needed to be the calm, level head who made sure we succeeded. Somehow.

Getting up again, I looked at the faces around me. Everyone was exhausted. Thankfully there was food in the truck.

"Who thinks they can drive?" I asked.

Minsheng raised his hand. "It wouldn't be the first time I've handled a military vehicle."

"Great. Everyone else but Zephyr and I are going to rest in the back and eat."

"What about the two of you?" Erlan asked.

"I'm going to eat while flying with Zephyr," I replied without missing a beat.

*I can fly alone,* Zephyr said. *We established this. Or, well, we had it established at some point.*

*You can, but we need to be careful. And I need to be following the trail to help pick up on this air elf.*

Zephyr didn't argue any further as I ushered everyone toward the vehicle. I grabbed food, then I lifted myself onto Zephyr's back. We needed to follow this cult and try to work out how to get the tablets from them.

Of course, that was going to be a lot harder than we'd prefer.

## CHAPTER FIVE

After several more hours of flying, Zephyr and I were tired. We had a trail to follow, however, and I was determined to keep us on it. Despite my best intentions and my surety that this was the best course of action, several times we almost lost the trail, and I had to fly lower and scan the dark forest.

Yet on we flew.

*We should get reinforcements*, Zephyr said, when we'd been doing this for a couple of hours.

I wasn't inclined to argue, knowing we'd gotten steamrolled because of the sheer number of powerful enemies and there not being enough of us for anyone to truly go on the offense.

I could only hope that the Sanctuary and the elves in it were willing to help us further. We needed something if we were to rescue that crate of materials, and I was sure we needed to. It wasn't a good combination.

Settling onto Zephyr's back again, I thought of the best way to tell everyone that we needed reinforcements. We were flying toward the base in Texas. Or closer to it. But that didn't mean we'd get a chance to land, pick up extra people who would keep this secret, and then catch up again. No, we had to keep on as best we could.

I ate as much as I could stomach of the energy bars and chips. Unhealthy snacks, but it was better than no snacks. Most importantly, it replenished my energy. I had some more substantial food on me, but I wanted to be sure of needing it or not.

There was no way to tell for sure if the elves we were following knew we were coming after them or were aiming for anything specifically. I also had no way to know if they were also resting and recuperating.

*We'll stop them*, Zephyr said. *I'm sure Minsheng will be calling for help.*

It was a good point. Not everything had to be on my shoulders. I wasn't alone, and we had a good team, even if it wasn't as big as we hoped. We needed a way to pick off their numbers, taking prisoners or reducing their abilities so far they dropped back.

As we flew, I noticed several vehicles and elves riding on horses and mythical animals ahead. It was part of the group we were chasing. I pointed them out to Zephyr, and he swooped lower. In the dark, I wasn't sure they'd seen us, but they were still moving fast and trying to stay hidden at the same time.

I'd gotten lucky to see the flash of light off a vehicle as someone had briefly used a flashlight. They were in the dark again, but Zephyr had them in his sights, and he could see far better than I could.

*Sen, Roth, let the others know what we're seeing*, I said,

feeling the bond stretch out between us as the vehicle they were in fell farther behind. Zephyr was flying faster than ever, trying to catch up and also adjusting his course to make us harder to see if they looked back.

We were traveling quickly, but I was growing tired, my energy spent during the fight. It was clear that many of the elves we were trying to follow were also resting, and that would make it harder on us to fight them again.

Despite that, we had to do something. We couldn't let them get away with the tablets, especially if they could do what we thought.

With Sen and Roth guiding the others and Zephyr flying without my aid while I ate, I hoped we could even the odds again, but before we could do much more, Zephyr slowed.

*What is it?* I asked, swallowing the mouthful of my sandwich and hesitating to take another one.

*I've lost them. They went past a thick patch of trees and didn't come out the other side.*

*Circle back?* I suggested.

*Already on it.*

I exhaled, relieved that Zephyr knew what he was doing in this unknown situation. Sometimes I panicked about things I shouldn't be worrying about, but I needed to know what had happened to these elves.

As Zephyr banked, I looked toward the last location where he'd seen them, but I couldn't see anything. They were gone.

*Looks like we might need to land*, I said to him.

*All right, but not too close. They might have spotted us and be trying to lay a trap.*

It was a good point, and once again, I was grateful for Zephyr. I had a habit of rushing in, and he helped keep me alive.

We landed in a nearby clearing as I reached out for Sen and Roth and warned them to be careful. It wasn't ideal, but it would have to do.

Once we were on the ground I dismounted, intending to lead the way. I took control of the air around us again, hardening it and making sure a barrier moved ahead of us, just in case.

Even in the dark, there was enough moonlight and starlight out in this wilderness that I could see ahead. I could also feel the air around the clearing farther ahead. I reached forward, probing for anything moving in the dark or anyone else controlling the air or plant life.

There was nothing. Not an animal moved around the patch of trees where the elves had last been seen.

*They've disappeared somehow*, I said into Zephyr's head.

*So it would seem.* He strode forward, coming past me and walking with more abandon. Not wanting to get too far from him, I quickly followed until we were standing in front of a wide hole in the ground, a tunnel that burrowed deep and away from the forest.

In it were tire tracks and the prints of various mammals and mythicals. The cult had gone underground.

While we stood staring at the gaping hole, the elves were putting more distance between us, but I couldn't follow. I had no flashlight, and the thought of wandering around in the unknown darkness made me want to puke.

I'd been trapped in one dark enclosed space recently. Another was too much to handle.

Even Zephyr hesitated, although his body would fit down the hole. If he went down it, there would be no backing out. We'd have to keep going, at least while he was in dragon form.

Thankfully, Minsheng pulled up, and the headlights of the truck picked out the entrance. It was an interesting tunnel that looked to have been made by an elf in a hurry.

It was wide enough to fit a vehicle and a little extra. I could assume that it was elven made. The lights of the truck showed there was more darkness farther in.

I also got the impression it was a relatively unstable tunnel. There was no shoring, nothing that showed this was supposed to hold up. It had been made by the elves to get here, and it was the way they'd left. Who knew how far it went, or if it stopped somewhere else?

Trying not to panic or show my fear, I had to endure as everyone got out of our vehicle and came to similar conclusions. It was a tunnel that we needed to investigate, though I didn't truly want to. I didn't hesitate beyond looking at Zephyr to check how he was feeling. He'd been there alongside me at every turn. Did he feel what I did?

*Yes. But we've got to keep going. We can't let them get away with those tablets. Not when we don't know what they can do. Are they the same kind of tablet, and how will that change things? The Earth needs us, and that means we have to push past our fears and go for it anyway.*

Roth and Sen sent waves of encouragement and solidarity to me and I assumed that they did the same for Zephyr, his large body visibly relaxing beside me.

*Okay*, I thought. *Let's take the plunge.*

I took a flashlight out of Minsheng's outstretched hand

and moved toward the open, cave-like entrance. Without another outward sign that anything was wrong, I pushed onward.

The dirt walls soon welcomed us into their embrace, the air getting colder as we descended. I shivered, and not because I felt the coolness of the environment. I thought of the cold, pitch-black stairwell in the mountain and the desperate way I'd clung to Zephyr in human form and needed him close to stay sane.

*It's okay. This is entirely different*, he said. *We're the hunters, and we're not alone.*

As soon as Zephyr finished speaking, I realized he was right. Not only were we not alone, but I could hear the constant gentle background noise of a group of eight other allies and our mythicals as they had low-key conversations or talked about what we might find. At the same time, several were working together with their flashlights to illuminate as far ahead as possible and to help us see and avoid obstacles.

We walked together for what felt like hours, passing several areas where the walls had given way a little. The earth elf with us often quickly patched them, walking near the front of the group. I was nearer the back, my eyesight not good enough for me to feel like a useful person to have at the front of the group.

Zephyr had come dead last, no one wanting to walk behind his large bulk. It was hard enough as it was to walk down here without being blocked off from most of the rest of the group.

Despite these problems and the very real possibility that Zephyr might get stuck unless he took human form, we pressed on and bypassed the large rocks and areas starting to grow unstable.

I was beginning to yawn, pretty sure we had used almost the entire night and would need to defend ourselves in a sleep-deprived and tired state if anyone attacked us now.

"We'll get the upper hand again," Minsheng said when things had been quiet around us for a while.

"How did you know that I was worrying about that?" I asked.

"I'm your Shishou. It's my job to worry about how happy you are and what might make your life difficult. I know you've not mentioned everything that happened during the time you were taken. But if you ever want to talk about any more of it, I'm here. As always."

I glanced at Zephyr as his wings brushed on the roof again and sent a shower of dirt and debris raining down. He shook it off as soon as he was clear, but it made me very aware that we still needed to defeat something or get out the other end of this tunnel we were in.

"I've messaged the organization and Ronan has contacted the Sanctuary," Minsheng added a moment later, keeping silent about the possible conversation I'd been having and what he might be able to work out of it.

I was grateful and expressed the sentiment, trying not to sound too wishy-washy.

"Least I could do. Call more backup for you."

I laughed at the offer and explanation. It was so like Minsheng to realize I needed something more and make it happen for me, but we still had a long way to go if this went wrong.

Trying to focus on the positive, I followed the group. Still lost, I didn't notice that the tunnel was blocked until I almost walked into my Shishou, the dwarf stopping with nowhere to go.

I swore under my breath and moved past him as the flashlights lit the wall. It wasn't a cave-in, but a deliberate end to the tunnel. Someone had either blocked it, or they had never come this far.

I angled my beam down, looking for tire tracks or any other sign that the elves we were following had come this way. There was nothing on the floor but our tracks and Zephyr sitting in dragon form in the way of me checking any farther than the bulk of his body.

I heard a deep rumble in his chest as it became clear that we were either going to need him to back up or show his human form to the entire group.

Before he could do anything drastic, I sent calming emotions his way and thought through the problem. I reached out with my mind to work out what might have happened here. There was nothing beyond the wall we'd reached as far as my control could go. No tunnel in any direction, the surface about a hundred yards up.

Wanting to get angry, I thought about what we could do next. The other earth elemental, Serfina, felt outward in different directions to help me figure out if there was any way to continue from here.

Everyone else took a break and passed out snacks from the ration packs the soldiers had and the gear that everyone had thought to bring with them. I was extremely grateful for them as they still shared with me and considered my needs from using yet more magic, something I didn't do very well myself, let alone do for others.

There was nothing for it, however. If the elven cult had come this way, they had hidden signs of their passing so well that we couldn't figure out what had happened.

"I think we need to work out the best way to get to the truck," Minsheng said a moment later, his eyes meeting Ronan's.

I wasn't sure what was being said between them via their body language, but there was no way I was going to argue. I wanted to get out of here now.

"Can the earth elves, Aella, and Serfina create us a path to the surface from here? It would be easier to travel on the surface," Ronan added.

I nodded. It wouldn't be easy to make something large enough and stable enough when we were tired, but it stopped Zephyr from having to, and it stopped him needing to take elven form. If someone wanted to mock me for a mistake, so be it.

I took Serfina's hand, and we stepped closer to the wall to minimize the strain on our abilities and pushed outward with our minds. It was time to get back to the normal world.

## CHAPTER SIX

As we broke through the surface, I noticed we were still in the woods, but this time we could hear the sound of birdsong. It looked like any other national park or protected forest in the US countryside.

I tried not to think about much else as everyone filed out, and I finally managed to breathe some fresh air. It took longer to make it wide enough for Zephyr, and by the time we had him out, it was daytime in the forest. I couldn't see any signs of the cult among the trees either. It was as if they'd vanished somewhere along the tunnel.

Although I wanted to walk to the trucks along the tunnel route, I was exhausted, and the trees were too close together for Zephyr to do anything but fly. Instead, I climbed onto his back again, and he flew upward. Rested, Roth and Sen joined us, and everything was well as we climbed into the morning sky.

The sun shone down through clouds, and the landscape stretched out beneath us. I could have forgotten our troubles and why we were out here and flown on toward whatever horizon we wanted to.

But the nagging feeling that we'd missed something or could have handled that fight better wouldn't go away. I'd hesitated in the heat of battle. That wasn't something I'd ever done before.

Killing an elf had made me worried I was turning into a monster, and I had begun second-guessing myself. For so long, we'd been holding ourselves above killing anything and anyone, but in the kinds of battles and wars we'd found ourselves in, it was clear that wasn't always going to be possible.

Leaning into Zephyr, I let him get higher before I took more of an interest in what was around us.

*We're not that far from the Texas portal*, Zephyr said. *This tunnel might have been one they made to get closer undetected. Or to try to find it in the first place.*

It was an interesting thought, but I wasn't entirely sure I trusted it. There were still so many possibilities. Not knowing where those tablets were or who the air elemental was who had been challenging me was beginning to consume my thoughts.

Even though I wanted to rest, we couldn't yet.

As if sensing my thoughts and feelings on the matter despite his desire to go to the portal site and rest, Zephyr banked and flew lower so we could follow the trail of the tunnel to the warehouse.

It was much harder to follow the tunnel from the outside, even with me reaching down with my abilities to follow the line of it. I wanted to be down on the ground, but my body was exhausted and I had to fight off sleep, my eyes trying to close every few minutes. It was going to be a lot quicker this way than with me walking.

With little other choice and no sign of the cult, we opted to leave the others behind for a while again, the walking pace they'd set was not enough to keep up with a flying dragon.

It was surprisingly quick to reach the entrance to the tunnel where the vehicles were parked. There had been no sign of the cars or people leaving the tunnel on the outside on the way back either.

Once again, Zephyr landed in the small clearing we'd used half a night earlier, and I got down. I pulled some energy drinks out of the food stash in the back of the truck and more snacks, helping Sen eat.

Roth quickly chowed down on the grass and living plants around us, leaving Zephyr still hungry. I apologized to him, but we knew there was nothing either of us could do about it. Our life required sacrifices of us. I was often sleep-deprived and blamed for everything, and Zephyr was often hungry and feared.

It was something we were sadly used to in life now.

As soon as I'd finished eating and drinking and Zephyr said he was ready to keep on, we got into the air again. We still had to fly to the warehouse, the pursuit we'd been on after the cult elves having taken longer than we realized and having covered a much larger distance.

Still, we made it to the warehouse, the four of us standing together as we approached it. It looked very different in the light of the sun instead of the moon. Less like the set of some horror film and more what it truly was. An old, abandoned building in the middle of the forest.

Neglected and alone. Something to be pitied for the lack of use.

Except it had housed a treasure trove to the elven community. And it had been the site of a battle I had a lot to learn from.

It made me respect the place as we got closer. The side door still stood open, and there were a multitude of footprints on the ground in front of it. I walked carefully, treading a new path where I could until I reached the door and had to go inside.

Although there were some windows in the building, they were so begrimed with dirt from the inside and the lack of use or care of the outside that it barely illuminated the interior.

Forced to flick my flashlight on again to see, I kept on.

The ground was covered in dust and dirt, a layer thick over most of it and the machinery that had been left inside when the owners had abandoned it. It was almost crazy to see so much left to rot, but more importantly, we could see the route that had been walked, plenty of scuff marks and footprints in the dust.

I followed it as it wove through rows and columns of old desks until it reached an office near the back of the building. The door was shut, but I couldn't let that stop me after I'd come this far. Pushing it open, I was grateful I had Zephyr, Roth, and Sen to back me up when I faced the unknown.

Being tense and tired made me jumpy, and I stifled a squeal when a rat that had been chewing on the bottom of the door scurried toward us. It didn't react to us in any other way, but I had to calm my racing heart before looking around again.

My eyes fixed on a strange object.

There, on the floor, was a strange contraption I'd never seen before. It looked to be a plug-in device for the tablets. Or like a weapons rack. Either way, it was an interesting setup and I was very curious.

Moving closer, I shone more light at it and noticed that the tablets were indeed gone. The cult had taken every single one.

I exhaled and wondered why they couldn't have let us be. A part of me knew the answer to that, of course. They were a valuable find for a cult that didn't appreciate my stance on not letting them do what they wanted and resisting them at every turn. They kept pissing me off.

*They'll learn*, Zephyr said, and I nodded, not sure what would get them to understand there was no way the portals were being opened.

I wanted to keep looking, but I yawned again. There was little more I was going to find out from what appeared to be an empty building. Maybe Minsheng or the others might have a better chance of working it out, but I needed to find another lead more than I needed to work out what and why the tablets had been in this warehouse instead of somewhere else.

Moving to the open area, I contemplated our next move.

*Sleep in the truck*, Zephyr said. *I need to rest too. And it will be another couple of hours before we can get to the portal site anyway. On top of that, we might need your abilities at some point.*

It was sensible except for one thing. The truck was in the forest to our west, and it wasn't going anywhere any time soon.

Before I had finished thinking this, I heard the unmistakable sound of the engine. I could see it moving through the trees as the soldiers returned with it.

I sighed, knowing Zephyr had probably heard it first and known it was on the way here.

I was pretty sure I saw him grin as it pulled to a halt and Seth got out.

"The others are trying to work out what happened to the cult and where they must have gone. Reckoned you'd want a lift to the portal site to properly rest and research something for Minsheng," the fire elemental explained, looking pretty tired.

There was no argument from me. My mind had become mush sometime around the middle of the flight from the tunnel exit to the warehouse, and I had barely taken much more in.

I was going to have to trust the people I worked with and call family to help me figure out what to do next. And hope that one of them found a clue about the man I'd gone to find in Canada. Thankfully, Minsheng knew how much that meant to me. With any luck, he'd be able to find me another lead.

*If he doesn't, we will*, Zephyr said. *I won't give until we know who your parents are and why they thought it best to give you up.*

A rush of warmth and support came from Zephyr, and I sent the same back. This was one of those moments that made me want to cry, knowing he cared so much and I was never alone. But I held it together as I climbed into the back of the truck, and Roth and Sen joined me.

Zephyr came closer, hesitating before he took human form. I frowned as Seth and the soldiers gaped. None of them had seen Zephyr in his human form.

*I'm too tired to fly more*, he explained. *It's either this or you leave me here.*

*I'm sorry*, I replied, knowing I'd asked a lot of him already. *You're right. We can't keep it a secret forever.*

*It's okay. I wanted to keep my appearance in human form a secret. I can't fly anymore today, and I don't want to be that far from you. Not when the cult is out again. They need you, and if anything happened to you while I wasn't there...*

As Zephyr trailed off, I took his hand. The two of us curled up in the back of the truck. Someone had moved the seats and put out blankets to make it more comfortable. It wasn't a massive help, especially as the truck lurched over uneven ground, no true road about for miles, but we were exhausted enough it didn't seem to matter.

I woke up when Zephyr did, his eyes going wide as he sat up.

*What is it?* I asked, the movement of the truck smoother.

I thought I felt the presence of another elven mind. An air elemental. Somewhere near the road.

I sat up too, wondering if it had been the same air elemental I'd been challenged by earlier, but though I reached out with my mind, I couldn't feel anything. If Zephyr had felt someone, they were behind us or had pulled back to also avoid detection.

Briefly considering asking the soldiers to turn around and go to check, I closed my eyes and felt as far out as I could. I could stretch out a lot farther than many elves, and I put it to good use now, but I still couldn't feel anyone controlling the air.

*It was probably me imagining it*, Zephyr said as the others noticed we'd woken up. I sighed, aware I probably wouldn't get any more sleep and feeling paranoid. But I wasn't going to let the others see either emotion.

Leaning into Zephyr as he wrapped his arms around me, I replayed the events of the last twelve hours or so and figured out what we'd done wrong and what might have worked to stop the cult. There had to be some way to find the elves again, but it wasn't going to be easy.

There was a good chance they were taking them to Mexico, but there was also the possibility they'd keep them somewhere nearby. A safe house. Ready to take on the portal here in Texas. Hopefully, the others would have answers for us. I could only hope that we made some progress soon.

Zephyr requested the truck pull over a short while later and made me wonder what he was thinking. Had he decided to get them to turn around anyway? Before I could ask him, he moved out of view of the road and morphed into a dragon. I considered getting out to fly with him, not liking the idea of him flying above us.

*Stay there and rest. This gives me a chance to see if anyone is moving out here, and it keeps my human form from as many people as possible.*

I couldn't argue, still feeling tired. Stifling a yawn, I settled down again.

*Let me know if you see anything.*

*Of course, I'll be calling for your backup. Whoever that air elf was, they were powerful. And I like it when we outnumber and outmatch the bad guys.*

I smirked, feeling the usual tug on my stomach as Zephyr and I were separated by a larger distance. It was never going to be something I got used to or liked.

*One day we'll go everywhere together,* he said.

*I'll make sure of it. We'll live and die together.*

I'd barely thought this when the truck turned into the base and we were admitted to the portal site. By the time I had gotten out of the truck, Zephyr was on the ground beside me, and I felt his closeness again. Roth and Sen came with us as we strode to the main building.

There was a huge possibility this base would be attacked, and I was the only one who could bring such bad news to the general in charge. I had to hope that he wouldn't hate me for not being successful so far.

## CHAPTER SEVEN

Trying not to worry while the general sat in stony silence, I finished my tale. It had taken some time, and I'd been interrupted many times to answer questions and clarify elements. Zephyr had done a fair bit of the talking, lending his ancient knowledge and experience of the cult to make it clear we had done our best.

I could tell the general wasn't pleased, but it remained to be seen if we were the problem or something else was. I tried not to worry as the man got up and walked to the window of his office.

"It seems I have underestimated the capabilities of your race. I know the President said you had more to you than it appeared when he assigned me here, but this is more than anything my mind could imagine."

"I'd say I'm sorry, but I love a lot of what the elves can do and change. I do know it can be scary when the elves have a goal that doesn't align with what you're trying to do, however. But you have us on your side, and we're going to do everything we can to stop anything bad happening."

The general gave me a nod at this, his jaw set and his torso straightening. It was the look of a man who was finding his backbone again and preparing to do what was needed.

I might have gotten off on the wrong foot with him, but it was good to see that we were working together now. And I had meant my words. I was willing to defend this portal and everyone on the site to the best of my ability.

More than once, the men and women had stood beside me in battle, trading blows with our enemies. I was seeing more friendships blossoming between humans and elves. After the rocky road we'd had to get here and have the human world accept mythicals, what we'd created here was worth fighting for.

Before I could say anything else to the general, there was a knock on the door, and the major appeared.

"Everyone is back from the little excursion. Minsheng was hoping to have you in the portal room, Aella." The major saluted the general as he spoke and looked at me after.

"He found something?"

"I believe so. And he didn't want another elf to be the one to help."

I lifted an eyebrow at the strange information, but the general waved toward the door as if he had no intention of keeping me and my mythicals any longer, and I was curious enough to go.

All five of us made our way to the portal site, finding Minsheng standing near the air pillar, something small resting on the palm of his hand and a device in the other.

Moving closer, I studied what he held. It appeared to be

a fragment of a stone, and by the time I was beside him, I realized that it had some of the air runes on it. As the tablets in the crate had done, it seemed to draw me in, pulling on my mind and abilities.

"Found this outside the warehouse. I think it fell out of the crate while everyone was fighting over it. It might give us an idea what the others in there will do."

"Want me to try to connect to it?" I asked, part of me wanting to as if it was calling me and my abilities. It felt as if it was the right thing to do. As if nothing else should be considered.

Minsheng stared at me and the readings.

*Careful, Aella,* Zephyr said. *This feels as if it could go wrong very easily.*

*You're right. But we have to try something. I'll do my best to be careful,* I replied, not sure I'd thought the words, my eyes still stuck on the fragment of rock.

"I think it's interacting with the portal and pillars. So go easy with it," Minsheng said as he brought it closer, offering it to me.

I slowly took it, my hand reaching out without me needing to tell it to. It felt warm and smooth except where the runes were carved, each one intricate and precise, etched with delicate swirls and strokes. This was crafted with love and care. And I got the impression that it would stand the test of time, never showing signs of wear and age.

As it sat in my palm, it grew hotter, my body and powers connecting to it a moment later. Minsheng's device showed a difference.

I could feel some of my power flowing into it, the stone somehow made of rock but feeling as if it was made of air.

As I connected, I also felt an understanding flood my mind. It was something that would help concentrate my abilities. But also something that had a purpose of its own.

Slowly it seemed to fill up, my body feeling the strain as it sucked power despite how small it was. It didn't take long for me to notice that the runes on the stone glow, getting brighter as I fueled it.

*I think that's probably enough*, Zephyr said a moment later. *We don't know what it does.*

It was as if his words came through fog, and I struggled to comprehend them.

"Aella!" he snapped, the word coming out a deep growl that made me jump. I'd never heard Zephyr yell.

My mind finally cleared, however, and I stopped the flow of power, breaking the connection as quickly as I'd begun it. It pulled at me once more, as if it wanted me to keep filling it, but I did my best to resist it.

"That is a piece of the tablet," the major said, looking over Minsheng's shoulder.

"Yes. It is," Minsheng replied. "And I think, even with that small piece, someone who isn't an air elf could act as if they were."

"Are you kidding me?" I asked, fear and awe making my voice sound higher pitched. "Are you telling me this is, like, an air-elemental grenade?"

"No. Something far more sophisticated. It's more like an air elemental battery. It still needs something to plug into. Probably an elf. I don't think a human could do anything with it."

"I'd be willing to try, but I don't think I should do so

until you know for sure what it can do." The major grinned, but he also looked nervously at the stone.

Minsheng nodded, and I tried to think of something to say to express my gratitude that he'd be willing to embark on trying some crazy experiment.

"So, what now?" I asked. "And why are we in here?"

"I wanted to see how it would interact with the field and the pillars. I confess I didn't expect it to draw so much power from you."

"Okay, so I'll keep doing my best to be careful with it, and let's see what it can do."

Zephyr moved closer to me, concerned. I reached out and rested my hand on his shoulder. He leaned into my touch, lowering his head and giving me a sense of approval even if he was worried.

After taking a deep breath to help steady my emotions, I reached out with my mind again. As soon as I connected with the stone, it attempted to suck more power out of me, but I did my best to fight that part, biting the inside of my lip to give me something else to focus on and stop myself from giving in to the temptation.

When I felt as if I could handle that, I turned to the pillars and the forcefield they created. Standing this close to the portal, I was strong enough that outside the field, I could reach for the pillar and the center of it. If I'd wanted to, I could have torn it apart. But I didn't, so I simply reached out to control the air around it.

At first, the stone seemed to do nothing, happy to let me use what was left of my power as I fought to get closer. The air pillar was strong. Stronger than the one in Mexico, and it wasn't easy to fight its control. Of course, I was getting practiced at taking ownership and keeping it.

My powers were still drained compared to their normal level, and I was soon feeling the dull beginnings of the headache that let me know I was taxing myself too much. It wasn't long before I felt the stone kick in, the power coming out of it matching what I was doing. Instead of it giving me control of the air element in the field, however, it seemed to take it for itself.

I frowned, not sure what to do with air that neither I controlled nor the pillar. After activating the stone, it didn't make sense for me to fight its control, but I didn't know how to manipulate what it held onto.

*It makes sense that it would take control itself if non-air elementals are supposed to use it*, Zephyr pointed out. That helped me feel better about it, but as it took control of more, seeming to hold it with ease, I worried.

While the stone was draining, I could feel it beginning to tug power out of me as well, as if it were far easier to resist when it was fuller. Not sure what to do, I stopped and let go of the air I'd taken, but I noticed the stone continued to hold on, not using anywhere near as much energy to keep control as it had taken to establish the connection.

I briefly explained what I thought was happening to Minsheng, noticing he looked at the device and how the readings had changed over the same length of time. Although I was fascinated, I was also growing more uncomfortable again. This tablet seemed to be both trouble and something amazing.

Before Minsheng could suggest how I proceed, there

was a spike in the readings. I noticed the familiar fluctuation from the forcefield, the not-quite-dormant portal suddenly emitting a lot of energy.

Without thinking, I stepped closer to the barrier between me and the portal field. I had connected to the air not too far from this edge, and I felt someone reach out. Another mind in the space between worlds.

It had been some time since I'd connected to anyone through the portals, the knowledge that something evil lurked on the other side having kept me from daring in case I was latched onto by the presence that had barged its way into my mind.

Now, however, the stone seemed to make that decision for me, whoever was on the other side finding the connections easily and latching on to us.

I gasped as pain ran through me, knowing this was exactly the evil we'd feared. Not only was it holding onto me and my mind, but I could also feel the bond between my mythicals and me taking strain, and as one, the four of us stepped a fraction closer.

"What happened?" the major asked, his voice full of panic, but the sound somewhere at the back of my mind.

The stone in my hand grew hotter, burning and hurting to hold. But I couldn't let go of it either. The creature on the other side of the portal was drawing from the fragment of the tablet, taking control of the air pillar and attacking it as the stone and runes fed off me.

With whatever was happening to my mythicals concerning me far more, I merely held the tablet and pushed at the connection I'd been forced to endure. It held fast, seeming to dig in tighter, exactly as it had done the previous time I was connected.

The pain grew, and I could feel my bond weakening in a way that added to the ache in my body.

"Aella?" Minsheng said. "What's happening? The forcefield is weakening, and the stone is doing strange things."

I couldn't reply, just gritted my teeth and fought harder. Whatever this was, I didn't plan to let it keep doing this.

"Aella, you need to drop the stone." Minsheng came toward me, but the major put out a hand to stop him, pointing at the forcefield and then the air pillar. It was beginning to glow too, but a different color. And the whole area was shaking.

"It's breaking," Minsheng added and came to me again.

I could briefly register their words, concentrating on fighting the connection to my bond and me. It was as if it was something trying to steal them from me and bond with them. There was no way I was allowing that.

Finally reaching around and attacking from a side, I felt some of the pain lessen, but I was also draining fast.

"Aella. You need to stop this right now!" Minsheng yelled.

The words finally cut through to me as I pushed the grip off my mythicals and noticed the pain in my head and hand. The stone had burned me, but it was also still drawing power from me.

While I refocused, my mind swirling with the desire to keep feeding it but the understanding that Minsheng was insistent about something important, I could barely do anything but stare at the fragment I held.

Before I could do more than blink in what felt like slow

motion, the major pulled out a dart gun. The sound of it firing came to my ears as if out of a mist. A moment later, I noticed the feathers of a dart sticking out of my chest.

It added to my woozy state and stung, but I could still feel the stone drawing my power, the elven metabolism I possessed stopping me from succumbing to the same dose of this thing as the humans would have done.

*Shut it off, Aella*, Zephyr's voice demanded, but it was as if he came to me in a dream, the burning sensation in my hand the only clear part.

I blinked as another feathery dart appeared in the center of my chest, and the world started to go dark.

As I crumpled, my eyes closing, I found my hand letting go and the stone falling out of it, leaving behind a strange mark.

Fighting the sleepy feeling that threatened to overwhelm me, I looked at Zephyr, Roth, and Sen, wanting to check they were still okay. I felt as if my bond had returned, but I wanted to be sure.

Zephyr's scaly face was the last thing I saw before I passed out entirely.

## CHAPTER EIGHT

Waking with a start, I sat and bumped my head into the side of Zephyr in dragon form. I didn't move or say anything, checking that I hadn't gone crazy and that Zephyr was still bonded to me and I still had ten toes.

*No, you've lost one. We had to cut it off. It's still numb, and you're getting phantom feelings from where it used to be*, Zephyr said.

I couldn't figure out if he was serious and wriggled my toes before finally opening my eyes to check them.

Hearing Zephyr chuckle, I frowned when I realized I had all my toes, and they were fine. It had been a silly comment, but it had distracted me from the real pain.

My hand was on fire, and I had a strange ache in my stomach. As I stared at my bandaged limb, I felt the memories come flooding back.

*I'm sorry*, I said to my three mythicals near me. *I was careless, and I let things get out of control. And it hurt all of us.*

*You had no way to know that was what would happen.*

*Whatever was on the other side of the portal turned up when they don't normally.*

*As if it sensed us,* I added to Zephyr's words.

*Possibly.*

*We need to be more careful. We can't let something like that happen again.*

*No. I think all of us agree on that.* Zephyr got up, his tail slowly uncurling from around me.

The movement made the pain worse, but I couldn't lay here forever. Slowly I got up as well, easing myself with the other hand and standing.

*How long have I been out?* I asked once I was on my feet and the pain had faded to a dull background ache again.

*Most of the rest of the day.*

*Shitsticks,* I thought.

It probably meant we'd lost the hope of recovering the tablets from the cult. I dreaded to think what they would do with them and be capable of. Did they know what the tablets could do? What a single fragment was capable of?

I shuddered at the thought of taking them on now, even if we could find them before they got back to Mexico with them.

*Ronan thinks they're nearby, and they're resting too,* Zephyr continued.

*He's come back?*

*He used the communication stone while you were sleeping. Asked if we'd put together a group of elves and soldiers to take them back.*

I exhaled, not sure if we had enough between everyone on the base. If the elves in the cult knew what to do with the rune-covered tablets, we were in a lot of trouble.

*Not if we attack swiftly. They won't have time to charge them and still have anything left to attack*, Zephyr pointed out as he backed up and motioned to the door.

A soldier had come to knock, but the door was ajar, and our eyes met before he could.

"The major sends his apologies and thought you might be hungry," the soldier said.

I lifted my eyebrows as I spotted the tray the soldier carried. It bore the largest plate of food I'd ever seen. A large steak dressed in mushroom sauce, fries, salad, and a large array of different drinks. Finally, there was the largest slice of chocolate cake I'd ever had the fortune to discover.

*We all ate a little while ago*, Zephyr said. *You should get your energy back.*

Needing no persuasion, I motioned for the soldier to come in and put it down. He did so, and with more care and kindness than I expected, cut up the meal for me so I could eat it with my one good hand.

Not wanting to wait, I decided to eat my meal in the wrong order and started with the chocolate cake. It tasted divine, and much to the soldier's amusement was soon gone.

Despite the others having eaten already, Sen happily ate some cake, her small face and eyes lighting up at the rich taste.

If I hadn't been in pain, the meal would have been perfect. It was the escape and calm I needed to relax and recharge.

By the time I was done eating, word had traveled

through the base that I was awake again, and I received my first visitor.

Minsheng looked apologetic as he came to me.

"It's okay," I said before he could open his mouth and say sorry. "We did what we thought was for the best. I'll live, and so will everyone else."

He nodded and sat down, filling me in on everything he'd learned despite the danger.

It was clear the tablet fragment was effective and that it could be used to power all sorts, but it had limits. It was hungry, and while it was efficient and potent at certain tasks, I had a feeling that it wasn't going to be the things useful for creating hard, sharp blasts of air in battle but more used to generate air shields and barriers. Things that didn't tend to go up in a hurry or require too much maintenance.

"I also spoke to the organization again while you were out," Minsheng continued as I finally finished eating and sat back, stuffed. "They had some more information they found in their archives. They think these tablets were created before the pillars and before the portals were ever shut down. They're not the same as the one the cult had several months ago."

"So they have a different primary purpose." I nodded; it made sense.

"There's a bunch of theories. But the organization thinks the cult probably wants them for various reasons and might not be aware they can help to open the portal."

I wasn't entirely sure that was a comforting statement, but I was pleased that my Shishou didn't sugarcoat it. I was going to need all the information I could get.

A part of me was excited about these tablets. Once I could work out how to use one without hurting myself, they could prove exactly the useful thing we needed.

Most importantly, however, with the information the organization had on the tablet uses, how they could be detected when used, and Ronan's information, it appeared as if we could not only find the cult elves again to retrieve them a second time but track the elves if they moved on.

It was the good news I needed to wake up to.

Not wasting any more time, I took the painkillers the base doctor had given me and grabbed my away bag again. It was time to get the troops in order.

As more people had realized I was awake and getting ready to head out again, I noticed there were plenty milling about, packed bags obvious. The major was organizing something and giving orders as food, equipment, and more weapons piled up.

"Looks like you're planning to come with me," I said when I noticed he also had a pack at his feet.

"Of course. I don't like being defeated, and someone needs to be around to shoot you with a trank dart if you get sucked into something dodgy again." He winked at me as he finished speaking.

I instinctively lifted a hand to my chest where the darts had hit me and rubbed the spot. It was still tender, but the pain would soon fade.

"I've never met anyone who needed three of these things to take them out, though."

"Three?" I asked. I only remembered two.

"Yeah. I knew you elves could take two, so I hit you with those pretty quickly, but you didn't go down, and the pillar was still shaking. I did the only thing I could think of and hit you again. That did the trick. Made the doc panic, though. Apparently, that's too many in a normal situation."

"My elven nature probably handled that too," I replied as I surveyed the list the major had and noticed he had names as well as equipment.

It seemed someone had been putting my team together for me while I slept. Grinning, I approved the list and added more names, hoping no one would object to me volunteering them. Mostly they were elves, but I included the two soldiers who had seen me right so far. Frank and Rick were starting to feel like part of the family.

"The general said he wanted some of those to stay here, but I don't think he'll argue with you requesting them personally," the major said. "And the President has said he'll send more men."

"The Sanctuary said more elves were willing to come here so others with more experience could aid you," Minsheng said as he came to join me again.

This time I noticed that Daisy was with him. She grinned, carrying a new shiny rifle that fired tranquilizers.

"I showed them how good I was with a gun, and someone found me this to use," she said, grinning from ear to ear.

I chuckled, hearing Zephyr do the same, and gave her a hug. While I'd slept and been recovering, it appeared more of my friends had volunteered, and we were about to make the elves wish they'd not taken those tablets.

Feeling ready for battle and the pain fading in my hand enough that I could ignore it and almost forget about it while busy, I helped everyone get ready, physically lugging ammo, weapons, food, and camping equipment onto several large trucks the Army had provided.

As I surveyed everything and the efficient team loading, I marveled once more at how much better it was having the US as an ally and how far I'd come. I might not have united everyone or changed the minds and hearts of the entire population, but I'd begun making a difference. *We'd* begun making a difference. Every mythical and soldier had created a tolerance and respect that I hoped would bleed out into the whole population.

By the time everything was loaded and everyone knew where they were traveling in the convoy and who they reported to, we had approached another mealtime.

Although I was eager to move out, I didn't want to push everyone so hard that it was detrimental. We opted to eat one more meal together, and everyone else who was off-duty came to join us.

The mood while we ate was strange. Almost party-like, though we had danger ahead of us and not something to celebrate. As if everyone wanted to make sure they lived and enjoyed something on the small chance they didn't come back. Or came back less whole.

It was something I could also get behind. And someone must have told the chef that we had a tradition with pizza and battles because the largest pepperoni pizza was brought out and placed in front of Zephyr, taking up an entire round table.

His mouth fell open in a grin, and he didn't wait for it to cool before he began devouring it. Before it was gone, he let Sen, Roth, and I have some, but normal-sized pizzas kept coming too, and I ate more than enough of those.

Only after everyone sat back, full and beginning to quiet down, did I decide it was time to go. The major and I got up. Neither of us needed to say anything as everyone else responded. After clearing the mess we'd made, our team headed to the waiting vehicles.

We knew what was going to be required of us. Knew we could be walking into something unknown and painful. Knew the elves were going to be as determined as we were, if not more. But we also knew we had each other's backs.

*Is this what it's like to be part of an army?* I asked Zephyr as I walked beside him out into the main courtyard.

*Yes. To know each person with you will fight and die for you if need be. And to know you're fighting for the same thing. To protect everyone else.*

A ripple of pride and anticipation went through me. I could do that. I could fight alongside these men, women, and mythicals to protect everyone else.

When I looked at Zephyr, I saw the light in his eyes and didn't need to be connected to his head to know he felt the same. As I turned my attention to everyone else, it wasn't just us either. Everyone felt it.

Now we had to make the cult feel it.

## CHAPTER NINE

Flying above the convoy on Zephyr added to the pride I felt as we moved out. The large dragon glided effortlessly through the sky, barely having to use any energy to keep up with the trucks as we rolled out.

Minsheng had the communication stone to talk to Ronan, as well as the device that would help guide us toward the cache of tablets and the centaurs keeping an eye on them.

I looked down at the troupe coming with me this time and knew there had to be over a hundred lives between us all. It was the best of the elves except for the masters in the Sanctuary, and it was some of the best soldiers as well, the base already full of the Army's most skilled members.

It felt strange to think we'd gotten to this point in only a few short years, and I found myself thinking back to the days I'd been a struggling waitress in LA, barely making enough to pay my rent. No safety net and no major friends.

*Whatever happens, finding you was the best thing to ever happen to me,* I said to Zephyr. *I wouldn't ever change it.*

*Hatching in your arms was the best beginning a dragon could have hoped for,* he replied. *So many of my ancestors didn't get to bond at all, let alone bond with the most powerful elf to ever live. The honor is mine.*

*Sen honored,* the dryad added.

*And I am also very honored.* Roth's musical voice followed the others. *There may be danger ahead of us, but I feel as I know Sen and Zephyr do. We are by your side, to work with you to protect this planet and everyone on it, mythical, human, elf, dwarf, it doesn't matter. We will serve.*

Grinning and ready for battle, I settled into flying, gently testing my abilities, reaching for the air around, the earth below, and the water vapor in the clouds above. I didn't do much with it, not wanting to drain my power at all, but I made sure I was in top form and ready.

My reach was still growing, and with each day I pushed and practiced with my mythicals, we became a better team, faster, stronger, and more in tune with each other. I was blessed, even knowing that there was a large cult I was up against.

We traveled as a group for a couple of hours, the sun setting as we did. We had to slow near the end of our journey as our course took us down another dirt track and we discussed the merits of waiting until nightfall once more. We wanted to give ourselves every advantage we could.

As the trucks pulled into a small clearing in a wooded area to one side of the road, Zephyr landed, and I slid off his back. With Roth coming down on the other side of me a moment later, I hurried over to Minsheng and the major.

They were looking at the map and the device Minsheng held.

"How far away are we?" I asked.

"A mile or two, I think," Minsheng replied. "And we're not far from finding Ronan."

"Then we should get everyone to wait here. It's not long until full dark. I want to get closer and liaise with the centaurs. Work out what we might be up against if possible," I said.

The major didn't disagree, giving some orders and putting another officer in charge of the camp.

"Cover the trucks as best you can and hide yourselves in the trees. Get the elves to help with that. And don't kill anything."

The soldiers saluted, and I had Seth come to take charge of the rest of the elves and gave a similar command.

"We'll see it done. Be safe and let us know when you need us. Ronan can communicate with me if needed."

"Good to know. Make sure the soldiers are included in any conversations you have," I said, motioning to the officer who had been put in charge of the human contingent. It was unexpected, and I doubted a human had been invited into a connection stone conversation with a centaur in a long time, if ever, but the trust had to keep flowing, and I hoped Ronan would understand.

Seth gave me a nod, though he glanced sideways at the soldier he was to work with. I hoped that neither of them would screw anything up as I went with several of the warehouse elves, Daisy, Minsheng, the major, and my mythicals to find out what was going on.

We moved quietly, but just in case, I used an air barrier

to keep the sounds of our passing from traveling forward. I also reached outward to feel the air in every direction, wanting to know if we came close to an air elemental. Emily did the same with the water and Erlan with fire, leaving me to feel for the earth.

It wasn't the easiest way to move, but I wanted to know the second we came close to the cult or any lookouts they had. In our recent training, we'd focused on our range, knowing it was one way we were more powerful than the cult and intending to make use of any advantage we had.

After about a mile, I felt movement ahead, the trees thinning and the creatures less active. It didn't take me long to make out the shape of a centaur, looking away from us.

As we moved closer, I could feel more of them spread out in an arc that bent around a target. It made me relieved. If Ronan had his centaurs watching a single location, there was a good chance our quarry was still in place.

I let the others know in a whisper, and we made a direct line for one of them. It didn't take long for Dyneira to hear us and turn, the grin on her face making it clear she was pleased to see us.

When we were close enough to see each other clearly, I bowed low as the centaurs did to show respect. She stepped closer, however, placing a hand on my shoulder and bowing to me. I leaned in until our foreheads met, aware this was another level of honor.

"Blood sister. Henera," Dyneira whispered. "I am honored to be aiding you once again. Ronan would see you. He's two centaurs over and has much to tell you."

"Thank you, Dyneira. It is you who honors me with

your trust and faith. We will all act the stronger for you being with us."

Her eyes lit up at my words, and we bowed to each other one last time. When I turned to head toward Ronan, I noticed Minsheng was staring at me, a smile and a look on his face that spoke of happiness. It was almost overwhelming, and it was the first time anyone had looked at me like that. I tried not to cry, knowing something I hadn't before. Someone was proud of me.

*He's not the only one*, Zephyr said. *No matter what happens, and even when you make a mistake, you do everything you can to make things right and protect people. You've got a good heart.*

I nodded, knowing I'd made plenty of mistakes, but I was surrounded by people who were helping me overcome my flaws and make this work as a whole.

Feeling as if we might be able to do what we needed after all, but still very in the dark about how these tablets worked and what we might be facing, I made my way to Ronan. An entire troupe of mythicals and soldiers came with me.

Ronan heard us coming. He glanced our way, his eyes on the building ahead. I moved to his side, aware he was only this focused when there was something important in his line of sight.

"I think they're on the move," he whispered. "But it's hard to tell. It's as if they know we're out here."

"They have a powerful air elf. One they didn't have the last time I clashed with them," I replied. "It's the only explanation for events so far."

"That does complicate things somewhat."

"Tell me what you know?"

"They left the tunnel partway through and then traveled light to here. They've got some good earth elves helping cover their tracks, but once we knew we were looking for something an earth elf had cleaned up, it was easier to follow them. The area they'd traveled was...too clean, with animal tracks that crossed the path but vanished in between."

I blinked, taking in Ronan's quiet words as he explained. This was a way of tracking that hadn't occurred to me. Once again, I was grateful for the centaur beside me.

"Then Minsheng told us what to look for with the tablets they're carrying, and the rest was easy. It led us here. They've been here all day and we've seen some of their scouts, but they're too quiet now, even for the time of night. Something is going on, and I don't think it bodes well."

"You mentioned that you think they know we're here. What do you think they might be waiting for?" I asked, not sure of the answer to the question but knowing it would be something useful.

*Charging the tablets*, Zephyr said. *They're resting in shifts after charging the tablets.*

My blood ran cold at the thought of it, making me shudder. I hoped my dragon was wrong.

Ronan looked over to me, taking in my reaction and then glancing at Zephyr.

"I take it I'm not the only one who has a theory," the centaur whispered.

"No. We need to be prepared for the tablets to be in use and loaded."

"Then we shouldn't wait any longer," Ronan replied. "If we are to stand any chance, we must make our move before they get stronger or can recharge any further."

"I'm inclined to agree," I said, but the major frowned, and Minsheng didn't look as convinced. It was going to be difficult to persuade them if they were not ready.

"I don't think it's worth pushing ourselves if we can't win this. We need more information, Aella," the major said.

I frowned. More information would be useful, but I wasn't sure of the best way to get it. While they were sitting there, I didn't think I could walk away and let them run again.

"I'm going to get closer. I want an earth elf with me. A good one. And the device," I said, holding my hand out.

Before anyone could volunteer or suggest an earth elf, Zephyr morphed into human form and came to my side.

*I'm not letting you go toward danger without me, and I can use the earth as well as if not better than you can*, he explained, not looking at anyone else although the major gaped. He'd not seen the dragon transform the last time, although everyone else close by had seen it at least once.

I wasn't going to argue with Zephyr, so I nodded and refocused on the task. Minsheng handed me the device that would let me know what was going on, then I reached for the air.

I hesitated, knowing this could be a bad idea. After all, they wanted and needed Zephyr and me, and we were going straight to them without much in the way of backup.

"If it looks like we're going to get ourselves in trouble and you can do something about it, do so. But otherwise, get everyone safe," I said to the major, Minsheng, and Ronan.

"We won't let them take you," Minsheng replied, but I saw the look on Ronan's and the major's faces. Both were battle commanders, where Minsheng was our guide and the closest thing we had to family a lot of the time. Ronan and the major would do as we asked.

With that done, I turned to Zephyr again and slipped my fingers into his.

*Keep the ground from betraying our movement, and I'll do the same with the air.*

*Got it,* he replied, giving my fingers a gentle squeeze.

Not needing to talk had its uses, but we still left Sen and Roth behind, controlling the air around us and once again feeling for the mind of the powerful air elf who lay before us.

Every few yards, I glanced at the device I carried, not sure what it would do but noting that Minsheng had put it into a recording mode. Although I didn't know what it was telling me, my Shishou would.

Moving as quietly as we could, we crouched lower as the cover grew sparser, moving between bushes and other vegetation to hide.

When we'd crossed about half the distance between Ronan and the building ahead, a large barn by the outline of it, the device came to life, the display it had showing readings fluctuating and moving. I turned it, pretty sure it was pinpointing a specific location as well as indicating to us what it had picked up.

It was telling me that the tablets were in that building and that they were at a certain strength, but I wasn't sure what else. We got fifty yards closer. From this distance, my abilities were strong enough that I could feel the air inside the barn, but I had to be careful.

If I could detect when other elementals of my type were present and reach out to control their affinity, there was a good chance this air elf they had could do the same.

That said, there hadn't been any sign of air elves, or other types, holding onto anything outside of the building. It was almost as if they didn't care who might be around and if they were detected at all.

But that wasn't likely to be true. These elves had a plan.

*We're going to have to take the risk. If we do it from here, I can be prepared to turn back into a dragon and fly off with you before they can unleash too much on us.*

A rush of warmth and determination came across the bond from Zephyr, and I nodded. It was worth the try. We needed to find out what was on the other side of those walls.

Taking a deep breath, I sat down and concentrated. This was going to require a greater deal of precision and a softness to my approach, something I had not practiced as much as I should have.

Not sure I was doing it right but knowing it was my best, I reached out again. I couldn't feel anyone outside the barn. At least, not on this side. I didn't dare wrap my abilities all the way around when I wasn't sure where the air elf was. Instead, I focused on the area the tablets were in, finding a slight gap between two wooden panels to link to the air inside.

I had barely moved forward when I felt the edge of another mind. Quickly I retreated, hoping they'd not felt me intruding. It was strange to be so cautious when normally I was the stronger elf who challenged those around me, throwing my weight around, but I couldn't afford that approach this time.

Knowing it was my fault if I found this difficult, I took another deep breath and closed my eyes. I had to work out a way to feel what was inside the barn without getting caught doing it.

Once more I reached out, looking for another way into the building. I had to find another crack farther over, but this time I reached out and found a clean space of air, no mind or other elf in the space. Slowly I reached deeper until I brushed against the mind of another again.

This time I didn't withdraw so quickly or as fast. Instead, I hung out of mental reach and worked out if it was someone I recognized. Given that the tablets also reached for the elements and controlled them, it was possible that it couldn't detect me.

Slowly I inched closer until I could feel that it wasn't the tablets, however. It was the air elf. They were controlling the space around the tablets if my mind was detecting it correctly.

*I believe you're right*, Zephyr said. *Can you push past their control in a way they won't notice?*

*Maybe. It's a risk, though.*

*Everything we're doing right now is a risk, but if we're to get what we need and the information needed to attack, we must take it. We have always been willing to risk our lives for others in the past. This is no different.*

I nodded, knowing Zephyr was right. We were doing something we'd always done. It was a new way of doing it.

Knowing I was almost there, I reached out again, skirting down to the ground and trying to find a route across the floor where the air elf might have been lazy, or there might be a draft that wasn't being monitored.

It seemed to work, my mind able to catch a breeze and follow it to where it moved and lifted over the crate the tablets had been in when we'd first seen them.

I could feel the power emanating out of the crate, the clear draw of more air tablets inside, almost begging me to connect and offer more of what I had. I could fight it as if the barrier between them and me made it easier, but I was still wary.

With enough information in that regard, I once more retreated my control. As I did, it was as if the air elf came to life. I felt the reach pursuing me as I pulled back.

*We've been detected*, I said to Zephyr, knowing I sounded panicked.

*Keep going. Feel how many of them there are, and then we'll get out of here.*

Part of me wanted to argue with Zephyr, but we had to get the information if we could, and I didn't want to let the others down. I kept pushing back at the elf inside and searching for the number of elves and their outlines.

I quickly counted, moving faster than ever.

## CHAPTER TEN

*Time to go*, I said as I counted thirty-two elves inside the barn and then retreated with my mind. There was no way I was sticking around any longer than I needed to.

*If they've not spotted us, we should continue to be stealthy,* Zephyr replied, taking my hand in his again.

I wanted to argue and run, but Zephyr was right. It made sense to evade what was coming if we could and have time to brief the others on what we'd learned.

Inside I had the nagging feeling that there was a chance the elves would run rather than fight, however. Then it would make our lives harder. But there was no way we could get our entire unit here to attack fast enough. Most of them were over a mile away, where we'd parked the trucks.

Moving as swiftly as we dared, Zephyr and I kept low and moving between vegetation again. It was harder to be careful and mask us when I was also trying to reach out to find the air elf and his control and work out if they knew where we were or not.

Zephyr focused on keeping the ground around us from betraying our movement while we hurried back.

I was relieved when we got to Ronan and the others and there was still no sign of the elves from the cult coming in pursuit, but it made me worry that they were fleeing rather than trying to fight us.

"We would need backup, anyway," Minsheng said when I voiced this and what I'd learned.

"We need to take those tablets back before they can run with them all," I replied. "Even if we only get some of them or stop some of their elves."

"Aella has a point. If we never attack, we will never stop them," Ronan's deep voice added to my request.

Eventually, the major nodded.

"Okay. Can you communicate with everyone we left behind and tell them to get here as soon as possible? We'll go in for an attack as soon as we can organize one. With the aim to capture tablets and reduce numbers, but not at the expense of any lives of our own."

I nodded. It wasn't as aggressive as I'd have been, but it was an attack, and it was better than nothing. By the time I looked at Ronan, he was in a trance. I waited, wishing I knew what was being said in his mind.

At the same time as the conversation was happening, Zephyr turned himself back into a dragon. Sen and Roth also prepared for battle, arming themselves. Sen donned her suit of dragon-scale armor, then came to my side.

There weren't many soldiers with us, but I suggested Minsheng and Daisy stick with them while I gathered the elves we had and the mythical creatures we sported.

We quickly agreed to split the focus. Our job as elves

was to counter any attacks and defend everyone, especially anyone out in front and the centaurs. The soldiers were to use their weapons to knock out elves, and the centaurs would make a collective run on the tablets to try to collect at least one of them each.

It was a rough plan, and I had no idea if it would work, but I was soon in the air on Zephyr's back, ready to lead the group into battle.

By the time the centaurs had come close enough together, forming two groups on opposite sides and everyone else was ready, I was sure we would have lost hope of catching anyone. But the moment we were ready, we moved with a speed that took me by surprise.

The last time we'd closed the gap between us and the building, it had taken several minutes and felt tense and as if I had to focus. This time we flew across it in less than ten seconds, and I was intent on one thing: following the centaur group led by Ronan and keeping a barrier of air around them and the ground steady under their feet.

Emily and Erlan were focused on protecting them from the other two elements and followed, Emily riding on a large centaur's back to keep up. Roth and Sen also rode with them, making sure they could work with Emily, and Sen could fire darts if needed.

Zephyr was focused on flying us ahead of the group, intending to use his body to deflect attacks as he often did for me.

When we reached the barn, we didn't find it empty, but some of the elves had left, and it was very possible that all the tablets had gone with them. I wanted to swear, but I concentrated as the centaurs, soldiers, and elves were spotted.

This created panic among the cult elves, but they soon formed up around something I couldn't make out. It gave me some hope back, and I pointed it out to Zephyr. He dove in that direction.

The centaurs also responded, powering forward as I did everything I could to keep my air box around them and the earth steady under their feet. I could feel the assault of the other elves as they wrestled past my control. At the same time, the earth elf must have been working on something as I found myself having to steal control from another.

Pushing and feeling forward with my mind I butted against a powerful earth element but noticed they had a weaker ally in their midst. Someone whose mind gave almost instantly when I came knocking. It gave me more control of the earth, but the centaurs weren't far off the elves and the soldiers were close enough they could see and fire their weapons.

The fight seemed to explode into a flurry of activity that threatened to break my concentration and overwhelm everyone below us, as we attacked a smaller group of elves.

With our backup still a long way away, the soldiers had their work cut out for them and despite them aiming well, there was one air elf who seemed to know where to blast the air so it knocked the darts out of it before any of them got as far as the Amcika elves.

It was frustrating but couldn't be helped. As Zephyr flew back again, circling to keep over the battlefield, I took a deep breath and focused. I was going to have to break this stalemate.

While still protecting the centaurs who had slowed while they were under scrutiny, I unleashed a barrage of air on the cult elves. Some of them staggered backward, and others fought it, but it broke the group and allowed the centaurs to rush in.

Facing eight of the large mythicals, the cult elves broke their formation further, several darting out of the way of the thundering hooves and aggressive presence of the centaurs.

I used the air to give the parting elves a helping hand, pushing two of them off their feet and out into the open. The soldiers, Daisy, and Minsheng seized the moment, and before long, three darts were sticking out of one of them and two out of the other.

It turned the tide in our favor, but the centaurs lost their momentum, something invisible appearing to block their path. Something I'd not noticed before now.

Reaching with my mind, I found a barrier forming across most of the elves. It was made of air and what felt like ice. Something cold and frosty, but also only air. It was a technique to make a barrier that I'd not seen or felt before, and I studied it.

The warmth had been slowly sucked out of the area and it had been almost frozen. It was strange but effective at making it harder to get through. I wasn't sure how an air elemental could do something like it alone, but I tried not to let that distract me.

Aware I still had a lot to learn about my powers and feeling the familiar connection of the elusive air elf who had to be hiding nearby, I broke through it, pushing for control. I was resisted at every turn, and it didn't help that

I was riding Zephyr and having to keep changing where I looked.

Thankfully, Zephyr soon picked up on what I needed to focus on and began circling the spot. It left us vulnerable to other forms of attack, and it meant we weren't protecting the centaurs as much. There was nothing else that made sense. I wasn't the only elf on the battlefield, but I was probably the only one who could deal with this.

I felt the air elf slip his control out, giving me a portion of the barrier. I tore it apart, making the area warmer and getting the almost stationary particles moving again. I then blew air through it, unable to communicate with the centaurs to let them know they had a path to get to the elves as they regrouped on the other side of the box, meeting the eight centaurs who had ridden in from the opposite entrance.

They couldn't detect what I had done, and I thought we were going to miss the chance to make use of it as the air elf attacked my mind and grip, trying to force me out again. Before he could, Sen and Roth rode up together, the small myconid leaping down and getting through the gap before anyone could stop her.

Despite my attempts to hold on, I was pushed out of the area by the other mind, a pain stabbing into my head momentarily as if I'd been hit by the full power of another strong elf. I growled and concentrated again as Sen darted about, trying to help from inside the barrier.

Although there were loads of cult elves in the barrier-protected area with her and she was without backup, they mostly appeared to leave her alone, one or two trying to half-heartedly grab her with their hands as she darted around them, but they focused more on attacking the centaurs with their abilities than they did anything else.

I swore as I noticed they were edging toward the door and a way out of the field behind the barn. We were throwing everything we had at them, and it wasn't having much of an impact.

As Zephyr circled, I could feel his response as he also grew frustrated, little more he could do when a barrier rendered his breath weapon useless, and we couldn't have him take human form yet.

Not wanting to waste his ability and knowing we needed to find this air elf and stop this barrier, I flew off Zephyr's back and landed in the middle of the field. I held the barrier around the centaurs and Roth, protecting them while the other elves countered direct attacks, but as soon as I landed, more of them came my way.

The elves turned on me, but I held the air around me, mimicking what I'd learned until I stood behind an ice-like wall. None of the attacks got through, but a slight tremor almost knocked me off my feet.

*I'm going to find that elf*, Zephyr said. The tug in my stomach grew as he flew to one side.

I didn't reply, having to concentrate too hard on defending myself and attacking the barrier that protected the elves.

The group was still moving away from the building, but their progress was slow. If this continued much longer, I would win since I and Erlan and Emily would last longer than the elves fighting us.

It looked like they were going to waver, and I could feel a slip in the barrier, my mind creating another small opening as Sen managed to grab a tablet out of a shoulder bag and jump clear with it.

She ran for the opening as I directed her, and I formed a bubble around her as the centaurs charged in again. Ronan scooped her up as they ran past and handed her off into the center of the pack, along with Roth.

Feeling better for having taken one of the ancient tablets and aware two elves still lay unconscious by the doors of the barn, I prepared to turn the tide. I moved closer to the elves and put everything I had into breaking down more of the barrier. Once more, the air elf fought back, his mind hitting me far harder than before.

I physically reeled as not only was I pushed out of his barrier, but my control of the barrier protecting me was challenged.

*They must be using a tablet*, Zephyr said. I had to stop moving and fight to keep my defenses up.

Not sure what to do but endure and hope it was drained soon, I felt for Sen and Roth. The cult elves reached for the tablets they each had. This fight was about to get a whole lot harder.

*Get everyone out of here. Retreat.*

*We're not leaving you*, Zephyr roared, hurtling back toward me.

I didn't reply but tipped my head to yell retreat at everyone else when I heard a commotion from the other side of the barn. More soldiers and elves appeared, pouring around both sides and quickly assessing the situation. Seth led one side, and the officer in charge led the other. They began giving orders.

Several air elves rushed to my sides, using their abilities

to move effortlessly and at a phenomenal speed across the ground. At the same time, Seth and Erlan joined their attacks to hurtle fire at the barrier around the elves.

Feeling the grass grow longer and seeing vines creep in made the cult elves react with fear of their own.

Instead of attacking us, they refocused on using their abilities to flee and defend themselves. I watched them speed up as the young female air elf with them used her tablet to power them forward. At the same time, an earth elf cut down the plant growth in their way and the fire and water elf hurled attacks and raw power, doing anything they could to distract us.

I kept the fires from spreading, dousing them with water, boxing them in with air, and sucking the heat out of that, but it was barely enough.

The tablets kept the power flowing and seemed to enhance everything the cult elves were doing. There was no way we could win this fight until they were drained, and I was aware there was a good chance that we were going to lose several of our elves' abilities before then. I could also feel my strength dwindling.

The cult elves were simply trying to run now, however, and there was nothing we could do to stop them as more attacks came from behind us where the rest of the cult must have been.

Zephyr landed in front of me, taking the brunt of several attacks to buy me and the air elves with me a breather, but it was all it did as more plants grew up, some trying to ensnare us and others trying to do the same to the cult.

It was chaotic and hard to tell what I should be

attacking or not. At the same time, the centaurs were caught out in the open, the tablet Sen had their priority to protect.

I focused on defending them again as more attacks came their way.

Zephyr and the air elves shifted with me as I encouraged Sen and Roth to bring their herd closer. The centaurs soon got the message, Ronan noticing Zephyr acting like a large shield and the three of us air elves working together to extend the barrier I'd created.

After quickly giving the elves instructions on how to make it cold, we finally bridged the gap, bringing the centaurs in behind Zephyr.

By the time they were safe, the cult elves were on the edge of the field. The soldiers had come up, still shooting despite the lack of hits. I was pretty sure they hit an elf now and then, but if the Amcika elves were anything like me, one wound wasn't enough to do anything more than slow them down. It wasn't going to get them to give up when they had the tablets fueling them.

The major called the fight off and ordered everyone to stand down as the attacks on us vanished and the elves fled, sped by the air elves among them. I watched them hurtle through the thin section of forest before they faded from view until Sen came to me, holding out the tablet she'd taken.

Looking around, I noticed a group of exhausted and spent elves, soldiers, and centaurs, one of the latter limping. On the ground were two elves, and in my hands was a single tablet.

This battle hadn't gone according to plan.

## CHAPTER ELEVEN

I connected to the tablet. The earth power it contained called to me to add more to it and encouraged me to let it out and use it for something, but I ignored both sensations.

"Hand out some food," I said as soon as Minsheng, the major, Seth, and Ronan were close. "Especially to the elves."

At the same time, I held the tablet out to Seth.

"Get this to your most controlled earth elf. Tell them to slowly fill it, but never to use their power."

Seth lifted his eyebrows as he took it. It seemed to glow less as if it sensed the lack of compatibility with him, which reassured me. If the tablets proved too addictive or problematic, I could get an elf of a different element to carry the tablets when they were not being filled in a controlled way.

The major didn't look happy, and I knew Ronan was concerned for his injured centaur.

"I'm sorry," I said. "That was unlike anything I expected, and I led you into a far greater danger than I'd realized."

"It happens," the major said. "You did your best to let us know what we were up against, but we should go back to the vehicles now. We can't follow them on foot."

It was my turn to be shocked, surprised that the major wanted to keep on, but Ronan slowly nodded, his chest heaving as he calmed his breathing down.

"My injured will need to ride in a truck. I would not ask them to run, and I think half my team should rest while the other half of us track. We may have been up against worse than we feared, but we still gained a small victory. One of the tablets is ours, and we have reduced their numbers, even if only by a little."

At the same time as Ronan spoke, Minsheng came forward with the device he carried. It was currently reacting to the tablet Seth was carrying to the elves he commanded, but now and then, it swung in the direction the cult elves had fled. It was picking up on them. It was his impetus to keep going too.

"If we attack them again, we will have a better strategy," I replied, setting my jaw as I lifted into the air and onto Zephyr's back. "In the meantime, we'll make sure we don't lose them. Get everyone ready to move out as soon as possible."

*Roth, stay with the centaurs, and Sen, stay with the soldiers. We'll keep everyone going in the right direction and plan another attack as soon as we can.*

I almost winced at the tone in my words, sending a wave of apologetic affection to my mythicals as Zephyr flew upwards again and took me with him. They weren't soldiers of mine to command into battle or wherever I wished. They were my bonded mythicals. Companions. Family.

*It's okay. Sometimes you are our general in battle. And that's right too. This is going to be one drawn-out war over those tablets with multiple battle sites. This is going to be the hardest thing we've faced yet. We'll have to keep thinking on our feet and hope it is enough.*

There was no argument from me as I hunkered down on Zephyr's back, reaching out with my mind to see if I could feel movement ahead and pinpoint the elves we pursued. The device in my hands was still torn, but it also slowly flicked more forward and to our right. I had Zephyr adjust the path we were flying, and we kept going.

I regularly checked in with Sen and Roth, making sure they were okay and getting updates.

The elves had helped everyone get to the vehicles with so much speed that they were soon on the move again, Sen riding with Minsheng in the first. I let what she could see fill my mind and smiled as I saw that Minsheng had begun working with one of the Army technicians to make something similar to the gadget I held.

Before long, we were going to be able to track these things.

Roth rode with Ronan, the centaurs helping find a path for our vehicles and working with two of the earth elves to make one if need be and at the same time making sure no more elves left or joined the party, tracking the old fashioned way.

I was grateful for the team of different mythicals and friends I had with me. It had been a difficult battle that had almost overwhelmed me on several occasions, but we should learn to combat it fast. With any luck, we'd hit them harder the next time.

Despite this gratitude and faith in everyone around me, I had a nagging doubt that wouldn't go away. This air elf was still an unknown. They were powerful and had knowledge and skills I'd never seen before. Who were they, and what had brought them into this ongoing war between the cult and me now?

It was an unknown that I truly didn't like. Another enemy like Jacobs who operated in the shadows and got others to front the fights for them. It was something I detested, but more than that. It was a riddle. Someone who had motives I couldn't fully work out. That made them an extremely difficult threat to deal with.

*We'll find them. And we'll stop them*, Zephyr said, his voice sounding determined as he continued to fly onward.

*I hope you're right*, I replied. *Because if we don't, they could potentially open the portals alone.*

*No. They might be able to break the air pillars, but not the others, and the others wouldn't be any easier. Not really. And whoever this is, they were also using a tablet. I'm sure of it.*

It had felt like it. I'd thought I had them beaten, and then they had hit me harder than ever. Even thinking about it, the pain seemed to come back and make me feel it again. Whoever they were, I'd not faced anyone quite like them before.

I tried not to worry too much about what they were capable of. Instead, I rested on Zephyr's back. After we'd been riding a while, I realized I'd forgotten to get any food before letting Zephyr carry me away. My powers would regenerate anyway, but food always made it faster, and now I'd thought of food, I was aware of how hungry I was.

We were flying out in the middle of nowhere, however. The elves we pursued appeared to deliberately be moving through the countryside, skirting towns and cities.

After flying for an hour, Zephyr and I detected something shifting that could only be elves at the same time, my mind touching on the outline of an elf in the air ahead as Zephyr spotted movement to the right of them.

He swooped lower, slowing and concentrating on flying as silently as possible. The sun wasn't up yet, but it wouldn't be much longer until the darkness would no longer hide our pursuit. As we got closer, I quickly realized the elves were joining the back of another group, the latter standing around what felt like vehicles.

Zephyr swung around, bringing us away before we could fly over, and then found a spot to land. As we set down, I used my abilities to help Zephyr land more slowly and stop the noise he made from traveling toward the cult. With that done, we crept closer, and I focused on the air.

I could feel the elves as they loaded the vehicles with supplies and the tablets, so many of the stones calling to my mind as I glossed over them. There didn't appear to be any sign of the air elf or their control. Had I worn them out?

There was no way to be sure, but I hoped it was true. If they were worn out, there was a good chance all I had to do to defeat them was endure. I still had energy left, even if it wasn't as much as I'd have liked.

As soon as I was sure the elves were going to be a little longer, I backed away with Zephyr.

Part of me wanted to attack them, but it wasn't a good idea. It would put us in trouble. If we'd been fresh and the air elemental hadn't been there, I might have stood a chance at working with Zephyr to take out another elf or two and maybe steal a tablet from someone. But as depleted and tired as I was, it was a bad idea.

On top of that, I was aware that pretty much everyone with me hadn't slept since the previous night, and it wasn't going to be long before dawn. Several of the soldiers had spent some of the previous night up and fighting alongside me in the first battle against the cult.

Everyone was tired, and we had far less to show for our attempts than I'd have liked.

We backed up as far as we dared while still being able to tell what was going on ahead of us and waited, watching and hoping that our cavalry arrived before the opportunity to attack a caravan in disarray presented itself.

Thankfully, it wasn't long before Ronan joined us with Roth. The centaurs were tired, their strong, lithe bodies picking their way through the forest. As they came closer, they covered the ground with their collective gaze.

As soon as I was noticed, they slowed, and Ronan came to me. I put a finger to my lips as I bowed to him. He bowed and then came to my side. Putting a hand on my shoulder and looking me in the face, he studied me.

"This fight weighs heavily on such young shoulders. It is almost as if they want to remind you of your age at every turn. Remind you that you are young and they have experience. But we will do what we can, and this will end one way or another with me knowing you have done your best. The centaurs are proud to stand beside you."

Ronan's words made tears want to fall from my eyes, but I held them back and very quietly told him everything we knew of the situation ahead and how it wasn't going to be easy to get the elves to give up more tablets nor reduce their numbers.

"It will be as it will be. It sounds as if you could do with rest also. And to eat. Go. Take the fastest method back to the main convoy and rest and eat with them as they come here. We will keep watch, and if they move out any time soon, we will pursue with Roth and have him send word to you, or I will use my stone."

I nodded, so grateful I couldn't speak. Although Ronan and the centaurs with him were tired, I needed to eat, and there was only one place I could get food right now. Hoping Roth didn't mind parting from me again, I gave him a brief stroke and sent another wave of affection across our bond.

After backing away from the group, Zephyr and I got into the air again, leaving the others behind as quietly as we could. I felt guilty that I was leaving them in the wilderness close to a dangerous enemy, but if I was going to lead everyone into battle again and do my best to protect them, I needed to recharge and be ready to fight.

I was also worried about Zephyr. He hadn't rested much, and while we were flying the way we were, there wasn't much opportunity for him to change that.

*Dragons don't need as much rest as humans or elves, remember. And I'm not doing much more than flying you everywhere you need to go.*

I was pretty sure I heard the frustration in his voice. It wasn't hard for me to work out what it was about.

*I couldn't do this without you. I know you want to play a bigger role, but what you are doing is invaluable.*

*And part of me knows that. But sometimes, I wish I was standing beside you in battle.*

*To be fair, sometimes you're standing over me, taking the hits I would otherwise be flattened by.*

*Good point. I make a good meat shield.*

*You make the best meat shield*, I replied, hearing him chuckle and grateful he'd taken it the way I'd intended it.

I lowered myself behind the large ridge on the back of Zephyr's head, letting his natural slipstream envelop me and help me stay seated with less effort, and rested, feeling him take me toward Sen, the small myconid letting us know exactly where we'd find Minsheng and the rest of the allies we had out here.

Within minutes Zephyr was circling again and getting lower.

*Fly off me. I'll stay in the air as long as you promise to bring me some snacks back with you.*

I chuckled and gave him an affirmative before activating my air abilities and flying myself down to land on top of the front moving truck. I wobbled, struggling to adjust from propelling myself to riding on the moving vehicle. As soon as I was stable, I shuffled to the back and knocked on the door from above.

Someone inside opened it as I felt Sen come closer, bounding through the length of the truck until she wasn't far from the door. I grinned down at her and used my abilities to swing down and into the truck. I landed beside Sen, and the nearest soldier pulled the door shut.

"Hi," I said as he stared at me, his eyes wide. "Thanks for letting me in."

I didn't give him a chance to respond before making my way through the wobbly truck to the front to talk to Minsheng and get some food.

My Shishou had a pile of sandwiches and assorted snacks to go with it on the seat beside him.

"Sen made it obvious you were going to be dropping in," he said as I lifted my eyebrows.

Grinning, I sat down and tucked in. I was surrounded by an awesome team.

## CHAPTER TWELVE

After a short rest and with a bag full of food and drinks, I was soon in the air with Zephyr. He'd told me not to worry about food shortly after passing a large cattle farm, and I had the feeling he'd found something he could eat in dragon form.

Not sure I wanted to ask what exactly, but respecting that he needed to eat a lot more while in dragon form to keep himself going, I didn't mention it. Instead, I asked Zephyr whether he needed to land any time soon.

*I won't deny that I'm tired, but we need to stop these elves. Have the others woken up yet?*

*No*, I replied, knowing Zephyr was talking about the few we'd captured. They'd been hit by trank darts and were out for the count still. It was a long time to be out cold for, but they'd been hit hard.

My focus was more on the Amcika elves ahead, however. They were dangerous, and every moment we left them was a moment they could fill the tablets and unleash hell on us.

Thankfully, the convoy of trucks and other Army vehicles had caught up to the centaurs following the Amcika elves and the rest of our allies despite the rough terrain. When I reached the centaurs, I understood why. They were standing, barely moving forward.

Zephyr and I landed as quietly as we could behind the line they were forming as they spread out. Roth was nearby, and he came close enough that I could stroke my hand down his flank.

I could feel the warmth and gratitude rushing off him, and I hoped this was the last time I had to leave him for a while. Zephyr and Roth with me, I made my way to Ronan, Dyneira, and another centaur who were deep in a discussion.

As I approached, they made space for us, and we bowed.

"They've stopped again. If they know we're here, then they're not reacting to us," Ronan said in a quiet voice.

"Then it gives us time to prepare and plan something better," I replied, grateful for the way he got straight to business.

"We'll know what to expect this time," Dyneira added, her eyes full of the same warmth as the last time we spoke.

I smiled back, grateful for the trust she was placing in me. Guilt filled me at not having been prepared enough or strong enough to handle the last two battles against this group of elves. This time, I had to be sure I had things under control and we were ready for whatever they could throw at us.

Within minutes, I was up to speed. The cult elves had found an abandoned building again. It was the middle of the day, and I didn't expect them to stay there long—perhaps until it was dark—but that gave us time to plan. Most of the soldiers had slept in the trucks while they had traveled, swapping out the drivers partway through the morning.

Although everyone had gotten far less sleep than they needed, they had fresh energy. The centaurs had been up for far too long, and I relieved as many as I could from duty. They were better trackers than anyone else, and I wanted them to take the opportunity to rest. In their place, I surrounded the building the cult was in with other mythicals, using the fire salamanders, Sen, Roth, Zephyr, and me to cover the majority of the area along with some other creatures from the Sanctuary.

It was less conventional, but most of the mythicals operated on less sleep than humans, and most of them were bonded with an elf who could raise the alarm far quicker than the centaurs could. It made the most sense for them to be our lookouts.

I was soon joined at my position by Minsheng, Seth, the major, and Ronan to figure out the best way to attack and take as many tablets as possible. We agreed that we needed to pin the Amcika members down in place and attack from multiple sides, and we needed to be prepared that they could use tablets to fuel their abilities further.

All of the elves on our side were going to need to preserve their abilities, using them only when necessary, except for the earth elves using the one tablet we had.

It was clear as our planning progressed that the major was reluctant to risk his troops. Part of me couldn't blame him. Although his soldiers had trained for war and battles, they had trained to fight people who at worst were as well equipped as they were. Not for a fight in which the very world around them could be used to break their frail bodies.

While I made it clear that I and many of the other elves would be doing what we could to protect them, he didn't want his troops in the thick of any area. But long term it was the soldiers who could win the fight and not the elves. When the elves were exhausted and down to the weapons they carried, the soldiers would be the ones to turn the tide.

Of course, everyone hoped it wouldn't come to that, but it was a huge possibility that it would. Especially if we pinned them down so they couldn't flee and they used power stored in the tablets they had.

I encouraged everyone, but doubts were appearing. Whatever happened, it was going to be tough to make it work.

*We're strong enough to defeat most of those elves alone,* Zephyr said as we finalized the plan and I returned to my post.

*Without the tablets, maybe,* I replied.

*Even with them, if we're careful and we use our abilities.*

*Are you ready to let them see your human form?*

*Some of them have already seen it.*

It was a good point. Zephyr had once been with them in human form as he tried to get to me. And they'd imprisoned him in human form. But none of these elves had been the ones to see him then. And there were still plenty of others with us who had never seen Zephyr in human form.

*We can't be secretive about it forever.*

I took several deep breaths as I thought through what he was suggesting. It was worth considering.

*If it looks as if you can turn the tide of this battle by becoming human, do it. But otherwise, you still bring a lot to the table when you're not in human form. You can defend many and work with the soldiers in dragon form.*

*Yes. I just hope they're worthy of defending.*

*You and me both.*

Over the next hour we waited, allowing the last few people who needed rest to get some and letting everyone else move into place ready for the attack. Everyone took their time, trying to be stealthy about moving into position. I helped where I could, blocking sound and movement from being picked up, but only where I needed to.

I rested for a short while when Dyneira returned and took over. It was strange trying to get sleep while on the edge of a potential battlefield, but I was exhausted enough that I slipped into the strangeness of the dreamworld.

Zephyr nudged me awake what felt like seconds later. My mind took a moment to catch up and process where I was and why I was asleep under some camouflaged canvas on the edge of a field with nothing under me but a small mat and a blow-up pillow.

*It's time to show these elves they messed with the wrong Henera*, Zephyr said, his eyes meeting mine.

The confidence in his voice made me feel better, and I got up and walked with him to the main area and camp the soldiers had set up. They were packing some of it down, making sure everything was stowed in the trucks so we could move out again swiftly if the elves broke the perimeter and fled once more.

I hoped they wouldn't, but I had no idea what would happen.

Having some more food, I waited for the rest of the team to assemble. Then we went over the rough plan one last time. Once more, I worried that the soldiers were holding back, but I didn't voice my fear. Zephyr was holding his power in reserve, and it could make a huge difference if he did join in.

With the discussion done, I nodded respectfully at the leaders standing around the small drinks station we'd created. Then I made my way to the group of mythicals and elves I would be working with. I had every bonded elf and their mythicals with me. We were responsible for getting as many of the tablets as possible.

The centaurs were responsible for reacting to danger this time. They were armed with modern weapons and other items that contained Zephyr's breath weapon or very small explosives and anything the Army had been willing to spare them. If any group was in trouble or overwhelmed, the centaurs would rush over, aided by an air elf.

Seth and Emily were leading the rest of the elves. They were our defensive line but would also form a barrier around the building. They would do their best to make sure no elves got past them and no one died.

Finally, the soldiers would hang back behind the barriers and the earth defenses that our single earth elf with his tablet was about to create and sustain. If anyone came close enough or presented as a target, the soldiers would take them out with feathered darts. They would also administer first aid and keep the path to our trucks open.

It was the best plan we could make in the circumstances, and it was one I was happy enough about to let it play out and hope it was enough.

As I lifted onto Zephyr's back, I nodded at Ronan. The centaur was several hundred yards away but was able to see me in the fading light.

Pushing into the air, Zephyr gave the signal that we were starting the attack with his presence in the sky.

*We should have brought a pizza oven with us*, Zephyr said as we rushed to the warehouse.

I had to stifle the laugh that wanted to bubble out of me and threaten to ruin the silence we moved with. Trust Zephyr to think of pizza at a time like this.

Concentrating, I reached toward the warehouse with my mind. It didn't take me long to find the cold barrier I expected in the air. As we approached, I noticed that it was getting colder as if we'd been seen and the air elf was forming a protective layer.

Zephyr exhaled, letting a large cloud of his breath out, and I moved it forward. At the same time, Erlan rode on Roth below us, reaching up with his hands. As I moved the gas in place around the barrier, pressing the one against the other as best as I could, Erlan set it aflame. The fire quickly spread, momentarily blinding me with light and making my face feel hot.

Turning to one side to avoid crashing into the barrier, Zephyr banked. I kept my gaze focused on the area I'd set aflame to find the barrier significantly weaker but still in place. Whoever the air elf was, they were going to have to expend more energy to try to make it cold again and stop the others coming running through it.

Once more, we did the same trick, Zephyr happily

circling until he could exhale again. While we were focusing on the barrier, I could see the elves on the other side of the fight creeping forward and the earth-based defenses rising out of the ground. The Amcika cult wasn't going to understand what had hit them.

With the second attempt to thaw the barrier taken in its stride, and an interesting and bizarre lack of movement or sign of anyone else, we were forced to circle once more.

*This feels too easy so far*, Zephyr said.

He wasn't wrong, and it made me hesitate, but Zephyr was still flying, and he had more control over how well I could avoid what was coming. At least, while I was riding on his back.

*If it is too easy, then I'm going to have to walk into that trap*, I thought in reply. *I have to retrieve these tablets, and I don't care about the clever ways they might be hidden as long as I can find them.*

*We need to find them. Our lives are all linked, remember?*

*Yes. How could I forget having someone like you in my head?*

Zephyr chuckled as he exhaled for a third time and Erlan once more set it alight. It was an effective strategy, and it quickly drained the barrier of its cold again. This time it was almost as if some of it fizzled out, but I felt the boost of energy that could only have come from a tablet.

It made me feel smug on Zephyr's behalf that we'd managed to drain the powerful air elf simply by surrounding the large barrier placed around the building by Zephyr's flammable breath weapon. It was a way Zephyr could be very useful, and it was a way I could attack the barrier without having to use any of my energy.

*I can't use the gas again for a while, but I should be able to again when we're farther through this battle.*

*If you've not decided to distract everyone with your sexy human form by then.*

*Distracting the enemy would be helpful.*

*Maybe, but just because they're elves doesn't make them stupid. Even if you're hot, it's only going to buy you so much of their attention and desire to have you close.*

Zephyr let out another rumble of laughter, and I felt a wave of affection spread over me.

*If any of them get too heated, I could always hose them down,* Roth said, chiming in from below me. I laughed and sent him a mental image of me and the other mythicals with him in the sea.

*If Minsheng could hear our thoughts, we'd be in so much trouble. We'd be seen as unfocused flirts right at the beginning of a battle.*

*To be fair, if Minsheng could hear our thoughts, he'd know we're just as bad in training and any other serious situation.*

*Good point.*

Grinning, I let Zephyr bank around again, but this time instead of jetting air, I lifted off his back and flew toward the ground while he circled, waiting for the barrier to fall or something to be done that meant he could aid us again.

It was time to break through.

## CHAPTER THIRTEEN

Trying not to let panic get the better of me, I moved closer to the building. I was one of a few mythicals who had come in closer and were currently concentrating on making the whole situation better.

I wasn't alone, Erlan and several other Sanctuary mythicals standing in a row as Roth and Sen joined us, as well as Newton and several of the fire salamanders.

*Okay, the coast is clear,* Zephyr said. *If you're going to attack, now is the best time to do it.*

I didn't need any more encouragement from Zephyr as I leaned in closer and unleashed merry hell on the elves without knowing exactly where they were.

I yanked the barn door open as hard as I could with my abilities. Feeling some resistance to my control, I amped up what I was doing, swiftly pushing past it. A couple of seconds later, I felt a mind trying to shut me out, but not before I'd managed to feel more about the elves in control and what they might be capable of.

The air elf was growing familiar to me now, but I still

couldn't work out exactly who they were or how they fit into this entire mystery.

However, another barrier of their creation blocked my way. This one was intensely cold, and it wasn't going to be easy to get past in any way other than direct control.

Outside the warehouse, the majority of the combatants were still waiting, defending against elemental attacks, but otherwise unable to get close enough.

There were some windows on one side that could be reached from the roof, but it was supposed to be our last resort if we couldn't get in the door.

*Let them know to get the elves on the roof,* I said to Zephyr as Roth came close to my side and Sen scurried over to a small broken section of the wall near the corner. As soon as the earth elf had finished with the defenses, he ran to my myconid. He carried the tablet under one arm, and it tugged at my mind.

It was probably the most dangerous part of our attack, bringing the tablet so close to the battle, but Sen needed another way into the building where she might go unnoticed, and the tablet she'd grabbed in the previous battle was hopefully going to get her the recognition in combat the myconid deserved from others.

I sheltered behind Roth, one of his wings almost entirely over my head as I closed my eyes and focused on the air barrier in front of the open doorway. The air elf had a firm grip on it, but despite their practice and ability, I was still the stronger elf. I didn't do it quickly, and I had to use every ounce of my strength and focus, but I eventually had control of the air and dissipated and blasted it apart.

This wasn't how I'd envisioned this battle going. No

one attacking us in person, but the cult hiding in the building we were attacking. It was strange, but if it meant we got closer and had a better chance of picking them off or snatching tablets away from them, I was all for it.

As soon as the barrier was down, I fought to keep control of the air in the doorway and looked toward Sen. The earth elemental had almost made a way into the building for her, so I strode forward and flew onto Roth's back.

I'd never ridden my pegasus into battle before and it felt strange, his wing joints naturally sitting where I would want to put my legs, but I crouched, my feet going back and behind them. With a rush of warmth toward me, he picked up speed and thundered toward the door we had forced open. I could see the fire salamanders rushing along the ground and through the thick grasses to join us.

As one group, we rode through into the first room. It was what appeared to be a front office, but the desk or reception area was long gone. Instead there was an interesting combination of empty crates, dust, and discarded food wrappers.

I wrinkled my nose at the smell. It wasn't going to be fun being in here for any length of time.

Before I could get much farther, I felt another barrier form. At first, I thought it was merely in front of me and blocking my path forward, but as I struggled to breathe, I realized something else must have happened and I had been boxed in.

Feeling panicked, I powered forward and out of the space, but it was chillier, the night temperature settling in, making it easier for this air elemental to make things difficult.

I was left with no choice but to challenge for control as I inhaled and yet still didn't feel as if I'd pulled in much of anything I needed. Feeling panic coming from one of the mythicals nearby, but unable to process exactly which one, I tried to remember what I was supposed to be doing.

*Break out, Aella!* Zephyr yelled.

The words crashed through the brain fog, and I could think more clearly. I focused again, fighting this air elf and the tablet that fueled him. There was no way I was letting him suffocate me.

Concentrating on one small part of the barrier near Roth's head, I could feel the pegasus standing firm beneath me, not needing air like I did. I soon had a small hole punched through, and I pulled in air from outside. This time I inhaled and felt the delightful rush of the oxygen I needed.

My fingers tingled as I returned to normal, but before I could keep on moving, the barrier was snatched out of my grasp again, and I was smacked so hard that I almost fell off Roth. He adjusted to catch me, and then I righted myself. Once again, the air was sucked out, and once again, I was forced to focus on saving myself.

I put up the best fight I could, but it was as if the air elf was using something stronger because, despite my best attempts and the way I pushed and tried to manipulate the elements, none of them would come under my control.

Starting to feel sleepy and as if I wanted to lie down on Roth's back and close my eyes, I noticed I was no longer alone, several elves coming inside the building with me. It seemed to take them several seconds to wonder why I was standing there. I could make out that they were speaking but not what they said.

While I desperately fought on, getting weaker with each passing minute, I saw two of the air elves come closer and try to put their hands on the barrier in the way.

I moved my focus to a patch near them, but my vision soon grew blurry, and the friends that had come to rescue me faded from view. Before I could go to sleep, it was as if someone slapped me again, but this time, the sting remained on my cheeks. I lifted my head and blinked, my mind clearing again as an air elemental stepped back from Roth and me.

*You need to move out of that area*, Zephyr said, and I couldn't have disagreed with him if I'd wanted to. But I had other elves with me and no sure way of progressing.

There was a door, but it looked to be welded shut, and I wasn't sure how quickly we'd get through. Somewhere ahead, I could feel Sen, but I wasn't sure where the myconid had gotten to.

*Sen have tablet*, she said, the glee in her voice evident.

Grateful something was going well, I got off Roth and ran to the door. Putting my hands on it, I felt the strange construction the cult's earth elves must have done. I swiftly undid it, making the connections brittle and thinner until a combination of brute strength and my abilities helped us yank it open.

Erlan and the fire salamanders ran through first, giving me a moment to get a breather.

We were in what looked like a massive storeroom where the shelves had once been lined with parcels and boxes. There were empty boxes here and there, and the interior was mostly dark, with very little light coming in the windows.

I was wondering if the panes grimy with years of dust and neglect could be broken when there was a shattering sound, and the whole room grew a fraction lighter. A moment later, the noise and effect came again. By the time it happened to a third window pane, I was hoping it meant the arrival of more reinforcements.

Pushing onward, I used the air to feel for whoever it was inside and wherever they were. I'd expected an army of elves, especially given how well the elves inside the building were attacking, but there was no one in sight.

We stopped, looking around, going up and down different aisles of shelves in small groups to see what we'd missed. The attacks also dwindled. The resistance had gone, but I didn't feel entirely at ease. Something was going on here. Sen had found a tablet somewhere. There had to be elves in here.

*I think there's another room at the back.*

Zephyr's words soon had me turning toward the rear of the warehouse, feeling forward with my mind and encouraging Roth and Sen to come with me. I still felt wary that something wasn't right and we were going to come across something like a trap. But for now, I could breathe, and the elves were nowhere to be seen.

I was beginning to wonder if they'd fled, unable to feel the air elf who had been holding us back with barriers, until I spotted a small door in a back wall almost buried behind shelves.

The shelving units had clearly been moved recently,

and I had to signal for more elves, centaurs, and soldiers to come and help. Most of our forces were in the building. The elves and soldiers worked together to move a shelving unit out of the way, trying to use strength over abilities where possible so it didn't drain any of us more than necessary.

Before anyone else could face the danger and get closer, I did, feeling past the door with my mind and trying to get it open. It was welded shut, heat having melted it into its frame. Once again, the earth elf with the tablet came forward and used it to break away the metal and reform it.

He wasn't quite finished when he and the rune-covered stone ran out of capacity. I waved him back and finished it off myself, then I pulled it open and rushed inside. I was hit with a blast of air. The barrier around me dissipated, and I reacted swiftly enough with my abilities to jet air out behind me and keep my body upright.

As my eyes adjusted to the dim room, I saw the outline of a cloaked body as it dropped into a hole in the floor, pretty much flying. Then he was gone, and someone was attempting to shut the hole from inside.

I reached out and fought for control with whoever was closing off the path. It was a struggle that made my head hurt. Whoever was on the other end of it was powerful and probably using another of the elven ability storage stones. At the same time, I rushed toward the hole, my mythicals joining me.

The tunnel was almost closed by the time I broke through the control and started trying to open it again. I crouched by it, unable to dive inside yet as Ronan and Sen appeared at my side. Sen dropped into the hole with her dart gun out, and Ronan crouched, trying to get a good angle to shoot the earth elf we could see in the flashlight beam.

Sen hit them with a dart from her blowgun before jumping and grabbing the tablet he held in his hands. At the same time, Ronan fired, and I made the hole wider again.

Sliding down beside Sen, I was in time to see the earth elf collapse, Sen having to steady the tablet and save it from shattering. The tunnel beyond me was dark and went along and away from the building for some distance. I couldn't see anyone ahead, but I felt forward with my mind and went to run down it, using the air to guide me, when I felt Ronan's hand on my shoulder.

"Remember that it is you they need. You shouldn't run toward danger alone," he said, his voice deep and respectful.

I exhaled but listened. He was right, even if I didn't want him to be. I couldn't go running into danger alone, especially when Zephyr and Roth would have a hard time following, and I could once again find myself at the end of a section that was closed off. Or worse, fighting for my life underground while elves cornered me and attempted to do things like cut off my air supply.

Picking up Sen and careful not to touch the tablet she was holding, I focused on what I had gained from this attack.

The centaur reached out to help me out of the hole and I let him, using my air abilities to take the weight off until I was standing beside him.

"They got away again?" Minsheng asked, standing beside the major inside the doorway.

I nodded. A soldier appeared with a much brighter lamp, and the room no longer needed to be illuminated by the little flashlights the soldiers carried. Looking around, I took in the small office. This was where the people in charge of the warehouse had worked, and oddly, it was still mostly intact.

As I looked around, I saw computers and all sorts of stationery lying out on desks. This warehouse wasn't as abandoned as the last one had been. It had been used until very recently.

Just as others did, I went over to a nearby desk to see if there was anything that might shed some light on what was going on and why these elves were taking the route they were and hiding in buildings like this.

I gasped as I noticed the piece of paper sitting on one desk and taped in place. It was an ownership deed. In my name. For the warehouse I was standing in. And it was dated the same day as the one I'd been given in LA.

Someone had been using yet another warehouse I owned and, given the deliberate way this deed had been left here, not only did the cult elves know I owned it, but they'd intended to tell me they knew.

Minsheng came to my side, his eyes going wide when he saw it.

This was a whole new level of crazy.

## CHAPTER FOURTEEN

So many thoughts ran through my head as I climbed onto Zephyr's back. I could feel the waves of comfort and warmth coming off Zephyr, Roth, and Sen, but I didn't know how to respond yet.

I'd let Minsheng take the deed to the warehouse, the confusion it caused making me walk straight out of the building and not look back.

*If the cult bought it and our warehouse in LA, I might have to tear it down,* I thought to Zephyr.

*You don't need to tear it down. Even if they did buy it, they gave it to you. It has not been theirs, and it never will be again. You shouldn't destroy something that you made pure and good. And we can do the same here. We can use this as another safe house for mythicals. There are so many now.*

Zephyr's words and the gentle, deep, calm tone helped soothe my storm-filled mind. He was right. It didn't make sense to throw it away, but I felt sick knowing the cult had anything to do with the buildings.

I had gone to Canada to find answers, and I *was* finding

them, but I hadn't expected this. Was the cult holding the man who had dropped me off? Had he bought the warehouses for me? Was this an elaborate setup to guide my life so I found Zephyr and fulfilled my destiny?

So far, for every half-answer, there were thousands more questions, and I still hadn't found the man who had started all this.

Sighing, I stayed on Zephyr's back, watching the rest of the allies I had around me go back and forth. We had captured another elf and taken two more tablets, but it wasn't enough. We had been tricked again, and the soldiers were tired and not sure what to do.

I could see the doubt on the major's face as he stood beside Minsheng, Seth, and Ronan, and they discussed what to do next. The centaurs needed rest and so did everyone else, but it was clear that the elves we were after intended to drag this out.

No one could fight a war like this, drawing it out across miles of American countryside for the tablets and elves to melt back into nature again as soon as we attacked them.

*We should go mediate*, Zephyr said. *Would you like me to do the talking?*

I appreciated the offer and sent a wave of affection Zephyr's way.

*We can both say what's needed*, I replied as he began walking closer.

"We can't keep doing this," the major said as soon as he spotted us approaching.

I nodded, acknowledging him before sliding off Zephyr's back again.

"You're right. This isn't working," I replied. "But they

can't keep the tablets either. The entire fate of the planet relies on us stopping them from getting the tablets to a portal and working out how to use them to break through the defenses."

"They're not heading toward either of them at the moment," Minsheng pointed out, showing the route we'd traveled marked out on a map.

I studied it, noticing the warehouse we were at was listed on there too.

"Everyone needs rest. And we have prisoners and other cult members I want to talk to," I said, my mind beginning to clear as I looked at the trail.

Ronan's face showed the shock he and Seth were feeling.

"I know it's not what most of you expected me to say, but I think they want me to follow them. I don't know if this is a trap or something different entirely. And I understand if some of you want no part of this going forward. But I intend to get more information and then keep on. And I'm sure they'll be waiting for me."

I felt another boost of warmth from Zephyr, and it made the sick feeling in my stomach ease. We agreed, at least.

"I should report back to the general. But I know the President will want to continue even if it takes time. This isn't what any of us expected, but the men can't travel like this without some respite." The major gave me a nod before hurrying away.

There was nothing more to be said after that. Although I sounded entirely confident, there was part of me that didn't feel it at all. The cult could do anything with those tablets. Every time I thought of the worst cases, my mind came back to the warehouse deed sitting on the desk and the person I was looking for. The cult was somehow tied to this, and it felt as if I were being led along a trail.

I watched the major go around the vehicles before leaving our makeshift camp, taking the soldiers with him. He left us two of the trucks big enough to carry the equipment we were borrowing as well as the elves and centaurs. He also left the tablets and captive elves with us, everyone agreeing that we could keep them contained more easily.

I had little to do but go and talk to the elves that were finally awake to learn something more. The newest ones were still out cold, however, and I wanted to go to the Sanctuary and talk to the council about what was going on. They'd banned the Amcika symbol, and I was pretty sure the councilors knew more than they were telling me.

With everyone taking the lead from me and surprisingly willing to take my gut instinct as the best course of action, we were quickly loaded into the trucks with the equipment. The tablets were in the first one, each one under the guardianship of an elf with another assigned to fill them up as swiftly as possible.

We'd gotten two earth tablets and a fire tablet, and I wanted to pick up the fragment of air tablet we had at the Texas site the next time we were there.

Thankfully this warehouse seemed to be in between and north of the portal site and the Sanctuary, so it was going to be one large triangle of travel to continue with our mission.

As soon as the trucks were underway, I flew into the air with Zephyr, Sen, and Roth. We were tired, but we wanted to be together after the craziness, and we would rest soon enough.

We flew as one unit, my mind automatically helping all of us. It was exactly what we needed, and my head cleared more the longer we were in the sky. The battles hadn't been total losses, even if they hadn't gone the way I'd hoped they would. I was getting stronger and figuring out what was going on bit by bit.

*We're all handling this better. With each fight, we and our allies become more coordinated.*

*We do, although they're getting practice too.*

*They are, but they're already a unit. They can't improve as much as we can. And we have the raw power. If we were as well-trained as a whole to fight as they are, they wouldn't stand a chance, even with the tablets.*

Zephyr's words bounced around my head, making me realize that, no matter how much we trained unless we worked well with others and they were also dedicated, it wasn't going to win a war.

Inspiring others to want to fight and forging the mentality and dedication to being the best were two different things. The latter was something that we had potentially overlooked. We had some very dedicated fighters. Dyneira, Ronan, Seth, Erlan, and Emily came to mind.

All of them had lost something or seen the way things could go wrong. Or they had the right personality. But others were hesitant to use their abilities on another person, preferring to use their abilities for sculpting, watering crops, or making something beautiful. I couldn't blame them either. There was part of me that would love to never need to fight.

The world had never given me that luxury, however. From the moment I'd had Zephyr, I'd been hunted, on the run, or fighting something or someone. It was my life, and we'd trained every day for it.

*There's plenty who want to fight alongside us. We just need to encourage them the right way*, Zephyr said. *And a few need reminding how badly this could hurt them in a way that inspires them to work hard to protect.*

*You saying I need to work on one of those inspiring leader speeches that makes everyone believe they're invincible and the enemy is sure to be defeated?*

*Yes. That's Army leader one-oh-one. You should have been practicing that too.*

*Sorry, I was a bit too busy learning how to make tornadoes and water cannons.*

*And how to keep unruly dragons in check*, Roth said, joining in the banter.

*And how to get dragons to behave*, I agreed as I heard Zephyr chuckle.

*Make pizza?* Sen asked, showing an image of us making pizzas one birthday when Grim had offered to show us how to prepare them from scratch.

I laughed aloud at the reminder that we'd also spent a lot of time consuming pizza, and pretty soon, we were laughing and thinking back to some of the fun things we'd done with our downtime.

We continued to remind each other of good memories until the Sanctuary came into sight and the trucks pulled off the road to head up a grassy slope to the Sanctuary border. The city had been built in a unique place, no part of it easily accessible by road or vehicle, but easy to reach if you knew what you were looking for.

Landing beside the trucks, we opted to walk the last of the distance to close the gap to the Sanctuary defense line and go inside. The guards quickly greeted us, seeing the centaurs who often took up the posts where they were and bowing low to them.

I smiled and greeted the Sanctuary mythicals, hoping to find the council quickly and ask them what they knew before doing the same to the elves who had joined the Sanctuary from Amcika. Finally, I wanted to see what I could get out of the elves we'd captured.

It was going to be a lot of talking, and I preferred training, but it had to be done. And I wasn't afraid of doing it. Weary of talking so much and never quite getting to the bottom of anything. There was always some piece of information missing or someone who was holding something back.

That needed to end. I needed all the information people had. And I needed it as soon as possible.

Ronan led the way to the council chambers, and we dropped off most of the centaurs, elves, and mythicals along the way to rest. I trusted the Sanctuary citizens and entrusted them with our captives while we went to speak to the council and let them know everything that had transpired.

I took the tablets with me, getting the elves of other elements to put the rune-covered stones into a bag and then into saddlebags that Roth happily carried for me.

When everyone was close to the cave network that housed some of the more important buildings for the

Sanctuary, I spotted the four elven masters gathered together in a huddle. As soon as they saw me, they broke their circle and turned their attention my way. At first, it seemed as if they were simply going to smile and move on, but instead, Ruehnar threw out his arms to hug me and made it clear he was pleased to see me no matter what.

I hugged him and smiled at the others before pulling back and looking them over.

"What is it?" I asked. "What has happened since I last left the Sanctuary?"

"It's the orbs. Someone has taken all of them."

"All of them?" I asked, my eyes going wide.

Knowing how hard it was to do anything with the orbs but use them to get to the Sanctuary, I felt compelled to ask for more details.

"Many were dormant when they left us, waking up in the hands of mythicals. Sadly someone has found a way to circumnavigate this. And they've taken as many orbs as they can get their hands on."

"For themselves?" I asked, but I already knew the answer to the question.

"It would seem they are still trying to isolate us."

I sighed. It was something that didn't entirely make sense either. I was getting tired of riddles and games. Of not knowing enough.

"I'll see what I can find out about it," I said, not sure what else to offer.

Aquilan reached out and squeezed my shoulder, giving me a confident nod. I appreciated the gesture, and part of me wanted to stick around to talk to him, but I had to continue after Ronan the centaur paused in the entrance to the cave.

"I'll come find you before I leave again," I said, noticing that Orthelo heard my words and nodded almost imperceptibly to me.

Figuring I'd better see him, I made my way into the Sanctuary council chambers. It took a surprisingly short amount of time to bring them up to speed. Dyneira had been communicating with them at regular intervals and already told them some of what had transpired.

I added the information about the cult and what they were possibly trying to tell me.

"I know they're not something you talk about here at the Sanctuary, but if there is anything you know about them and their interest in me. I need to know it," I said to finish.

There was a moment of awkward silence as none of the council seemed to want to answer me, but I could see Vestan looking more thoughtful than avoiding my gaze. I looked his way, wondering if he had something I ought to know.

"You're right that they're not something we like to focus on," Vestan said eventually. "For a long time, we hoped they had disappeared, but I do know they've been playing a long game. They are ambitious, and they truly believe that you're Henera. But...unlike the rest of us, they never wished to wait until nature and fate did their part."

"They wanted to make it all happen." Sierrathen gave me an apologetic smile.

"Make it all happen?" I asked, not sure what the elves were getting at.

"We don't know anything for sure," she explained.

"Simply that they would have been looking out for you. They'll have known about you from the moment it was possible you could be Henera. It's possible that what they have planned for you, they had planned for others too. Your birth... I know you've said you were given up for adoption. It's possible they have an idea who your birth parents are. Why you could be so obviously special. I could speculate no more than that."

I nodded gratefully, knowing it wasn't much to go on. It helped paint the picture I needed, however.

We talked briefly of the rune-covered stone tablets that had been discovered, but the council was happy not to see them, deeming them a device they didn't yet need.

There was little more to say, and I was aware that I had plenty of other people I wanted to talk to. After thanking them for their time, I turned to leave.

"Thank you for all you do for us," Vestan said, getting up before I could leave the chamber. "You risk a lot. If there is ever anything we can do to help you understand who you are and your possible future, know that we will support you. We've not always agreed on everything, but we do consider you not just one of us, but someone with a great burden. We will make it lighter if we can."

I nodded as Ronan would have in response, unable to speak and not sure words were necessary anyway. The Sanctuary had become an ally, and I was grateful I'd persevered in trying to get along with them and that I'd been able to tap into their strength and skills.

Without the Sanctuary, I would have perished long ago, and my mythicals with me.

CHAPTER FIFTEEN

Although I was still tired, I went to find the elves who had defected from the cult several months earlier. They'd told me plenty about the cult they'd once been part of, but there was a chance we'd not heard everything, probably far too much in their memories and minds for them to have told me everything already. At least that was the hope.

I wasn't sure they'd be up, but I found the pair sitting together by one of the guest houses, much as they had the first time the council had asked them questions. Sen bounded up to them, smiling and waving her dart gun in a way that made it clear she was showing it off and not threatening them. Roth and Zephyr came the rest of the way, one on either side of me.

"Hello again, Henera," the nearest one said. "I hope you and your bonded mythicals are well?"

"Well enough, but we have some possible puzzles to solve. We hoped you might be able to help us," I replied.

They looked at each other and then at me, and I could see the wariness in their eyes.

"Please don't panic. I'm not even sure how important it is," I added as I sat on the ground not too far from them.

Zephyr also plonked his body down, almost as if he was tired of standing and holding himself up. Seeing the wide-eyed look one of them gave Roth, the pegasus came closer and lowered his head.

I explained how I'd bonded with the water horse and that he'd been my companion for some time, then we talked of the many mythicals in the Sanctuary. Time seemed to fly by as we talked of bonding and what it was like and many conversations around it. I was surprised they were so easy to talk to and that they wanted to work with me on certain things.

"Do you know why the cult is so fascinated with me?" I asked when the conversation took a natural turn in that direction. "And I don't mean for the portals and opening them."

"Technically, they'd settle for Zephyr when it came to opening the portals," the female elf declared.

"I know. But it looks as if they've been tracking my life for some time. Before anyone knew I was the Henera," I replied. "They seem to know something that no one can possibly know yet."

The two elves looked at each other, but neither of them spoke.

"They have an area of the mountain that few elves go to. There they have gnomes, dwarves, and other mythicals. There's been a side project there that was responsible for monitoring the Henera and the possible elves. It's been part of Amcika's strategy for a very long time to be looking out for you. But very few believed you would truly be found."

I nodded. It was the same information as everyone else pretty much said.

"There is another area that many don't know about," the other elf said, looking like a deer in headlights when I looked at her.

"To do with me?" I asked.

She frowned, then tilted her head to the side.

"It's an area that most of the mountain don't know even exists. I only heard about it because I had to help another elf fix something in the lab with the airflow. They were researching and experimenting with some kind of science combined with our magic. They were developing something. Something to do with the Henera. To do with you. It was a while ago, though."

"Do you know what they were researching?"

"Not exactly. Just...they seemed confident that you were the Henera long before you ever used magic."

I lifted my eyebrows.

"Did they have Zephyr's egg?" I asked, not sure how else to interpret them knowing. It felt as if I'd been bonded to Zephyr my entire life. Maybe they'd known I was Henera from that. Or suspected. Maybe they'd looked after Zephyr's egg my entire life.

As I was thinking this, Zephyr leaned in and nuzzled me.

*I hope they didn't have my egg,* he said. *But if they did, I'm grateful they brought me to you and made sure we found each other.*

The sentiment and what Zephyr was choosing to focus

on made me feel a thousand times better, and I leaned back into him.

Gently, I asked the elves if they knew anything else that could be useful, mentioning the person who had dropped me off at the police station but not the exact role he played in my life. It was no good, however. I didn't have a picture of the man on me, and I couldn't describe him well enough to set him apart from the many elves in Amcika.

With nothing else to do, I had to move on, my feet automatically heading to the earth elf and his menagerie of animals. I wanted a familiar face who would be trying to help me as much as possible before I took on the difficult task of trying to interrogate prisoners.

The elder elf was where I had expected to find him, surrounded by sick animals and those healing and on the mend. He stopped feeding a small mouse-like creature liquid with a small spoon as I came inside. I was careful where I moved, and Zephyr stayed outside so we didn't hurt or accidentally trample any creatures, but Orthelo noticed us.

He smiled as he stopped what he was doing and then came over to me.

"I hope this isn't a bad time to disturb you," I said, not sure how else to start a conversation when I wanted to ask so many questions, but I also knew I had been asked there for a reason. This wasn't the sort of thing you interrupted.

"It's never a bad time to see you, Henera." He smiled and waved me over to one side of the building where there were fewer animals.

In one corner, curled up in blankets, was a golden

foxlike creature with a bandage on its front paw. He picked it up and brought it over to me almost expectantly.

"Worth a try," he said with a grin.

"Fire mythical?" I asked, unable to keep from smiling.

He nodded as he placed the furry creature in a small bed and gave it a gentle stroke. Seemingly used to him, it curled up and went to sleep again.

"Not why I asked you to come here, although it would make Bialan very happy if you bonded with a fire mythical. I know he desperately hopes he'll have something to teach you soon."

"What do you need of me?" I asked as I got the impression he was trying to find the courage to say something.

"I've got something for you to possibly find. It might help, and I'm sorry I've kept it from you all this time, but... I didn't want to hurt Bialan with it."

I raised my eyebrows as Orthelo pulled out a small notebook and placed it in my hands.

"It's the whereabouts of the fire belt Zaos had made. In theory, the great four elementals were supposed to hand down their artifacts to another of their element. But someone in the line Zaos chose decided there was no worthy fire elemental in the past. The earth elementals ended up with it. It's one of the best-kept secrets of the few of us who know."

"And you want me to fetch it?" I asked.

"Not exactly. It's in the hands of an elf in Amcika."

I blinked again, too stunned to speak.

"How? Surely Zaos wouldn't have wanted that?" Zephyr said for me, the growl in his voice evident.

"No. I don't think he would have done, but sometimes

we think we know someone. I know Bialan has been searching for the belt. And I know he suspects it moved to another element of elf, but I'm the only person in the Sanctuary who knows where it must be. Everything I know is in this notebook. Forgive my English, I'm used to writing in Elvish, but it should help you work out exactly who in Amcika holds it. You should take it back."

"But surely it should be given as the other three artifacts have? And after I have shown I can wield the element."

"Zaos would want you to have it. The elf who had it before would give it to you were they still the owner now. That's all I can say. Take it. By force, if you have to."

I swallowed, not sure how to respond to the determined sound of Orthelo's voice. I had many questions, but a bird squawked, and his attention was gone as he shuffled away. I watched him tend to the phoenix he'd had under his care for some time. It had been an egg when I'd first met Orthelo, but it was now a young bird, almost majestic.

Hoping the answers I sought were in the notebook I'd been given, I retreated with Zephyr, Sen, and Roth.

*For what it's worth, I agree with Orthelo*, Zephyr said. *Even if you never develop a fire ability, you could potentially give it to Bialan.*

*We've still got to find it,* I pointed out, not sure how I felt, or if I truly had time for something that appeared is if it was so much like a wild goose chase. There was so little detail on what this could mean.

Tucking the notebook away in my bag and trying not to worry about it for now, I went to make my last stop on this strange tour of people in the Sanctuary. I had been talking so much lately that I was neglecting my practice and training, but I also knew that I was likely to need my abilities again soon. The cult wasn't going to wait around forever for me to follow. When they did begin moving again with me giving chase, I would want every bit of extra power I could get.

Thinking of what might come made my heart rate pick up again and my shoulders tense. I had no idea if I could do what was expected of me. Stopping the cult from opening the portals wasn't going to be an easy task, but it felt as if this time, I was close to not being able to prevent them. I'd worried in the past, especially when I'd been in their mountain and had little choice about cooperating and no way out, but this was a new level of cut loose.

I made my way to the few elves we'd taken prisoner from the cult and the area they were being held in. The Sanctuary had never needed to hold elves in captivity before, but I'd talked them through the way the cult had held me. It wasn't ideal, but it meant pairing up each elemental prisoner with several guards of the same element who had a great deal more power.

On top of that, there were several natural elven concoctions that could help an elf slip into sleep or rest when troubled by pain. The Sanctuary was keeping the prisoners in a half-sedated state. It made it harder for them to focus their minds and their abilities. Of everything, it made me thankful once again that I was so much stronger than most other elves.

As soon as I stepped into the prison-like area, I was aware of the eyes on me. The elves here were awake and more alert than I was expecting, but I tried to look as unbothered by this as I possibly could, walking deeper into the building and trying to get a good footing.

"I've got a few questions," I said, trying to get straight to the point. "Now, I know you don't want to answer my questions, especially ones about the cult and the portals, but I think there's something more that no one is telling me."

"There's plenty. If you think it's us who need to be talking to you, you're mistaken," one of the women said, her body lying on the floor of the cell, one of the Sanctuary earth elves standing outside.

I walked closer, suspecting that if she was willing to say something, I might be able to get her to talk enough around the subject that she'd let me have enough bits and pieces of information I could put some more of this puzzle together.

"You're the ones leading me on a wild goose chase, however. If I didn't know any better, I'd say you're all hiding something."

"We've got nothing to hide, but it's not our fault if you can't see what we're putting right for you to pick up on."

I frowned at the response. Had I missed something or was this earth elf just being obtuse? There was no way to be sure, but I thought about everything I'd seen of the cult and everything I knew. What was obvious?

"You've done nothing but withhold information since the beginning," Zephyr said as he stalked closer, his powerful dragon body making the words seem more menacing than they were.

Of course, they weren't, but I wasn't going to say anything to them. Let them think that the dragon was a killer and willing to put the cult members out of their misery.

I watched the ripple of fear as it made the woman shuffle over to the back wall before she sat.

"Whose job was it to look after me as an egg, and what happened to my mother?" Zephyr demanded.

The question and the anger in it took me by surprise. We'd talked about his genetic memories and how they continued to the point the egg was fertilized. Then it was as if the next few days began a life capable of thought and his new, younger body kicked in. I stepped closer to him, sending him concern about his question but unwilling to interrupt him.

It was obvious I wasn't the only person surprised by this. I watched the elf lift her eyebrows.

"It was a gnome responsible for your egg," one of the other elves said, the guy's middle age not blending very well with the punk rocker attire. "One of the gnomes that came and went a lot. He was always keeping a lookout, scouting for things, sometimes clashing with Cherisse too. But the egg was something he knew how to care for like no other."

"So Cherisse kept him around," I added, acting as if I was getting a picture of things. "The gnome with the silver streak in his eyebrow."

"Yeah, made him look different, even for a gnome who took the time to try to fit in. That's all we know. They don't let elves like us know more than we need to."

I hid my grin as they confirmed the gnome. The one who had stolen my hairbrush and started all this. The one who had led me to my dragon. At the same time, I felt the wash of confused emotions from Zephyr.

*We'll find the gnome and get him to tell us what happened to your parents too*, I promised Zephyr, knowing our lives had become linked in a whole new way.

*And we'll make sure we find out what they know about yours,* he promised back, our eyes meeting and everyone else melting away.

*Yes. We were going to find out everything. And we were going to hunt Amcika until we'd got every last bit of information out of them.*

## CHAPTER SIXTEEN

I stood beside Zephyr, Roth, and Sen, the Sanctuary elves in front of me, and the elven masters off to one side. After learning everything I could, I'd gone to gather the masters to talk to them about the problem I was facing.

They'd agreed that I needed more elves, especially elves who could handle the heat of a battle and work together. Also elves who trusted me or Seth and Ronan.

Seth was also present, standing with the fire elves and Erlan. They'd come with me rather than to the portal base. It left the Texas portal more vulnerable, and it was our duty to protect that, but within hours, we'd be out in the wilderness, hunting down the cult elves and the tablets they carried.

I looked out over the elves and then stood forward as Zephyr lifted his head higher.

"I know many of you have lived in the Sanctuary all your lives, and for the most part, your lives have been completely peaceful with no need to challenge or fight others. And then I came along, and I brought danger with me. I didn't mean to. I'd have kept the Sanctuary safe and hidden if I could. But danger has come. And it's not gone away yet."

I paused as I looked around at the faces and thought about the best way to phrase this next part. While danger had come and it wasn't all down to me, I felt responsible. This was my fight and a fight over my life and who I was. Asking anyone to join me in that was hard.

"You all know what Amcika wishes to do and why that means danger for us. I won't exaggerate the threat or focus on it. What I will focus on is this. You have all come here day after day to be taught by four of the most amazing elves I know. And although they never taught you directly to fight wars or use your abilities against other elves in combat, they have prepared you in ways that no others could. Now there's a threat out there that would take all this away. Will you come with me to stop them? It won't be easy, and you're likely to find yourselves tired and spent beyond anything you've ever felt before, but we'll be alongside you. Will you stand with us?"

There was a deafening roar from the elves as most of them raised their fists and called out.

I exhaled, so much emotion filling me that I realized I was shaking. As the elves came forward, I had the masters help me assign them to groups, pairing up an elf from each element into squads that were fairly evenly matched until there were ten groups of four standing in front of me. In terms of an army, it wasn't a lot of elves, but with the elves from the warehouse and the commanders I had like Emily, Erlan, and Seth, who had been training for war with me, it was a significant improvement.

When we found the Amcika elves again, they weren't going to know what hit them.

I quickly gave the troop some instructions on how to get ready to leave and what to pack. Then I motioned for Seth to follow me. We went to find Ronan, who was doing something similar with the centaurs and other mythicals in the Sanctuary.

Several council members stood with him, noticing us as we approached.

"We'll be ready," Ronan said as he bowed to me.

"And the council has given their blessing for you to take whoever volunteers for this mission," Sierrathen said.

"Will the Sanctuary be safe enough?" I asked as I saw the group of over thirty centaurs, dwarves, gnomes, and a couple of fairies who often guarded the Sanctuary borders and generally kept the city safe.

"Given the biggest threat is the elves you're going after, I think we'll be just fine. And the council has a lot of power. If we need you, we'll be able to let you know."

I nodded, grateful for their understanding. I wanted to be able to forge ahead and protect everyone, but knowing that the Sanctuary was willing to work with me when we'd been at odds in the past was something that made me feel better.

With Ronan briefing everyone and prepping them to leave as I had done the elves, I had a rare few minutes to relax with Zephyr, Sen, and Roth.

*Pizza?* Sen asked before Zephyr could.

All four of us burst into laughter, drawing looks from the mythicals around us, but we didn't explain, our feet having directed us toward the main eating area of the city where we were bound to find food. We'd probably have to eat whatever was being prepared, but it would still be something yummy.

Within minutes we were sitting in the canteen, surrounded by food and able to stuff our faces. Despite the serious things that had happened and the notebook I kept thinking of tucked in my bag, we still managed to have fun. More of the mythicals came to us, finishing getting ready and joining us to eat.

By the time we were done and I was on Zephyr's back at the border of the Sanctuary, I was surrounded by a small army. We'd had to find more vehicles capable of off-road travel, but it was a place to begin.

Everyone loaded in the vehicles, including Sen and Roth, and Zephyr and I launched into the air together, circling as everyone else started their engines and got moving.

The centaurs and mythicals good at tracking were in the back set of vehicles, and the elves and everyone going to the portal with us were in the Army-loaned trucks at the front. We were going to split the group as we reached a fork in the road. Ronan and the centaurs would find our elves again while I went to persuade the general to give us as many of his soldiers as I could.

It wasn't an ideal plan, but my phone call to the President earlier in the day hadn't gotten through or had a response. I couldn't wait.

We soared through the air so naturally that I soon felt calmer, close to Zephyr and in our element, but I could feel the seriousness under everything.

*I know we're worried that Amcika had more to do with us*

*coming together than we'd have liked. But whatever's happened, know this. I wouldn't change it,* Zephyr said. *I wouldn't change meeting you. I wouldn't change being your bonded mythical. Whatever got us to that moment is okay. It might hurt, but being your bonded dragon is worth it all.*

Zephyr's words took me by surprise, but I felt the same.

*Whatever Amcika did, they brought us together. And I love you. Entirely.*

*Completely.*

*Always.*

*Always.*

Warmth spread through us as we continued to fly, nothing more needing to be said. We were united, and we were going to get answers.

The portal site came into view more quickly than usual, my mind having automatically helped us speed up, leaving the convoy behind us as we came in to land. The soldiers spotted us and waved, friendly and making me feel welcome and hopeful.

By the time Zephyr and I had touched down, the convoy was pulling up to the main gate. The major had come out to greet us again.

"The general would like to see you," he said as I studied his face.

Unable to tell if it was a good or bad thing by the look in his eyes, I reached for Zephyr with my mind, hoping he'd come with me. The general seemed to respect us more now, but having Zephyr at my side wouldn't hurt.

We came closer together and I rested my hand on his shoulder, the feel of his warm, smooth scales comforting.

He leaned into me briefly before we found the general's office.

"Aella, Zephyr. It is good to see you've returned. It has been a strange twenty-four hours since the major returned from your mission." The general's businesslike tone was almost unexpected, but it made me feel easier.

"What's happened?" I asked, wondering why the major hadn't said anything.

"The portal has been acting oddly again. The major has the scientists here monitoring it, but the anomalies you associate with the presence of another on the other side of the portal have increased. They're no longer...predictable. And a couple of times, they have been stronger. One of the barriers was sucked into the forcefield and torn apart."

I lifted my eyebrows, feeling fear ripple through me. Did the evil on the other side know that something was happening on this side? Was it trying to reach out to the tablets it had felt the time before?

"Has anyone been hurt?" I asked.

"Thankfully, no, but it has me concerned. Are these cult elves likely to be returning here?"

I thought before I shook my head.

"No. I think they're leading me somewhere. I'm not sure where, but they have something to do with me finding Zephyr as an egg, and they seem intent on trying to screw with me emotionally."

"I hope that won't be a problem?" the general replied, suddenly studying me.

"It shouldn't be, but we've got plenty of level-headed people with me, and I respect their judgment. I want answers, but I'll still listen to them when it comes to winning this war."

This seemed to satisfy the man. He nodded and looked down. When he looked back up at me, however, there was sadness on his face.

"In the heat of battle, anything can happen. And I know sometimes we can find ourselves standing effectively alone, facing an enemy we only know we have to beat. When that moment comes, we can't always know what we're going to do, but we'll have to live with it afterward. It's clear you're doing a better job than a lot of people would do. I hope if that moment ever comes to you, that you act in a way that you can live with."

"Thank you," I replied, knowing I'd been offered acceptance and at the same time respect and a confession. I was honored by his words.

"Now, tell me what you're planning and how we can keep defending these portals best."

Zephyr and I spent the next half an hour swiftly going over the plan. We hinted at what Amcika knew of Zephyr and me and what role they might have played in our early lives, but we didn't go into detail, focusing on the strategy for facing them and how we intended to win.

The general had advice, but he mostly approved what we were intending.

"It sounds as if it's going to be tough on the troops, but if the first battle goes well enough, you can pull it off. I've had more soldiers assigned here over time, and I can talk to the President about getting more. Take your pick and work with the major, and you've got yourself a mission. But I want to ask one thing."

"Name it," I replied.

"If it looks like the elves are going to attack here, or whatever it is on the other side of this portal makes even more of a dent in our defenses, bring everyone straight back."

"I'd do that anyway. This portal is clearly the more important one. They might have one of their own, but...this one is what they truly want open."

"It would seem that way."

With this, I wished the general well, made sure he could contact Zephyr and me and returned to the folks outside. The general's orders were relayed to the major, who appeared at my side again mere moments after I'd greeted Minsheng.

Already many of the soldiers were ready to move out, the major having anticipated my request to take a larger team than before, and there were more trucks ready to go.

A part of me wondered how this was possible and how we'd truly thought we could take on the US government in previous months and years. We'd gotten lucky in many ways in our earlier battles, and I was grateful I didn't have to fight the many men and women lining up to accompany me to the fight.

By the time they were ready to head out, I had talked to Ronan again. The centaurs were pretty sure they'd found the trail and were on their way to find the elves again. Minsheng had also briefly had a look at the portal once more and the information from the previous spikes. He'd confirmed that someone seemed to be trying to punch through.

I shuddered as I thought about the evil I'd connected to.

It couldn't be allowed. With any luck, it never would. But we were going to have to do something about Amcika once and for all. With the team I had and the mythicals I was bonded with, we would hopefully stop them forever.

Flying on Zephyr's back, I put the fears and thoughts of the Texas portal behind me for now. It was time to find some elves and the tablets they carried and hope that we could stop them before they unleashed hell on earth.

## CHAPTER SEVENTEEN

The wilderness was almost a blur beneath us as Zephyr flew high in the sky. We could feel Sen and Roth. They were guiding the convoy as we went to join Ronan as swiftly as we could. They'd found tracks and something more interesting. More fragments of a tablet.

So many thoughts ran through my head about what that might mean and if something was happening in Amcika. I didn't understand what I was up against, and although we were making the best plan we could, this wasn't going to be predictable or easy.

Eventually, Zephyr spotted Ronan and the other centaurs, watching yet another building. We were warier approaching this one, the evening late.

Touching down a long way off, Zephyr and I moved closer as quietly as we could. My powers were once again deployed to keep the air and ground from giving away our movement as we got closer.

Ronan came toward us, something evident in his hand in the gloom under the trees. I felt the draw to it as soon as he came close. A fragment of a water tablet, the power wanting to leave me and fill it as if it was a dry well or a hard sponge that could be made to hold so much.

It took control not to react to it.

"These were found to one side of the path about a mile from here. An elf deliberately walked out away from the main group and dropped this before coming back into the path with the others," he explained.

"Like they wanted us to find it?"

"Like they wanted the group not to have it."

"But it's only a fragment."

*Maybe it's all they could get away without anyone noticing,* Zephyr's deep voice stated.

I frowned as I thought through the possibilities. This was unexpected. Did we have an ally in the Amcika group? Or was this another ploy to get me to follow them into a trap? They'd trapped me once, and they'd fooled me many times.

*There's no way to be sure. We can only do what we think is best and hope we don't break us. Or anyone else.*

*What do you think is best?*

*That we keep on,* Zephyr said. *If we miss an opportunity to take those tablets away from them and they use them to open the portal, we'll dislike ourselves. If they open the portal despite our best attempts, we'll be able to live with it, and we'll get ready for whatever comes through.*

*Just as the general hoped.*

*Exactly.*

"Okay, let's get ready to attack and try to take some more tablets. I want tablets, not elves, if we can help it this time," I said, lifting my head and feeling the determination grow in me again.

Somehow I had become the leader of an entire army, and I couldn't keep fighting it. I couldn't keep hoping someone else would take charge and tell me what to do. This was my war to fight. I wasn't alone, but I was the one giving the final orders. I was the one who had to step up and put everything I had into this.

Resolved, I asked Ronan to show me everything he could. While we waited for the rest of our allies to arrive and get ready to mount another attack, we began planning.

So far, the elves had always found an escape route, and they had seemed to know we were coming. This time I had everyone hang back from the building, and I went forward alone. I felt around the whole building, especially underground, to be sure that no one was running out of tunnels this time.

The building before us this time was an office block, built beside a large factory. The factory was wrecked and had been looted over the years, but the offices had been boarded up and protected.

I didn't need to look at a database to know this was in my name, no doubt bought the same day as the others. I might not know why, but I knew one thing: they were trespassing on my property. I was about to claim it back.

When Roth, Sen, and Zephyr gave me the signal to let me know everyone was in place, I reached out, pushing into the building and not caring if the air elf was there to detect me.

I could feel their control, the building under their watch, but I could also feel the tablets. Unlike the previous two occasions, they weren't in one area that called to me. They were spread over the building, one in the grip of almost every elf inside.

Again I counted approximately thirty or so of the elves, my mind feeling around them as they sprang from sleep or came rushing in from watch posts.

In the middle was one who was far calmer. Someone who had been sitting in the very middle, head bowed until our minds seemed to touch. My gut was pretty sure it was the air elf I'd been up against all this time.

Before long, they rose to their feet, not looking toward me but beginning to move.

At the same time, I could feel the army I commanded starting to head into action. Centaurs were working with elves and soldiers to form an almost perfect circle. As I continued to explore with my mind, trying to pinpoint the air elf, I felt their mind reaching out to me, probing as much as I was.

Slowly, controlled, and with the focus still on the office ahead of me, I rose into the air. Roth, Zephyr, and Sen came behind me, flying to me as quickly as they could.

As I rose, I took control of the earth underneath the office, making sure none of it could be used to tunnel except for one small area. If the elves fled that way, they would only be able to go toward the soldiers. The US military was waiting and ready to shoot first. If the elves ran out of the only two doors on the building, they would be met by two groups of my elves.

And if they flew out, they would be met by me. And a dragon, pegasus, and dryad.

This time we weren't letting them out without a fight.

As everyone with me got into position, the elves inside grouped up to make their move. I felt the earth elves trying to snatch control from me. I fought their minds, concentrating and wobbling in the air until Roth caught me.

Grateful for the support of the winged water horse, I closed my eyes and doubled my effort. At the same time, I reached into the bag I carried and touched the earth tablet stowed in it. I could feel it reaching to me to try to get me to fill it more, but I needed its power. Instead of using my power, I used the tablet to fight against the elves inside the structure.

While I held on for as long as I could, the pressure increasing as the elves inside pulled on earth tablets of their own, my earth elves tunneled with the soldiers ever closer. At the same time, Zephyr exhaled gas outside the windows and doors, and other air elves stepped up to hold it in place.

Before the cult elves could get out, Erlan and Seth, one on each side of the building, set fire to it. A rush of flames engulfed the space around the entire building, stopping anyone from being able to come outside. I could feel the heat as it blossomed outward, but the fire and air elves kept it contained and swirling around the building far longer than I'd have thought possible.

By the time it faded out, the elves had regrouped inside, the air elf in the middle still standing there. I was pretty sure he was giving commands, but I couldn't make out what they were or what he was waiting for.

There were two tablets on him. That much I could feel. And they didn't pull at my abilities, trying to suck me in the way that the others did.

At some point, the elf would unleash them, and I'd have to try to counter. It wasn't going to be easy, especially if the earth elves continued to drain me. Zephyr was on standby, flying around the building and making sure I didn't lose anyone. He was in dragon form, and Sen and Roth were sticking with me, but who knew how things would change?

As my elves got closer, tightening the net around the cult elves, my abilities waned. The tablet was almost spent, the energy that had been stored in it gone enough that the rune-covered stone was tugging at my mind again with an almost irresistible pull as it called me to fill it.

When it was too much to bear, I cut my contact and slung the bag with the tablet over Roth's neck. At the same time, I powered off his back and toward the building. My mind was still fighting the earth elves, some of them thankfully beginning to wane, but I was weaker in that regard and concentrating on flying once more.

I landed on the edge of the roof, feeling pain as someone stole control from me below the office. I frowned and tried to hit back at them. Instead, another of my air elves beat me to it, and then I felt the earth elves from the Sanctuary as they worked toward the bottom of the building floor.

Aware they were being hemmed in, the elves inside were ushered by their leader into a new formation. Some of them were gathered around the area where the Sanctuary group was going to pop up, preparing to attack. I was worried that this was going to be a shock, and I needed to do something.

Before I could defend anyone from possible threats,

however, there was also movement from the back door. The Amcika fighters had rallied water elves, put out the lingering fire in a circle around the building, and were keeping the area clear of magical abilities.

I ran across the top of the roof, heading toward that door, although I was aware that my power wasn't at full strength anymore, and taking on an entire group of powerful cult elves might be impossible. This wasn't an ideal fight by a long way.

I got there in time to blast a couple of elves inside and try to shut the door before I felt the creeping reach of the air elf inside the office. The time had come to face him head-on.

Trying to be in two places at once and struggling to know which way to turn, I hoped I was doing the right thing. I let go of the air by the door and ran to the center of the office building roof where a stairwell stood, giving access to the roof for whoever happened to be below.

The presence of the elves grew, as did the tug on my mind from the tablets coming closer. I took control of the air, knowing that the elves could potentially fly out of the building if I wasn't careful.

At the same time, a small group of my air elves landed nearby, having flown from the ground when they saw me land on the roof. If the elves couldn't get out of a tunnel and we were keeping the doors and windows blocked, that left the roof.

But I was the most powerful air elf I knew about, and I was in their way.

On top of that, Zephyr still flew around above me along with Roth and Sen. If anyone did get past me, they would come face to face with another mythical intent on stopping them.

Before I could take control of the air on the roof, I was hit with a large blast. It knocked me off my feet and pushed me almost flat as I took control of enough air near me that I could start building a barrier. It took me several agonizing moments to get to my feet.

The world around me was a blur at first, the air moving in strange directions, but I slowly managed to get it under control. The other elves I was with had to back off and regroup as I tackled the elf in the building below. Fighting him for control was quickly draining me, but I could feel him using up everything he was carrying to fight me mentally.

For a while, neither of us had the capacity to overwhelm the other, but then he began pushing harder in one area, and before long, I felt other air elves. I took a hammering and was not sure I could hang on. My body was focused on breathing and the exercises I'd been taught as I stood still and kept my grip as tightly as I could.

Wondering if the masters often felt similar teaching the rest of us, I opened my eyes and focused on my enemy once more. It wasn't easy, but I slowly regained my position, holding the ground steady and not feeling too overwhelmed. When I was seconds into this stage, I noticed there were more elves underneath in the building, and the fire elves in there hadn't yet done anything.

It made me pause and encourage Roth to get the water elves ready. The last thing we needed was for the fire elves to blast everything we had under control to pieces. At the same time as Roth flew lower to give the fire elves nearby time to see him reacting to the threat, I reached around beneath the office again, feeling rather than knowing that the elves had breached the floor.

There was a moment of respite as the earth elves and soldiers pouring inside caused so much chaos the air elf in charge was forced to go to the aid of his cult.

No longer under pressure, I lifted myself to my feet and straightened. Despite the fighting I'd done, I still felt fairly good. Reaching into a pocket, I remembered where I'd put my energy bars. It was a brief respite, and I was going to make the most of it.

As soon as I could, I was going to make these elves wish they'd never been born.

CHAPTER EIGHTEEN

I blasted the door open, then strode into the heart of the building. I could hear the sound of the battles raging inside. I hesitated by the door, wanting to block an exit but also wanting to go to the aid of the mythicals and human soldiers trying to do their best in the building.

Before I could make up my mind, I was hit with another blast of air that came from in front of me. Somehow the air elf had moved through the building and managed to find a pocket of air I didn't control.

I was flung back again, losing control of the earth once more as I had to concentrate to use the air to slow and protect my tumbling body. Managing to stay upright, I powered forward again, wrapping myself in a thicker barrier.

"Watch out on the roof," I heard a familiar voice yell before the very ground beneath me seemed to explode up and out, flinging my body along with it.

The blast burned heat through my torso as something exploded and flames jetted up after me. The air around me had kept me from doing more than flying back, cushioning me. Shards of concrete and metal came flying along with me as someone yelled in my head. Words I couldn't focus on.

I pushed up and above it all, flying clear as the familiar bronze scales of Zephyr flew past me and shielded me from the rest. I felt small bursts of pain as debris hit his underside, and then the roof that had been blown off the building rained down everywhere. Five more air elves tumbled upward and outward, slowly getting under control or landing. Many of them were exhausted now.

Knowing that it could hurt everyone on the ground around us, I called to Zephyr and focused on pulling the air in around the building, whipping it in circles hard and fast so it could help catch and contain it all. Zephyr caught me, flying underneath as I cut off the jets keeping me in the sky, and I concentrated on the debris.

I was too late to stop all of it and there was fire everywhere, but I did my best to land the larger of the rubble and broken parts out of the way, funneling it there. My body hurt and my head pounded, but it was a background feeling, the concern I felt and the need to help the others far too pressing.

By the time the air was calm once more. The fire elves were working to put out the fires, air and water elves joining them; the battle was over. The group of cult elves had flown out of the chaos while I was trying to stop the flying building parts.

Zephyr banked to see the Amcika elves as I spotted them landing in a clearing off to one side, but I only got a glimpse of the elves, the male air elf with them wrapped in a cloak and hidden from view by the elves with him.

I lifted off Zephyr's back.

*Turn. Let's get these elves once and for all*, I said to Zephyr as he continued to circle around to the building we'd been fighting in.

*No, we're needed here. The elves and soldiers underground are trapped.*

The last word Zephyr uttered made me turn and fly to the building, fear gripping at my heart. As I took in the final sight of the building, I felt worse. It had collapsed, and plenty of our elves were under there somewhere, along with most of the soldiers.

Zephyr and I landed beside each other as he morphed into human form. Everyone not dealing with a fire came rushing up.

"We need to get them out before more collapses," Ronan said, his hooves pounding on the ground as he came to a sharp stop.

I nodded, reaching into it with my mind and feeling for the parts I could control.

"Keep the fire and water elves putting out the fires, get me every air and earth elf," I said.

Most of the elves who heard me got into two groups, Zephyr adding to the earth elves and giving me a nod.

I moved closer to the air elves and focused on them, feeling Zephyr's control as he started creating a new tunnel, heading down under the foundations of the building.

"We need to get as much of this building safe as possible and make sure no more falls down on them. Work in teams of two, pulling debris out. Be careful not to knock anything down any further. Don't rush it, but let's take some pressure off and make sure they get some air down there. Spread out around the building and get to work."

An even number of elves in front of me moved out. I looked for the worst section alone and got to work. At the same time, I kept the entire area under surveillance, feeling the areas as the other air elves worked.

Minsheng organized the centaurs and soldiers we had above ground to help put fires out that were dangerously close to people and also used his device to help pinpoint anything tablet-based inside the building.

Our battle had switched into a rescue mission so fast that it was only as I helped catch rubble dislodged by another elf that I processed what was happening. I wanted to scream and rage, aware this battle hadn't gone to plan either.

Exhaling, I tried not to let my anger get the better of me. I had to focus. I was catching chunks of concrete and twisted metal and stopping the building from falling down.

Some of the earth elves joined me as one of the walls wobbled, helping to pull it down away from the building and giving it a more controlled landing. It opened up one side of the building and allowed those without powers to start working their way toward the elves underground.

I paused a moment to feel down into the earth, aware my headache was growing worse.

"Food," I said to a soldier as he came close. "Get someone to start passing all the elves some food."

I thought he was going to argue with me, but he watched as I reached into my pocket and pulled out the last energy bar I had. I tore it open while focusing on catching a piece of broken pipe as it fell off, saving the soldier underneath. This seemed to demonstrate the importance of keeping us fed and the soldier soon ran off again to do as I asked.

I could feel the group of elves and soldiers under the surface, many of them having been underneath the building in the tunnels we'd created when the building collapsed. There were some trapped by the rubble, however, and I was aware that a couple of them weren't moving.

Focusing again, I felt through the area and over the parts of the rubble on top of them. There had to be a good way to get them out and make sure no one else was hurt.

While Zephyr continued to tunnel through and get the elves and soldiers some air, I focused on guiding everyone else in from the top. Someone handed out sandwiches and soup, the elves having their hands free after all, we continued to work. Then an elf had to stop, entirely drained, but they rested only long enough to eat more and refocus.

I didn't stop, eating almost constantly as Zephyr continued not far from me. With the fires soon out, the water and fire elves joined everyone who couldn't fight with an element, and they formed several convoys of people hauling rubble away as the elves freed it. While we were working, rescue services people showed up, some of them specializing in this sort of thing.

They said very little, their eyes wide as I used my air power to catch a pillar as it went to topple. Quickly elves and mythicals moved in, taking pieces and breaking it up between them. Like ants destroying a piece of cake, it was soon a pile of rubble to one side.

I vaguely listened as the soldiers nearby filled the newcomers in and then the guy came to my side.

"I know you're concentrating and keeping a lot of people safe, but I think we can guide you on the best route in. Can you keep me safe as I get closer with some gear?"

"Yes," I replied, not wasting my words or doing more than glancing at the gray-haired guy.

He nodded, and we walked closer. As he stepped onto the rubble, I told him exactly where everyone was, my mind seeing it as I felt downward. We'd cleared about a third of the path to them, but he was almost certainly right that we weren't doing it in the best way possible.

*We've gotten air through to them*, Zephyr said a moment later. *But the earth elves are far too exhausted to get the tunnel wide enough or stable enough to bring anyone out this way yet.*

*We'll save them. One way or another*, I replied, momentarily ignoring the man beside me.

A moment later, Zephyr came over, Sen on his shoulder. She jumped down as the guy bent down, stopping on the last stable section of rubble. He had a camera attached via a lead on a small robotic device to a screen in his hands.

"Give it to Sen," I said as she came running up. "She'll get it where you need it, and I can direct her with my mind."

Once more the guy's eyes went wide, but he did as I suggested. I moved closer to him. I rested my abilities as we calmed down the process and waited to see if the experts could focus us better. Sen darted into a small hole with the camera, going where my mind guided her.

I watched the picture on the camera along with the rescue marshal beside me and let him suggest when Sen should backtrack or when he needed a better look at some of the debris in the way.

"How much control can you exercise?" he asked, a moment later, his eyes never leaving the screen as he got Sen to show him a large length of metal and concrete that was wedged across a path. "Can you get something like that out without brushing up against anything you don't need to?"

"With enough rest, I could say yes with no problem. If you give Zephyr or me enough time—"

"We can do it together," Zephyr said, interrupting me and coming close enough to take my hand.

I exhaled and nodded. Yes, together, we could feel each other's thoughts, control, and intentions. Together we would have enough power left.

"Okay, then I think we can get to them," the marshal said, but he kept asking me to direct Sen until we'd reached the first of the elves. I was relieved to see a smiling face and a pocket where an air and earth elf had worked together to create a small space for themselves. They appeared to be cut off from the elves underground, or at least, they weren't able to get through to them easily.

I exhaled, knowing this wasn't going to be a quick process. I wouldn't stop until it was done and we'd rescued everyone we could.

With Sen down there and a camera, the marshal had someone bring a second one. Sen retreated, leaving the first so we could communicate with those below while also making sure we were watching what we were doing as we went.

Zephyr stayed by my side and, with the direction of professionals who knew what they were doing in this situation, we began clearing the debris out in a more organized way. Several more earth and air elves came to join us as things were complicated, and we slowly opened the path again.

I was growing tired once more and knew that the hardest section was still coming up. I needed to find the focus and strength for it. In case it was going to cause a lot more of the rubble to fall, the earth elves gathered around, and Sen pulled out of the gap. Then Zephyr and I got as close as we could.

It wasn't easy to get it moving, but we acted in sync and reached out to connect to half each, our minds moving over each other intuitively. I felt my head pound, but no one else could work with Zephyr to get this done.

*Take a deep breath. We can do this. You can do this*, Zephyr said.

I did as he suggested, feeling the warmth and support from Roth and Sen as they came closer.

Without needing to nod to each other, Zephyr and I started lifting together, our minds controlling the large chunk of debris as we slid it out of the area. It had to move perfectly, not touching anything, but even then its passage caused other bits of debris and rubble to fall, some of it having been resting on top.

Other earth elves came to help, keeping anything from falling into the gap we were creating. The air elves came with them, clearing the air of the dust and finer particles by blowing it gently away from the building.

I tried not to be distracted by what they were doing and concentrate on keeping steady and confident, using earth and air in sync to move the large object.

We were about halfway when we reached a narrower section. We were trying to pass the largest section of the jagged column through it. We had to pause, the current orientation not going to fit without pushing something out of the way.

*Twist it*, Zephyr said. *It will fit through if we turn it upside down.*

I exhaled, not sure how easy that would be. We had to try, though. As Zephyr and I began turning, the marshal shifted the second camera and moved it closer with the robotic element of the arm so we could see what we were doing better.

The pressure increased, but I continued to ignore it, knowing that if I let go or stopped, it would go crashing down the hole and do more damage than it already had.

Slowly, gently, we rotated the pillar and kept it at the same angle in the hole. For a brief moment, one part rubbed against another large block of building, and the whole mound shifted ever so slightly. Zephyr and I stopped moving again and made sure the earth and air elves could keep everything out of the way.

I saw one of the pieces of debris that were making it harder for us to shift, another earth elf using the other tablet we had to boost their powers and make it safer in other ways. I exhaled again as I realized they'd stopped something we'd missed, grateful we weren't alone.

With our way clear and the pillar turned, we continued, easing it out of the pile inch by painstaking inch. The pain grew until I was gritting my teeth, the other subconscious uses of my abilities entirely gone as I focused everything on controlling the air and earth in front of me.

Zephyr's grip on my hand tightened as my focus slipped and the whole thing dropped an inch. I bit down on my lip and tried again, almost done.

We moved faster as the pillar was finally mostly clear until it was safe to put it down. As I let go of it and the elements I'd been controlling I swayed on my feet, my mind going blank a moment.

Zephyr's arms closed around me as my vision blurred. I clung to him, unable to feel my bond to him, Roth, or Sen despite them being close. I'd pushed my abilities to the endpoint. I had nothing left.

It wasn't the first time, but it felt as bad as it had the previous time.

For now, I was alone in my head.

## CHAPTER NINETEEN

Sitting beside the ruined building, I watched and slowly ate and drank as the rest of the elves and Zephyr finished the job and rescued everyone trapped underground. My bonds had faintly returned, but they still felt weak and tired compared to normal, and talking into Zephyr's head seemed harder.

There were several elves and humans sporting injuries and two were out cold, as I'd feared when the building had first collapsed. I couldn't help but get to my feet, my head spinning as I did.

As soon as I was sure I wasn't going to pass out myself, I made my way over to the injured elves, noticing that one of the unconscious pair was a cult elf and not one of ours. It made me feel sad for them that they had been caught up in everything, their side setting off the bomb that buried them.

I remembered what I'd seen and felt of the air elf. So far, he'd given me the impression that he was ruthless, willing to put his elves at risk to get away, but he was also playing a dangerous game with my allies and me. Was this the elf who had attacked my contact in Canada? There had been a fight in the man's apartment.

But if they had attacked him, then where was the person who'd taken me to the police station all those years so? Had they taken him somewhere else? Or worse? I still had so many questions and so few answers, and that wasn't likely to change anytime soon.

The moment everyone was safe and being tended to, I went to Zephyr's side again. In his human form, he put his arms around me and simply held me, the presence of his body and the feel of our minds as they merged, helping me feel calm again.

Roth and Sen came closer, and the four of us huddled together. I pulled away a moment later, however. We couldn't stay where we were much longer. We needed to figure out what had happened and make more plans. The elves were still out there, and the days and nights seemed to be flying past as we tried to catch them.

*We've gained some more tablets and another two of their elves*, Zephyr said.

I exhaled in relief, but it wasn't enough. We were slowly making them weaker, but it was costing us much more. It wasn't sustainable. We needed something that would make it easier. Another edge that the cult elves didn't have.

*They've been planning this.*

*And we're still just reacting*, I replied.

*We need a way to get ahead of them.* Zephyr's eyes met mine as he said what I was thinking.

The buildings they had been going to. They were all in my name. We'd verified it after they'd left the first deed, but they were following a chain of buildings. And each and every one belonged to me. Could someone find us more of them nearby? Could we beat them to a building?

We rushed over to Minsheng and the major, my body feeling tired and achy after everything it had been through but my mind overruling the pain and filling me with adrenaline.

Zephyr joined me in explaining to Minsheng and the major what might help, and their eyes went wide. The organization had been tracking the buildings for us simply because it made financial sense. With every building the cult had revealed to us, I'd essentially become wealthier, finding there was even more property in my name.

The major and Minsheng pulled out cell phones and called their contacts, making me feel better about the idea Zephyr and I had. If they were as excited as we were, it was a good sign we'd thought of something that might prove more useful.

Within minutes they were back, people on the task of finding out what else might be owned by me in a sensible radius. Once again, we called a meeting of everyone involved.

My heart almost broke again as I was informed about everyone injured and hurt and how exhausted everyone was. With the battle and the collapsed building after it, every elf had pushed their abilities to the extreme, me included. Every human and mythical ally had physically exerted themselves, either underground or above, trying to clear the rubble.

With the building taped off and the people safe, the rescue team had left, many of them getting a quick selfie with a mythical creature before they did. I couldn't blame their enthusiasm, but there were a lot of requests that they stayed off social media for now. The last thing we wanted was a bunch of folks descending on us, trying to get pictures.

Most of the teams were resting, sleeping in tents or the back of trucks, as night drew in. I wanted to rest too, but I was aware that some of the centaurs were out again tracking, and not everyone else could sleep yet.

No doubt the elves we were chasing were also somewhere resting, drained. During the last battle, most of the elves on our side had talked of moments when they thought they had the upper hand, and then a seemingly spent elf had pulled energy out of a tablet and hit back with it. It had been effective.

Now, of course, we had an array of different tablets, and there were fewer of them. But I had several injured soldiers and mythicals, and some of them weren't going to be able to fight a second time, no matter how much I might want them to.

*Rest*, Zephyr said. *We can't do any more right now. But I know the major and everyone else is willing to try at least once more, even with the building coming down on so many.*

I sighed, grateful for Zephyr as we found a spot near the trees and out of the way. In dragon form, he curled his tail around me as I lay down, and I was soon asleep beside him. His calm presence and even breathing were enough to make me feel safe even in the edge of the forest out in the open.

The sound of Minsheng and Zephyr talking woke me

several hours later, the moon high in the sky and the first thing I saw when I opened my eyes.

As soon as I stirred, Zephyr acknowledged my presence, and I sat up.

"We've found a couple more buildings. They're looking for more. But your idea worked," Minsheng said, the gleam in his eyes obvious in the dark.

"We won't know if it will work yet. Not until we beat them to a location. Where are they?" I asked, getting straight to business.

I was relieved when the major came a moment later, carrying a large bowl of something hot and a spoon in his other hand.

"Holfin said you'd want this, and Zephyr can get some too if he heads over to the main tent," the major said.

There was an appreciative rumble from Zephyr as he made his way over there, careful not to flatten anything with his large body.

Pulling up a map on the tablet he'd been carrying under one arm, the major showed me where the two locations were and filled me in on the details about them. It was strange to know that I owned these places, and no one had known until the organization and the government had pulled strings to unbury things long buried.

It made me wonder what other secrets were out there that no one knew about. What else did people hide in plain sight?

"And these are both abandoned?" I asked.

"As far as we can tell, they all have been the last two or three years at least," the major said.

I frowned as he finished speaking, realizing the significance of what he was saying. Had they been used until I'd developed my abilities and bonded with Zephyr?

There was no way to know for sure, but I did know I was about to make use of them now. All of them. It was time I took control.

After deliberating over it, I started putting together thoughts on how to use the information we had best. I didn't want to hit these elves again and fail.

"Do you think you can get the general to agree to send a small team to both these locations and just see what the elves do when they show up?" I asked a moment later.

The major nodded. "It would be a good idea. And if it means we have more information at another location, then I think he'd be all for it."

"Good, then do that and see if there are any more locations farther out. We'll make them think we're attacking the next one, but we'll have most of the team waiting at the place we drive them to."

Minsheng grinned as Ronan came up and showed he'd heard everything. With most of the elves and centaurs still resting, we didn't have much to do, but Ronan also looked over the map.

"I think they're more likely to choose this second location," the centaur said a moment later. "We're still tracking them. They're moving slowly and we're trying not to get too close, but they're heading in a direction that seems as if it will be the next target."

The major quickly called the general again and let him know. With gratitude flowing through me, I coordinated his men so the elves would have some silent watchers waiting for them. I then went to find Roth and Sen, feeling them nearby and awake.

Finding them with Daisy and Emily by another small tent out of the way, I smiled as Roth and Emily worked together to control some water in a large bucket. I felt a pang of jealousy. I'd been so busy leading this little army that I'd not had much time to talk to any of my mythicals or train with them, and here were Roth and Emily, working together as if they were the bonded pair.

As I came closer, they stopped and I smiled, wondering if I should offer to let Roth go so he could bond with Emily.

*It wouldn't work*, Zephyr said, coming toward me from the other side of the clearing.

He licked around his mouth as he met my gaze and made it clear that he'd heard my thoughts. I didn't know how to reply.

*Roth is bonded to you. If you let him go, there would be no bond for him.*

I don't want to cut him loose, but I don't want him to be unhappy either.

*He's happy. You can feel it coming off him in waves. We'll all have others in our lives and people we get along with better. And Roth is very much a water creature. And you're still getting to grips with water. It's not your strongest element. Even with him having fun with Emily, that doesn't mean he wants anything different from the life he has now.*

I nodded before I realized that several of the others were staring at me.

"Sorry," I said out loud. "I was trying to understand something."

Emily smiled and looked between Zephyr and me. It made me once again wish that she could have a bonded mythical. That all the elves could.

"Have you got time to come and sit with us?" Emily asked. "There's some cool stuff Roth and I were working on that might help in the next battle."

I nodded, willing to sit down and give them my time even if I didn't really have any. Sometimes people had to come first.

Over the next few minutes, Emily and Roth showed me a way of passing the water between them, Roth using his body to soak it up and supply it for Emily to then control and manipulate.

It was impressive. I made sure they both knew how cool it was, then I got them to show me the trick again. After watching them a few more times and feeling what happened to the water with my mind, I was ready to try something similar.

I helped Emily put the water in the large bucket Roth was standing in with my abilities. Then it was my turn to try controlling it. I focused on the element as Roth pulled it into him and prepared to jet it out again. It felt strange to be trying to take control of an element still inside him, but he assured me it didn't hurt as long as I didn't do anything with it until it left his body.

As it came blasting from the center of his forehead, I helped narrow the spray, turning it into a blast that could be directed in all sorts of ways. It was incredibly powerful, and I made it more so until the bucket ran out and the water was in the forest beyond.

"Wow," Emily said a moment later. "You did that even better than I can."

I blinked, having not expected it to be true. Zephyr had been right that the water element was my least effective. I didn't feel as if I understood it the way I did the others at all. And I frequently worried that the fire element would be harder to learn to control.

Emily quickly worked with Roth to collect as much of the water as possible and get it into the bucket. At the same time, Minsheng appeared with another large container full, pulling it along the ground with a cart.

Not sure I was entirely impressed that this had turned into an impromptu lesson, but feeling the delight and excitement in Roth and not wanting to disappoint him, I prepared to do the same technique again.

Minsheng hooked the container up with the bucket, making sure that it would flow fast enough to replenish the smaller vessel as Roth sucked the water up. At the same time, Daisy and Emily made a set of makeshift targets about thirty feet away in the forest using empty food wrappers, cans, branches, and rocks.

I tried not to panic at the increased difficulty of the task and focused on simply doing as I'd done before. Roth was grinning as he lowered his head and started sucking the water. I concentrated once more. As the element opened up to my mind, I felt Roth move it through his body. He jetted it out of his head.

This time I didn't just focus on narrowing the spray of water, helping to keep it flowing in a focused burst, but I helped Roth direct it. The pegasus aimed pretty well. Within ten seconds, we had knocked everything off the platforms and out of the trees where it had been placed, each jet of water passing cleanly over everything until it hit the obstacle.

The rocks were the hardest to move, the largest needing me to concentrate the force more and having Roth do everything he could to boost the amount of water flowing. As it flew off the branch Daisy had put it on, everyone clapped.

It was only as Roth stopped the water from flowing and I looked around that I realized an audience had gathered. We had been performing for several of the elves and many of the soldiers.

"Impressive," the major said. "I'm really starting to see why you elves and mythicals are so feared. Glad you're on our side, Henera."

I nodded as I blinked, aware it was the first time a human had used my elven title. It felt strange but also right.

Beside me, I could feel the pride and delight in Roth, and I promised myself I would train with him more in the future. I'd been so focused on what I could do that I'd lost sight of what my team could achieve if we worked together.

## CHAPTER TWENTY

As I sat with Zephyr in the shade, the group still waiting for news and information, I pondered the best move for us to make. The camp was almost entirely packed up, everyone getting ready to move out again.

I felt guilty that I wasn't helping much, but after training some more with Roth and filling the fragments of tablet we had, I had been out of energy again.

The fire tablet had remained inactive when I'd tried to connect to it. It was frustrating, given Minsheng had expected the tablets to let elves with different elements wield them.

I had a look through the notebook Orthelo had given me while there were few people to see what it contained. There were all sorts of things either copied or stuck into the pages—letters and sections of lore books.

All of it had been translated to English. Not necessarily perfectly, but well enough that I could understand what it said. It was clear that the belt of the great fire elemental from Tuviel's time had been passed to an elf of another element, and they had taken it somewhere else. That was where the journal grew vaguer, the writers unsure which direction it had gone in.

Given the importance of the item, it was either still in hiding with the elf who'd received it or it was hidden somewhere, but the notebook didn't give me much of an idea of which one of those options might be the truth nor exactly which elf held the belt in the first place. It was clear someone thought they had joined Amcika, but there were a lot of elves in the mountain.

*I'm sure we can figure it out*, Zephyr said as I read a letter about the choice of elf to see if it gave me any information I could use. *If it's in that mountain, we'll find it.*

I sighed and nodded as I put the notebook away. It was just in time to hide it from Minsheng as he appeared.

"More news. Looks like it's time to move out," my Shishou said.

Scrambling to my feet, I tried not to look too excited about his words. I was ready to get to tracking down the cult and getting more answers of another kind.

Minsheng led me to the other commanders. I joined the group, Zephyr, Roth, and Sen with me. There was a strange expectancy in the looks they gave me, but I merely looked to Minsheng to explain.

"The organization and the government combined have found more locations. Some have fallen into disrepair and are no longer close. One is under an ownership dispute, but there are a couple more nearby."

"Great. Can we narrow them down?" I asked.

"Yes. We can now that our teams at the other two buildings have reported in," the major said before Minsheng could reply.

I lifted my eyebrow, hoping we finally had some solid information.

"They've gone south-east, and they're hiding in an old pig farm building." The major pointed to the location on the map and then looked at me.

"Tell me everything we know," I replied, glancing at Zephyr to check that he was listening. I might not remember everything later, but Zephyr would. He would help make sure I didn't forget anything important.

I listened as the major described everything he'd been told. How the elves had approached without caution, one of them having keys and many of them acting as if they had been there before. Most importantly, they were tired and drained, having used their abilities to get there. It appeared as if they were low on stone tablets too. It was a good time to strike them.

But we weren't entirely ready yet, and by the time most of us reached the location the cult elves were at, they would have recharged themselves if not the tablets they carried.

*We can go with the ones who can fly and those we can carry,* Zephyr said. *Scare them to move. Use the tablets we have. And everyone else can go lie in wait at the next location.*

It was a good idea, the best one we had.

Given their location, it was obvious where they were going to head. One of the other two sites was near the Mexican border, and they were trying to get what was left of the tablets and elves to their base and portal.

We quickly made plans, deciding to send the elves we'd

captured and one of the tablet fragments to the Texas portal along with enough soldiers and elves to make sure that happened smoothly. We'd captured so many elves we didn't want to keep them with us where they might get free and rejoin a battle.

I also knew the general would want to hear how we were working our way away from him and have a tablet fragment and some of the elves and soldiers who defended his portal back again for peace of mind.

"Okay," I said once the commands had been given. "Let's make sure everyone stays safe this time and we get ourselves as many of those tablets as possible. And then we get out again. No one takes a risk they don't have to. And we all rest as much as we can between now and then."

Minsheng frowned very briefly, but he didn't say anything, and everyone else prepared to go where they were needed. The elves needed to think they were being attacked, and they wouldn't believe that unless Zephyr and I were there to challenge them. We couldn't go that distance without Sen and Roth.

With that in mind, we needed to pack up and prepare for a long flight. We would have to keep flying after we'd gotten the cult elves moving. They would be on their way to a location where we were going to be needed to fight when we arrived. That meant we wouldn't get a rest until this was over and done with, and neither would anyone with us.

As I thought over the plan, several more air elves joined us with their away packs and determined looks on their faces. There weren't many of them, and we had a trio of weaker earth, water, and fire with us, loaded with the tablets we had in each element. They were going to be responsible for making it look like we had the entire army.

At the same time, there was going to be a group of centaurs meeting us there, heading from somewhere Ronan knew. I hadn't been able to ask how he knew where more centaurs were and why he hadn't told me about them, but they were a secretive race, and the Sanctuary wasn't the only place they existed.

I wasn't about to pry. I didn't have the right. Thankfully, Ronan handed me another stone.

"It will help you communicate with my brother. He knows of you, and he commands a unit of centaurs who have trained for aiding mythicals to get from Mexico to the US and the Sanctuary. They know how to travel fast, and he can make it look as if he were me."

I blinked, stunned by the confession and explanation.

"Thank you," I replied a moment later, recovering enough to understand the honor of what I was being trusted with.

I bowed to Ronan, and he did the same. As he walked away, I took a moment to acknowledge the enormity of what we were doing and how many people were relying on us.

Before I could get in the air with the elves riding on Zephyr, Roth and Sen intending to fly alongside me, I noticed Minsheng still lingered. I hurried over to him, thinking of his reaction earlier.

"Be careful, Aella," he said once I was close enough that he could talk quietly. "This is a lot to ask of you and even more of everyone else."

"I'll be as careful as I can," I replied, not sure what was

different about this battle compared to the many we'd faced before.

"I mean it. They're trying to lure you in. And they're still likely to need Zephyr or you to open the portal, even with these tablets. You need to make sure you're not taking risks you don't dare ask other people to."

"I know. But we can't let them open a portal either. And I need to know what they know about me. How they've planned all this and how they knew I would bond with Zephyr. It's not as simple as keeping myself from harm. It never has been."

Minsheng sighed, but he also nodded. "I worry about you as if you're a daughter of mine. I know you're not, but I would protect you like a father should if I could."

I felt a lump form in my throat as his eyes grew wetter and he looked at me.

"Fathers have the difficult task of having to let go so their daughters can prove they were taught and raised well. It's not easy, but I hope I make you proud."

It was Minsheng's turn to look surprised a moment as he blinked away tears. "You already make me proud. All of you."

Zephyr lowered his head as Minsheng reached out and patted the scales on his neck before giving Roth a gentle stroke and rubbing Sen's head. It was a moment no one dared interrupt. Minsheng had taken me in at the beginning and been there at every turn, but there were some things we couldn't do with him anymore.

As soon as he backed off, I turned to the rest of the elves and met their eyes one by one. All of them were looking my way with determined expressions, even if there was a hint of fear in a few cases. We were ready to do this.

"Let me know if any of you are struggling. We just need to fly and get there with as much power left as possible. You all have plenty of food and the tablets we can spare, but we've got to make two journeys in one. If needed, we'll keep you in the air. Got it?"

They nodded, some of them uttering affirmative words of one kind or another. With that, I lifted into the air, flying toward the setting sun and the location we'd be scaring the cult elves from. I tried not to think about how far we had to go, instead lifting and letting Zephyr take the lead. He was carrying two of the elves who couldn't fly with the air element, and Roth was carrying the other. Sen was with the pegasus for now, but I suspected she'd end up curled up in my jacket before we reached the end.

Zephyr was leading the way, and the air elves fanned out behind him in a strange bird-like V. Roth was in the center behind Zephyr, and I flew almost directly above the pegasus.

More than once, as we passed cars, houses, or people outside, I wondered what they would think of us. Although there were areas of LA and some of the places on the route to the Sanctuary where people seemed to have grown accustomed to seeing us, we were a long way away now. People here wouldn't be used to seeing a dragon.

Even with that possibility, however, we focused on one thing: getting to the cult's location as efficiently as possible.

After we'd been traveling for the best part of two hours, the formation dropped a little. We were almost there, but we couldn't show up tired. I needed to make sure we were ready for battle.

I moved lower, studying two of the eight air elves with me. One was struggling.

*Bring us down to land*, I told Zephyr a moment later. *We've got some tired elves.*

*And a tired pegasus,* Roth replied. *I'm not used to carrying someone for so long in the air.*

I nodded, not sure what else we'd do with the female fire elf riding on his back if Roth didn't carry her. Only the air elementals could fly without the aid of a mythical.

*This body is strong enough to hold three*, Zephyr said.

Frowning, I considered arguing, but if I was to arrive at the building with power left, I couldn't fly them. My powers had limits, especially if I wanted to fight for a while.

There were several air tablets or fragments, and I was likely to need one of them if I was going up against their leader again. Mine was stowed in the bag at my side—another thing to weigh me down, as were the food and drink I might consume.

As Zephyr made his descent clear, everyone was relieved. I'd expected too much of them. The worry continued to fill my mind until I was on the ground and I saw them land, having enough strength for that. Most of us reached for food and drink as the elves who were riding slid off their mounts.

It was a strange party in a lot of ways, but I tried not to think about how different it was compared to normal humans and instead focused on eating enough and making sure that everyone else had what they needed. Zephyr didn't eat much, but he closed his eyes. I was worried about him, knowing he would sacrifice the most in terms of physical energy.

While everyone else was eating, I found a quiet spot away from everyone and sat down with the communication stone that Ronan had given me. It was subtly different from the centaur stone I already had, but it seemed as weighty in my hand. It made me wonder if the magic wrought on them made them seem similar.

Not sure how this one might work, I concentrated on it the way I did when I wanted to talk to Ronan, and then I was in a strange meadow. It was both there and not quite there. I looked around, having expected the darkened room I usually spoke to Ronan in.

"Hello," a deep voice said as a centaur entered my view, moving gracefully over the meadow toward me. He quickly slowed and stopped not far in front of me. "You must be Aella. I'm Donnacha."

"I am Aella. Forgive me for calling on you with so little warning and no introduction. I'm honored that you would trust me with one of your communication stones when you and I have never met."

"My brother speaks very highly of you and your selflessness. It was logical to aid you, and this is the best way to ensure we can do so. Tell me where we need to be and what to look out for and we'll join you in battle, even if it is more of a ruse than anything."

I bowed low at his words, mimicking the motion I'd seen Ronan make so many times. The centaur's eyes widened as I straightened. I explained everything I knew, and he listened with the familiar silence and the same mannerisms Ronan did. Donnacha barely moved, and I studied his face.

As far as I could tell, he was younger than Ronan, but on his chin was a long bushy black beard, the thick hair braided in three sections.

His skin was the same deep, almost black tone the majority of centaurs shared. And he had a similar build, the strong torso adorned with the same set of weapons and basic clothes.

As soon as I was done speaking, Donnacha backed up and studied me.

"It sounds as if it will be an honor to fight alongside you. We will be at this location you speak of as soon as is possible and await your presence and your command in taking on these vile creatures and people."

"We're not trying to do too much more than scare them," I pointed out, wanting to make sure none of the centaurs got too ambitious. "We need them to move on and believe they're being attacked by many. If we can capture some of the rune-covered tablets they use, all the better, but our priority is to drive them forward."

"This I can understand. We have used similar tactics with those hunting mythicals in the past. You will have the support of my team and me, and we will continue to the Mexican border with you. It is not in my power to go farther, however."

Once again I bowed, feeling as if I had been offered more than I deserved. "I can't ask any more of you."

With that, Donnacha let go of my mind and the meadow and faded from my vision. I blinked and returned to Zephyr. We only needed to look at each other to know it was time to move out. We had a cult to scare.

## CHAPTER TWENTY-ONE

After flying for half an hour longer, Zephyr dipped lower, his powerful body gliding ahead of me. He was carrying three of the non-air elementals, which meant Roth had regained some of his strength.

The air elves were flying lower, gliding in each other's slipstreams, Zephyr at their front and Roth at their back. Although it was more tiring, I was still flying above it all, but I reacted to Zephyr's movements as he went lower.

*I see the centaurs,* he said. *I think they're waiting for us not far from the building.*

I followed his gaze until I spotted the flank of a large centaur underneath the edge of a leafy canopy. As a unit we lowered, Zephyr guiding us to a place to land. We didn't have to wait for the centaurs to approach, several of them spotting the large dragon and the shadow he made before he landed. I touched down last, using some of my power to help the more tired elves.

It was an impressive landing, even if I hadn't helped— an entire squad of elves and mythicals flying in. I could see the awe on the faces of the centaurs, but they recovered fast and came to join us.

"It looks as if the elves are trying to...*charge* the rune-covered stones they have. We should attack sooner rather than later," Donnacha said as he came to the front of his small team.

"We need a few moments to rest and recover," I said. "And then we'll join you in storming the building and driving them out."

The centaur frowned almost imperceptibly but tilted his head down in a sign of acknowledgment. I tried not to let the frostiness of the reception bother me and reached into my pack to pull out a snack.

At the same time, I plonked myself down beside Zephyr and started munching while I rested against him.

*You should nap if you can*, Zephyr said. *It's going to take a moment for everyone to be ready to fly out again.*

His words made sense, but part of me didn't want to wait or let my guard down for even that long, however. I could feel the centaurs' surprise when we flew in, and rather than heading toward doing our jobs, we sat down and rested. I could also see how exhausted everyone was. Except for the three non-air elementals, everyone had been using their abilities the entire time.

Many others were eating or curling up to nap for whatever time they could get. It made sense for me to do the same.

*Zephyr, you're in charge*, I thought, closing my eyes as I swallowed the last mouthful of the energy bar.

I wasn't going to make this easy on anyone in the building ahead, which meant I needed as much energy as possible. Of course, I still had energy to spare, but more was never going to be something I objected to.

I was distracted by the noises of the elves and other mythicals around me, but I soon felt my body succumbing to sleep and the dream state that went with it. I was beginning to dream seriously, my mind not registering that I was anywhere but my bed when Zephyr gently shifted, his tail moving over my legs and gently waking me up.

My eyes flicked open to see Donnacha standing near Zephyr, the pair deep in a quiet conversation. I got up and made my way over to them, hoping I hadn't slept for too long.

*Only twenty minutes or so*, Zephyr said as if he had heard the question spoken, but it hadn't been a thought of mine. I grinned, grateful for the answer, the reassuring sound of his voice, and how he had been keeping everyone organized. It hadn't been long, but he'd allowed me to rest unhindered.

"Forgive the need to nap. We've taxed our abilities greatly in our ongoing war with these elves," I said as soon as I was close enough that I wouldn't have to talk too loudly.

"It is something I didn't expect, but if I understand correctly now, then it was needed. Given what we know of the elves, I recommend we continue, however. They shouldn't be given much time to prepare for us and can possibly detect the presence of so much magic in one place."

It was a good point and something we'd considered. Even if none of it was true, we had to push on anyway and do our best to get the tablets and stop the cult from opening a portal without Zephyr and me.

The unpleasant thought of being in the Mexican mountain where they'd held me made me shiver. I had no desire to go back there, but I wanted to know how they were involved in everything in my past, and I wouldn't back out of the chase now.

I encouraged everyone to gather around, then Zephyr and Donnacha talked about what to expect and the plan we were going to follow. Although we still wanted to do our best to further our goals, we needed to be more cautious this time and make sure we had enough energy to stay close on the cult's heels.

Any tablets we managed to win would be a bonus but not a priority. With that said, neither Sen nor Roth was a big part of the plan. Neither was able to do as much when there wasn't loads of water nearby or me to defend on land. Sen could control plants a little, but it drained her quickly, and now wasn't the time for it.

Instead, I instructed them to focus on stealing a tablet or two and working together. I felt the thrill of delight as Sen and Roth got ready, the pegasus opting to ride with the centaurs on the ground and give his wings a rest for the inevitable flight afterward.

It was sensible, and it would help Sen get closer to the tablets where she would stand a chance of grabbing one in battle as she'd done in previous situations. With the rest of the elves finishing off food and getting ready to fly in along with me again and the other three elementals being borne by gracious and understanding centaurs to various points about the area, I had another rare moment alone with Zephyr.

*Don't overdo it*, Zephyr said. *And remember, I can give you backup if needed.*

*We ought to save you for either the pursuit or the final part of this battle.*

I heard Zephyr sigh, but he knew I was right. Despite that, I could understand his desire to be more involved in the fights. There was something about being in the thick of everything and able to sling different abilities around.

*We'll make use of your breath weapon again*, I added, hoping it would make him feel better. It would help us hide what few we had attacking and make it look like more, and it would also make the elves worry that we'd set it alight again.

I moved to Zephyr's side and gave him a nod. As one, we rose into the air, his powerful wings beating down and causing a draft I helped dampen. I didn't make it quite so hard to detect us, although I didn't want to let my guard down too much.

The building ahead was shorter than previous ones, almost entirely one level. It smelled of old farm animals, the faint aroma of pig crap and mold lingering in the air.

Behind us came the other air elementals, and I could see them beginning to work their magic, the earth changing and moving, vines growing toward the building from multiple directions. At the same time, a pipe burst and water sprayed everywhere, and a fire erupted on one corner of the building.

It was an impressive display of power and no doubt almost entirely fueled by the tablets, but that was the point.

I'd wanted us to appear far stronger than the few of us were from the beginning. It was the only chance we had to convince them.

As we got closer, Zephyr exhaled his gas cloud over one side of the building and then circled to do it again. Before long, I was holding a large gas cloud over the only obvious entrance and exit to the building. It would give any mythicals with masks a way to approach without being seen and again hopefully make the occupants think there were more of us.

With that done, Zephyr swooped over the roof, and I reached into the building with my mind. I could feel the elves huddling in the corner of the building as if they were gathering around something. The same air elf was monitoring the area and holding defenses in place. I punched through, making it obvious I was there.

His mind fought back, but I was getting used to his techniques and the way he controlled the element. I was soon through the barrier he made, opening a section near the door. I let Roth and Sen know, the pair able to work with the centaurs. Zephyr was circling again, and I needed to consider the air elves and our part of the plan.

A moment later, I was in the air as Zephyr continued to fly circles and keep the gas he breathed out gathering in one place. I joined the group of air elementals to land on the roof of the building. None of us went inside, but I reached in with my mind again as the elves inside moved outward, as if they'd had a team huddle or something.

My control was attacked again, the air elemental working with one other to send me a message. I was glad I was standing on the roof as I stumbled back, feeling as if someone had thumped me. No part of me gave up, however.

I fought to keep control of the entrance, knowing that Roth and the centaurs were coming closer. I dreaded to think what would happen to them if I failed. The tension and pressure grew as I resisted the attack. I considered reaching for the air tablet I carried, but I might need it later. There was also a possibility that one of the others would need it.

*You've got this*, Zephyr said. *You've just got to focus and trust yourself.*

I appreciated the vote of confidence and sent a feeling of warmth to Zephyr. Then I focused on holding on. Even with them having tablets, I was confident that I could hold out under the assault. As the elf tried to keep me from working my way through his barrier and making the cult elves vulnerable to attack, I felt them moving.

Instead of them coming together in the middle of a room or heading toward another exit, they fanned out, pairs of them heading to different parts of the building. I followed them with my mind, trying to work out what they were doing as the air elves with me started working together on controlling the air outside. Slowly they boxed the building in another barrier.

This one was going to starve the people inside of air and make it so they had to get out. Of course, it had the danger of suffocating our team too, but they were sporting the equipment to deal with it. They were also going to hopefully be in and out before it had much impact. It took a while to starve an area that big of oxygen.

I moved nearer the edge with the door, noticing that

Zephyr had almost filled the entire area with a gas cloud so thick it was spreading out, including over the roof. Needing it out of my way a little, I took control of this edge and pushed it back.

It was all the strain the air elemental I was fighting needed to have me distracted. He latched on to the barrier inside the building, reforming the door as I attacked back. The air elves finished their barrier a moment later, trapping the centaurs and pegasus between the two temporarily. I could have sworn as I realized that was a bad place for them to be and to be stuck, deep in a gas cloud that I couldn't easily move out of their way.

A moment later, I felt the building wobble, and some of the air elves were knocked off their feet. I braced myself, but again I was distracted as the other elves rocked the building once more.

"Everyone lift up a fraction," I said quietly but hoping that they could hear me. Then I did the same myself, not looking back as I bore my weight.

It wasn't ideal, draining us and taking our concentration but giving us a similar boost at the same time, no longer distracted by the earth elves trying to do something dangerous with the building.

There was no way I wanted another set of mythicals to get stuck in something like a building if it could be helped. Of course, the centaurs were taking some heat for us.

As soon as I was flying, I returned my efforts to opening the barriers into the building and getting toward the air elemental I wanted to talk to. I could feel him moving inside and I matched him above, walking in whatever direction he went. It was strange, but he didn't stop fighting me as we moved.

Finally, either his tablet faded or something distracted him for a change. I was suddenly able to reopen the barrier. As I let Roth and Sen know, I pulled the gas mask I carried from my pack and pulled it on.

Flying down to the ground made me worry that I was about to lose the air elves above, my brain seeming to expect the worst, but in reality, I was unlikely to see the same strategy used as the first time. They were the ones trapped inside this time, not my elves. I was going to be fine with any luck. They weren't going to risk killing me.

I landed beside Roth and Sen as they rushed to the door again, Donnacha and the centaurs with him spreading out around us. It was obvious everyone was struggling to see, so I hurried to the front of the group, aware the elves inside were beginning to control elements as if they were trying to attack the elves outside.

Not that there were any obvious elves on our side except me, but I could feel their control, and areas of the forest were soon on fire. Within seconds we were inside; no gas in here. I threw up an air wall in front of us, still fighting the air elves inside.

I stopped, unable to move as I finally came face to face with the elf in charge. He stood in the middle of the room, an air tablet in each hand, gritted teeth as he fought me, a sheen of sweat on his face.

Locking eyes with him, I felt my blood run cold. I knew his face. It wasn't the first time I'd seen it, but I hadn't expected to be confronted with him now. This was the person who had delivered me, only a few days old, to the cops.

"Hello, Aella," he said as he relaxed. I felt his mind pull back, no longer challenging mine for control.

I didn't respond as I heard Zephyr roar and felt him land somewhere behind me.

"You've learned so much in such a short space of time. I knew I couldn't keep you at bay forever," he continued.

"How do you know my parents?" I asked, the words tumbling out. "You're Amcika. Why did they trust you with me?"

He laughed, shaking his head and looking down a moment.

"I can't imagine how confused you must be right now. And it's understandable. You've got a lot to learn still. The Henera is a big role to fill, and it's not been an easy path for you. The strength it gave you has been necessary, however. We all agreed on that."

"We?" I said, feeling my anger rise as Zephyr came behind me in human form so he could get into the building. His arm slid around my waist, and I glanced his way. The glare on his face as he stared at the air elemental reflected what I felt.

"I'm sorry. I'd love to say more now, but I think we all know it's time for us to go." He backed up a couple of steps. "But thank you, Aella. It has been wonderful to see how far you've come. What you're capable of. You've made all of us so proud."

Before I could do more than frown, the air slammed straight into me and everyone else, the tablets putting so much extra power into the attack that the air wall I'd put up barely took anything out of it. All of us were knocked off our feet, slamming backward.

Stunned, I lay on the floor a moment before hastily grabbing the air again and using it to get to my feet at the same time as Zephyr did.

I reached a hand to help Donnacha to his feet, and I used my air to help everyone else. Once they were stable, I looked around. The elves had moved as one, blowing several holes out of the building and then running together.

In my shock, I'd let go of the barrier for long enough they'd punched through. Somehow I hadn't seen any of that coming.

*We've got to go after them*, Zephyr said, taking my hand as we followed them out of the building. At the same time, I tore the barrier down and pushed Zephyr's gas away. He was right, but that didn't mean I wasn't angrier than I'd ever been.

I was going to catch up to this air elemental, and I was going to make him answer every question I had.

## CHAPTER TWENTY-TWO

Within minutes we were in the air again. Donnacha and his centaurs had questions, but they'd been satisfied to know that Ronan would explain as soon as I understood it all. No matter what happened, we couldn't get farther behind.

I had almost entirely wasted the opportunity to reduce their numbers or take any more tablets, and the knowledge made me want to scream. Once again, only Sen had managed to grab anything, the myconid launching herself at the air elemental and breaking one of the tablets he held. She'd handed me the chunk she'd come away with, and I could feel it pulsing with energy.

Somehow the fragment had kept its power despite being broken, almost as if they were individual units. I couldn't pretend to understand the magic behind them, but I did know that I was going to make use of it, if nothing else.

With the tablet I already had, it meant I could help everyone get back in the air, and we could make a speedy flight. Up ahead, I could feel the presence of the cult, and

Zephyr assured me he could see them as they fled over the ground. They'd made their way to several waiting vehicles and driven them down a dirt track until they'd come to a larger road.

It was the first time they'd not traveled to the next location using an off-road or earth elemental-made route, and it was also clear they were trying to travel more swiftly. As if they knew that we were pursuing them more closely this time.

At first, I feared that they were going to entirely bypass the location Minsheng and the others were waiting at, the road not going directly there. They were, after all, heading to Mexico or toward the border, but eventually, they turned down another dirt track that led closer.

Aware I needed to let Ronan know we weren't far away and that there were a lot of incoming elves who'd barely been made weaker on the way, I powered closer to Zephyr and landed on his back.

With the two elves he already carried, I was worried about wearing him out, but I couldn't fly and use the communication stone.

Getting the two elves to agree to hold onto me and warning Zephyr so he wouldn't let himself be pulled into the conversation with me, I reached out for Ronan. It wasn't long before I was in the darkened room, the centaur's comforting presence before me.

"Forgive the late notice, but we're soon to be upon you, and the cult is stronger than we'd have liked."

"I'm sure you and my brother did your best. And we will defend against them all as best we can. It's all any of us can do. You should expect no more of yourself."

I bowed, grateful for the kind words. "There's more to say, but it can be said after. We've managed to drain them a little, but we'll also be drained."

"Then we will see you in person soon. And stand together on the battlefield once more."

Ronan bowed low before cutting the communication. I was on Zephyr's back, strong arms holding me steady as we flew through the air. I blinked, trying to process everything that was happening.

*You can stay where you are if you need to think*, Zephyr said, his strong wings holding us up. *And rest your powers.*

I considered arguing, but I didn't want to fly if I could help it. The flight here and the battle had used a lot of my capacity. It would still be at least an hour before we arrived at the next location, and it would be beneficial not to be exhausted.

At the same time, I was aware that I didn't want to wear Zephyr out more than necessary.

*I'm taking human form for the next battle*, he added, taking away some of my reluctance.

He was right. It was by far the best course of action, and I knew I should listen to him.

After thanking the elves who had held me in place, I reached into my packs and pulled out the last of my food. The elves around took that as an indication they should do the same, and we looked as if we were having the strangest picnic, sitting on top of a dragon, hurtling forward at the best part of a hundred miles an hour.

I had to use my air abilities to shield us a little, creating a slipstream around us that kept the air flowing up and over. At the same time, I encouraged us to hunker down in the natural space that Zephyr's ridges and spines created.

A couple of times I glanced behind, feeling Roth growing more tired and noticing that he wasn't the only one. Some of the air elementals with us were going to arrive and be good for very little in the way of fighting. Of course, they had a dart gun either strapped to a leg or tucked in a pocket courtesy of the United States military, but it wasn't much of a solace.

Most of them had no experience firing a weapon, let alone aiming one.

I felt my stomach tie up in knots. Several times, it had appeared as if this whole chase might have been contrived or planned. I had wondered what was going on, but the truth was far worse. What did Amcika have to do with my parents and the future they thought I was supposed to be making happen?

Had my parents been involved in my decision to be given for adoption? Had Amcika stolen me and then hidden me? Or were my parents alive? I'd always hoped that one day I'd meet them. But I was suddenly faced with a situation that implied they could well be dead. And I could feel my dislike of Amcika grow at the thought.

The more I let the conversation I'd had with the Amcika elf run through my head, the more I realized that I wasn't likely to ever get to meet my parents. Somehow they were dead. A part of me seemed to know it now.

*They might not be. Chris wasn't always Amcika. And Orthelo mentioned another elf who joined them. There's a chance this air elemental we've been chasing defected and took you.*

*And your egg*, I replied, knowing Zephyr must also have

so many questions. This was a difficult situation for both of us, not just me. I had to remember that he was also worried about his mother.

*We'll find answers together*, I promised him, sending waves of warmth and comfort his way and feeling the benefit of the declaration and emotional intent.

Whatever happened over the next few hours, we needed to make sure we had answers.

The car ahead of us slowed as it came to trickier terrain, the dirt track heading uphill and becoming bumpier and harsher on the suspension of the vehicles. I didn't have much sympathy as I saw it lurching around, and I considered encouraging our group to attack and start this next fight here and now, but I managed to restrain myself.

A glance around at the air elves reminded me that we needed to wait and drive the elves forward toward a fresher set of mythicals and soldiers.

I didn't have much strength with me. Roth, Sen, Zephyr, and the three elves resting with us might have been able to put up a decent fight with me, but there were over thirty elves in the cars and trucks below. There was no way I was going to be able to defeat them. It was almost entirely suicidal.

Instead, I let us fly on, and everyone slowed, almost gratefully. It was possibly going to alert the group that we were waiting for something. I was sure they knew they were being followed. It couldn't be helped, however. We had to keep going and hope that we had enough of an advantage this time.

The abandoned ranch house that was their destination

soon came into view, the building standing out on the side of a hill. There was something almost majestic about it, and I gasped as I saw it, part of me falling in love with it and wishing I wasn't about to fight within its walls. Who knew what would happen to it before the day was done.

*We can try to make sure they don't knock it down. Attack before they get inside*, Zephyr offered, an almost amused tone to his voice.

It was part of the plan not to let them get into a corner they could defend easily as they had at every other turn. I took control of the air in front of the building as soon as my range would let me. Zephyr swooped in lower, speeding up again to close the distance between them and us.

Now we were going to find out exactly how much it would take to beat these elves.

I concentrated, feeling the presence of my people in the house and on the ground to the sides, hidden for now. I did my best to mask them with my control. It wasn't something I was going to be able to keep up as the battle began, but it might buy us more of the element of surprise.

As the first car pulled to a halt and the air elemental who had my answers got out, he looked at Zephyr and me and the air elves with us. I thought I saw a flicker of concern on his face, but if it had been there, it vanished before I could be sure.

Instead, he looked at me with calm regard. There was no hatred, no anger, just a reserved expression that was studying me. Almost thoughtful if it hadn't been too cold and calculating for that.

Zephyr landed us several hundred feet away as the elf

challenged my control of the barrier into the house. At the same time, the elves around him fanned out and took control of the elements.

"Now!" I yelled as loudly as I could, Zephyr's roar joining in with the last sound until I was almost deafening everyone. The elves below us hesitated.

Some of them were still getting out of vehicles, and I wasn't about to let them get away from me and make this harder. I boxed them in as soldiers lifted above hiding places and fired.

Several elves were felled, feathery darts sticking out of them. Zephyr landed as the cult leader called out something in Elvish and the earth elves he commanded started morphing the ground. They were going to defend the spot they stood in, earth walls beginning to form.

It wouldn't stop them from being attacked from the air, and I brought the barrier in closer, intending to take away their air if I could. At the same time, most of the other air elves landed behind Zephyr. It wasn't a great place for them to be given what we were facing, but they seemed unaware that Zephyr wouldn't be their shield much longer.

I walked forward, my eyes fixed on the cult's air elemental and thinking of the best way to get to him. At the same time, I saw a fire spring up not far from him, Seth's grinning face appearing at the ranch house window.

I wondered if he knew not to hurt the elf, but I had no time to think about it as someone hurled a ball of fire toward me. Roth met it with water, putting it out but momentarily blocking my view with a combination of steam, hissing water, and chaos.

As it fell to the ground, no longer a threat, I looked for

the air elf again. He wasn't there anymore, his body having ducked down behind something. I looked for him again, reaching with my mind and my eyes.

I flew into the air as Zephyr exhaled his gas. Another air elf took control of it and began moving it closer.

Zephyr then transformed into his human form and cruised beside me.

*We'll find him*, the dragon said, his words as steady and reassuring as I had been earlier.

With two of us working on it, we soon spotted him. The elves were trying to burrow down and make a sunken fort right where they were.

*We need some earth elves to fight them*, Zephyr said.

*Go around to the house. Coordinate them*, I replied. *I can focus on the air elemental then.*

Zephyr didn't argue, knowing it was for the best. We had to work together on this. Roth and Sen also came closer, the pegasus running through the gas, entirely unaffected by it. I grinned, knowing I had a powerful team. We were going to make them pay this time.

As Zephyr flew over and Roth and Sen ran closer, the elves threw the elements at them. It forced me to help defend them, seemingly being ignored as I blocked blasts of fire, air, and water and kept the ground steady beneath Roth's hooves.

At the same time, the soldiers advanced on the elves, taking careful aim and doing their best to take out the mythicals. Although the military knew that elves could take more sedative, it hadn't been worked out exactly how much more yet, and everyone had agreed that they couldn't justify upping the dose in each dart without knowing exactly how bad it could be on elves.

Admittedly, hitting someone twice was potentially worse than a larger first dose, but apparently, that was how the logistics worked. It also meant no one had to change anything and be blamed directly. That I could understand. It was hard to be the one everyone was looking at to make sure everyone was safe.

I watched briefly as a couple more elves succumbed to the darts, and more of the elves from inside the house came rushing out to push an advantage. All the while, I was trying to find my air elf and pin him down again. I still had so many questions.

The earth elves under Zephyr's guidance fought against the strange fort, taking control of some of it and pulling it apart before it could grow especially large.

It gave me the window I needed as I spotted the air elf again, giving commands near the center of the structure his elves had made.

Swooping in, I aimed for him, smashing through his control by using the tablets I carried and pinning him in place until I was close enough. I lifted him as I flew past and pulled him out of the fort by the roof. He yelled his rage, reaching for his stones.

After I landed with him to one side of the battle, Sen and Roth came galloping up, and the myconid managed to grab one of the tablets. She yanked it out of the air elf's hands and then I blasted him off his feet again, trying to make him drop the other.

It didn't work, but it gave Roth time to bear Sen away with the air tablet she'd stolen.

*Get it into the hands of an elf who can use it*, I said to Sen and Roth. Then I focused on the elf in front of me.

He chuckled as he got to his feet.

"You are becoming Henera," he said.

"What do you know of my parents?" I demanded. "And Zephyr's? Did Amcika put his egg in the warehouse for me to find?"

"That's three questions, and the answers won't have to be voiced if we don't want to. You can't make us do anything. Or say anything."

"I don't think you understand," I replied. "I can make you do an awful lot of things that you won't agree with at first. But I'm not like you. I don't play those kinds of games. So we're going to make this really simple. Whatever reason you think you have for hiding what you know, out with it. What makes you think you get to decide my future?"

Again he laughed. I could feel the anger rising inside me.

*Knock him on his ass again?* Zephyr suggested. *Won't make him tell you, but it will make us both feel better.*

I could hear the anger in Zephyr's voice, but I could also hear the amusement. I was tempted. If only to make my dragon smile.

"The cult has only ever wanted what's best for you and your bonded mythicals. You're our hope, even if you don't agree with us on everything," he said eventually. "But this isn't the place for me to tell you anything about our reasons. And in a lot of ways, the answers to your questions don't matter as much as you think they do."

"They matter to me. They matter to Zephyr."

"All that matters is you are becoming who you were designed to be. Henera. You are *her*. Everyone involved in your creation and your life is proud of you, Aella. All of us."

I blinked, shocked, the words coming out genuinely, almost tenderly. And I felt anger rising. I wanted to hate him for this. For everything. But he felt as if something else was going on.

Before I could do anything to stop it, there was an explosion from behind me. I was knocked off my feet, having to use the air to stop myself from being slammed into the ground like a rag doll. Zephyr roared aloud and inside my head as I slowly righted myself.

Stopping, crouched, somehow near the wall of the ranch house, I looked over the scene. The strange bunker the cult elves had made was mostly gone, a small crater where it had been. There were several dead elves, two dead soldiers, and Newton didn't appear to be moving, a short distance from me.

Erlan ran out from the house as I watched, my ears ringing, my mind struggling to take it in. The rest of the cult elves fled, the air elf whipping a barrier up and around them so fast that there was little I could do to stop it.

How had so many died so suddenly?

## CHAPTER TWENTY-THREE

I barely dared to breathe. Many of us huddled around Newton, willing the creature to open his little eyes again. Erlan was cradling the fire salamander to his chest, and Minsheng had a hand on the young elf's shoulder.

Erlan assured us the bond was still there and Newton was still alive. I could see the small stomach moving very faintly as he breathed, but still, I wanted to know the creature was going to be okay.

Zephyr's arm slipped around my waist, and I leaned into him.

*The only dead elves are cult members,* Zephyr said. *It's still tragic, but they blew themselves and several tablets up. It looks like it was an accident. A tablet exploded.*

*A tablet?* I asked, giving him some of my attention while I continued to study the small, frail creature ahead of me.

*From what the soldiers describe, the ones close enough, anyway, it was because an earth elf used a fire tablet and harnessed the energy somehow for something else. It wasn't a good idea.*

I tried not to react, but it was impossible. What had possessed the elf to try something like that?

With no idea, I could only absorb the information. I would have to convey it to as many as possible before the hour was out, but I wasn't going to do anything until I knew Erlan and Newton were fine.

Minsheng raised an eyebrow, his eyes meeting mine. I was sure he'd noticed my expression, but neither of us spoke.

I almost jumped when Newton finally opened his eyes and moved. A collective breath was released, and everyone relaxed a little. Erlan's eyes filled with moisture and relief, and Newton scurried onto his shoulder.

"You okay, buddy?" Erlan asked.

The fire salamander nodded and snuggled into his neck.

I gave them each a warm smile as Minsheng squeezed Erlan's opposite shoulder, then we made our way to the major. The soldiers were somber, and I could understand why. They'd lost two of their own in the blast.

"I'm sorry," I said as soon as I was close enough to the major.

"I am too, but it was an accident. As much as I wanted to get angry at the elves you're chasing, it's clear they're just as shook up and distraught," the major replied as he motioned at the cult elves they'd captured.

I stood, shocked about that. It appeared as if they had about half of the cult elves in one huddle. Some of them were still sedated and out cold, but others were sitting there, no fight left in them anyway. The major had ensured they were being given food and drink and a blanket and having their injuries tended to.

His soldiers were getting the same treatment. I was proud to fight alongside someone who could find their humanity in a situation like this.

"Get them all back to the portal site," I said before I could think about it further. "There's little more you can do to get those last tablets. They'll have gone to the portal in Mexico, and everyone here has done as much as they ought to."

The major looked as if he might argue, but eventually, he gave the order to his subordinate to start packing and getting everyone to return to base.

I looked at the pile of tablets we had. Using some cloth, so I didn't have direct skin contact, I selected several fragments of an air tablet. Some of them contained enough energy that the pull to connect wasn't very strong, but others made me want to reach into them and add what was left of my strength. I resisted, no matter how strong it was.

With them safely stored in a leather pouch and stowed in my pack, I looked around for the centaurs. Ronan and his group had managed to avoid the worst of the danger, having been firing from farther away, their height and team tactics making them better long-range shooters.

The centaur came closer as soon as he realized that I was looking for him. I pointed to the array of rune-covered stonework.

"Take these back to the Sanctuary along with all our injured and anyone who doesn't want to go any farther. I'm not risking the lives of your people anymore. And I think we've done enough for now."

"You're going on alone?" he asked.

"I won't be alone, I'm sure. But I will only take those I truly believe can handle the danger we'll be in. While the cult is trying to not majorly harm me, they aren't affording the same respect to any others."

"Your path is a difficult one, but I believe in you and your success. You will prevail, and the tablets will all be in our hands soon."

I bowed to the centaur, not wanting to take too much of his time or keep him too much longer. No sooner had he gone than Minsheng appeared, and my mythicals gathered around.

"Rest for a while," Minsheng said. "Don't do anything more rash than waiting until morning."

I opened my mouth to object, wanting to go after the elves right away, but Zephyr nodded.

*We all need sleep. And this ranch house is yours.*

I almost chuckled at the words, especially with the mental image Zephyr sent me of the bedroom. But I kept my outward calm. My body needed rest, and I was fairly sure my mind would benefit too. Although I knew there was only so much that I could do, I needed to get to the mountain soon.

There was also the strange response I'd had from the air elf. He'd implied that my parents had been happily Amcika like him. It made me wonder if I'd found them. Was this elf one of them? He'd been alone when he dropped me off, and he didn't look much like me. I had assumed he was a messenger, especially when I had found him living alone.

Could I have made one of the worst assumptions ever?

Had that been why he found my questions so funny? Had I been fighting with my father all this time?

*It's a possibility,* Zephyr confirmed. *But that doesn't mean you suddenly have to like him.*

*I know. I just...*

*You hoped they'd love you and be lovely.*

*Yeah. That.*

I felt the rush of warmth from all three of my mythicals.

*We're your family. Us, and Minsheng, and Daisy, and Erlan. And you do have two parents who raised you. They might not have gotten everything right, but to be fair, they had you for a daughter. I don't think you made it easy.* Zephyr smirked, and I chuckled.

I hadn't been an easy child to raise. Headstrong, fierce, and unwilling to bend for rules that made no sense to me.

*Perfect for the Henera.*

*Not so much for a kid in a middle-class suburban family.*

*No, but if you'd not been in one, we might never have come to appreciate pizza so much.*

*True. And pizza is everything.*

*Pizza and chow mein.*

I smiled and leaned into Zephyr's embrace, grateful for the way he seemed to always know how to lighten the mood again. He was my rock and everything else I could want. With my family of mythicals and friends and my adoptive parents, it did feel as if I had everything I needed. Sometimes it was good to be reminded of what was most important.

With that thought firmly in mind, we went to find more food and rest until we had to work out the final element to this whole pursuit. I'd been following this guy around the country ever since I'd found his house in Canada, and I was going to follow him to Mexico.

Although I needed to come up with a plan, we'd been chasing them for so long that I needed to rest first. It would bother me that I wouldn't know what I was doing the moment I was awake, but I'd been flying and fighting for so long on so little sleep that I was sure I'd decide on something better as soon as I had a fresh mind anyway.

Sleep was far easier to slip into than I'd expected. None of the thoughts I feared would keep me up were able to stop me. They came flooding back the moment I was awake, however, and I was vaguely aware of dreams of elementals from the cult hiding my parents.

It was still early, and everyone I needed to talk to was fast asleep. Not sure what else to do, and suddenly reminded of the notebook Orthelo had given me, I settled down to flick through it.

Mostly it was interesting rumors and accounts of possible sightings of the ornate belt, but it soon became clear that the evidence of a genuine nature pointed to the cult having it. I sat back, wondering if anyone knew it was there now. The original elf was likely to be dead. Who had they passed it to, and did that person know what they'd gotten?

It was up to me to find out. I didn't have much to go on above that, but there were drawings. Mostly extrapolated from descriptions and things like that, but there was one from someone who had once seen it.

Given I had nothing else to go on, it would have to do. I hoped I recognized it once I got my hands on it.

*All you can do*, Zephyr said, letting me know he was

awake. I tucked the notebook away and got to my feet. If someone else was ready to talk, that meant it was time to plan. Or eat breakfast.

We found Daisy in the ranch house kitchen. She'd worked with the soldiers before they'd left to get everything working again, the house previously unoccupied for a while, and she was cooking. I helped her, not needing to say much.

By the time we were done cooking, there were plenty of folks awake, and I was sitting at a table surrounded by the mythicals and people I cared about and worked with best. Once we'd finished eating, Minsheng brought up the cult and what we were going to do.

A part of me didn't want to think about it, but we were on a path I couldn't deviate from. I had to go to the Mexico site again, and I had to make sure they couldn't open the portal. And this time, I didn't plan to leave until I got answers.

Although I didn't want to risk the lives of anyone else, I could see by the looks on their faces that very few of them wanted to be left out of whatever I was planning. Ronan had insisted on staying behind, sending Dyneira to the Sanctuary with the tablets in his place.

I looked around the room. Erlan, Newton, Emily, Daisy, Minsheng, Ronan, and my mythicals were there with me, and they were my family, as Zephyr said.

"Okay," I said. "We need to get to Mexico asap, and then we have three tasks. I can't ask any of you to come, but I won't deny I'd appreciate you all."

"We're all in. We decided after you went to sleep last

night," Minsheng said. "And we've got some ideas and some tech that will help."

I grinned as Minsheng reached for a bag and pulled out some of the prototypes Chris had been working on. I noticed the little jet pack Sen could wear among them, and she did a fraction of a second later. There were also a bunch of the grenade-like devices that could store Zephyr's breath weapon and something for me.

They looked like strange gloves, but they were fingerless, and the back of the hand was mostly straps.

"What do these do?" I asked as I slipped one on.

"You'll want to test it outside, but if the organization got another gnome and a dwarf to finish them off right, they'll make your air blasts more focused, a bit like a superhero. You'll fly and attack better with them and use less energy."

A grin spread across my face as I put the other one on. That was something I could get behind. Before we'd finished making a plan, I hurried outside, then paused.

Someone had smoothed over the ground outside and there were plants growing, but it still felt strange and wrong that so many had died there the day before. It should be different. A lot different.

*We could put a marker somewhere. A memorial, so we don't have to have a broken-up driveway or lawn.*

*You sound like you are getting house-proud.*

*Well, it is the first house I've owned.*

*Technically, I own it.*

*We're bonded. Pretty sure that's a bit like marriage, and I own this too*, Zephyr replied, chuckling.

*If that's true, I have two husbands and a wife. I'm not sure polygamy is legal in the US.*

*It's not. But what we have is still awesome.*

I grinned again, entirely agreeing with that description before I reached out and concentrated. I soon blasted air out from my hand, and the glove seemed to work wonders, but it also had kickback, and I spun around and tumbled over myself. Instinctively, I blasted more air to catch myself.

It rocked me around. My limbs flailed, and I wobbled more.

*More subtle*, Zephyr said, his voice coming out panicked.

A moment later, Roth sent me a wave of calm, and I managed to fight through the panic enough to use air blasts from other parts of my body and steady myself instead. Once I was stable, I experimented until I was doing a better job of controlling the gloves.

Once I stopped, landing after a very short flight, I noticed I had an audience. Everyone had come out of the ranch house to watch me. They clapped as I came closer.

"They work then?" Minsheng asked.

I nodded but explained the difficulties I had.

"I'll let the organization know to keep working on them, but there might not be anything they can do about that."

"They're still awesome. Thank you for making this happen," I said as I hugged my Shishou.

As I did, I noticed that all of them had their away bags. When I pulled back, Daisy came forward carrying my pack.

"Time to move out," I said, nodding my gratitude and putting the pack on.

## CHAPTER TWENTY-FOUR

Flying high over the landscape on Zephyr was my favorite place to be. I'd done so in many situations and on many different days with many different landscapes beneath me. No matter where I was or what my troubles were, nothing seemed to make this moment any less special.

I could feel the tension leave Zephyr when he was flying across the sky. This was a natural, enjoyable activity, and I could feel the difference in him.

Up ahead, the mountain was visible and beginning to grow as we got closer.

There had been no sign of the elves we'd scared out of the ranch house. No sight of the man who held the secrets to my past and how I had come to be the focus. I'd hoped we'd find the team along the way and I'd get another chance to stop them, but either they had gone somewhere different, or we had left too long after them to be able to catch up.

We'd been flying for a long time, and I was tired despite my minimal involvement in the process to get this far. I had formed and held a barrier around myself and used slipstreams to make it easier on Zephyr and not much harder on me.

Below us traveled the small vehicle containing all the friends we felt we had, and for the most part, needed. I wanted to be down there with them in one way, knowing they were experiencing something different than I was. I loved flying, but I wanted to be there for my friends too.

When we grew close enough that we risked being seen by a scout, Zephyr and I looked for a place for us to rest until nightfall. We wanted to sneak into the mountain and the building within, and that meant being more careful.

While we were coming in to land near the side of a small town, I noticed that the view ahead had changed since we were last here. Before, it had been a mountain anyone could access, and houses had dotted the landscape around the base and up it. Now there was a large fence with Mexican soldiers patrolling it. There were also regular lookout posts.

It seemed the Mexican government had decided that the mountain and the cult within were a threat and hostile territory. It was strange to see and to think that we intended to sneak inside. I worried that we'd not be able to get close enough without clashing with the soldiers, but I soon reminded myself that we'd snuck past these sorts of things before.

With any luck, we wouldn't have much harder of a time because of it.

Zephyr touched down as the truck came to a stop, then we quickly grew up the plants and trees to shield the vehicle and us from view from almost any angle unless someone came within a few hundred yards of us. It wasn't perfect, and anyone who knew the horizon with a perfect memory would notice the difference, but Zephyr took human form and worked with me to make it as unobvious but effective as possible.

With that, we settled into various spaces to rest, eat, or keep watch until darkness came. There were plenty of quiet conversations, talking of happier things. Memories of some of the places we'd been. Now and then, one of the elementals with us poured energy into a tablet or fragment. None of us drained our powers, just used enough that we'd have it back before nightfall.

I tried to sleep, but it wasn't easy with so many questions. I'd have answers soon, however.

By the time I gave up, it was almost sunset, the sky to the west a gorgeous orange. I sat beside Emily as she stood watch alongside Roth, the two of them scanning the horizon and sky near the mountain between them.

"There's more activity suddenly," Emily said. "Roth spotted it first. Elves on the outside of the mountain. I think the elves we were hunting have come back. They're either about to start looking for us, or something has them active for another reason."

I looked where she pointed and frowned. She was right. There were more elves on the side of the mountain and it looked as if some planned to set out and fly somewhere.

While we watched, I noticed that they seemed to fan out in pairs, flying slowly enough they could see the horizon and search, but not too slow, as if they wanted to find what they could as quickly as possible.

I wasn't sure what to do. We wanted our attack to be

enough of a surprise that we could sneak in. That meant making sure we weren't seen waiting here.

When it was clear that a pair of scouts were coming our way, I had to act.

"Keep everyone as hidden as you can. Inside the truck if need be. Don't let them know how many of us there are, even if they work out there's something here."

"What are you going to do?" Emily replied.

"Make them as confused as possible."

Nodding to Roth and calling for Sen and Zephyr with my mind, I looked for a way forward that would keep us hidden for as long as possible. We could use buildings and more plants to get closer, but not masses.

Without hesitation, I led my mythicals that way and reached for the elements around me. I couldn't feel forward enough to detect the scouts in the sky yet, but I made sure I would be able to. At the same time, Zephyr took control of the earth, making sure we'd know if someone came close to us on foot.

The town we were near wasn't empty, but it was quiet enough there shouldn't be too much in the way of others for us to pick up on. I also did my best to guide us around the majority of the houses, using them to shield us from view when there wasn't a better alternative.

I kept going until we were as far from the truck as I could get yet still have a moment to choose to reveal ourselves on our terms. I didn't want to risk being seen before we were ready to make our move.

It didn't take me long to find a good spot between two houses to linger and jump out from. I felt farther out in the air and also found a water source to pump Roth with. Sen climbed onto Roth's head, wearing her armor and helping Zephyr as he began growing plants and moving the earth to better accommodate an assault on our terms.

As soon as the scouts came into view, flying past us, I grabbed control of the air around them, taking it away and blasting them toward us as hard as I could. They tumbled through the air, both of the elementals taken by surprise. I caught them when it looked like they might hit the ground too hard, and then Zephyr used the plants and vines to grab a couple of ankles.

He pulled them closer, lifting them so they were held above us and unable to do much. I focused on helping keep them still, blocking their attempts to get control of the air again. At the same time, I cut off the oxygen around them, lowering it bit by bit, hoping to have them pass out if we couldn't get them sedated another way.

At first, nothing seemed to happen. The elementals thrashed and yelled as they hung there, and I wondered if I had done something wrong. They were making so much noise I had to make a barrier to keep it deflected into our bubble. It wasn't totally effective, but I did my best, and Sen and Roth got a good angle to help.

Roth hit the elementals with a water blast. This shocked one of them so much that they went still, and Sen finally got a decent shot with her dart gun. Hitting the elf with two shots in quick succession had the desired effect. Within another second, he was limp, hanging by the ankle the plant was wrapped around.

The other elf grew more frenzied, but I could see fatigue and lack of oxygen taking a toll, and she grew more sluggish. After missing the flailing body a few times, Sen managed to hit it.

I pulled a dart gun out of my pocket and took aim. As I shot the elf for the second time, Zephyr growled a warning.

*More elementals incoming. On foot. Similar direction.*

Frowning, I looked out of the gap between the two houses. Zephyr was right. There was a group of four elves on their way. Once again, I reached out, feeling for the control and working out how many elves of each kind we had. I could feel earth, and I was pretty sure there was at least one water elf.

As Zephyr let the two flying scouts down, I thought of a strategy that would give us the upper hand against the four elves quickly and quietly. We had to lure them into the alley, and we needed to make sure they didn't make too much noise.

I was tempted to stand out and ask to be taken to their leader, get this whole thing over and done with, but instead, I held my ground, and I kept planning. As soon as they were closer, I reached out and surrounded them with a cold barrier, making sure they didn't see us. I sucked as much of the air out as discreetly as I could while making the surface of the barrier and everything within it colder and colder.

This time it had an impact on them more quickly, the elves growing weaker and one stumbling. While I waited for them to pass out, Sen found a small space and corner to peek around so we could see her projected view.

Now that I could see the elves, I could plan how to defeat them. They were moving cautiously and trying to work out what was going on as if they could tell something was strange, but not what. As they moved forward, I shifted the barrier with them so they never reached the edge, but that it kept any fresh oxygen out.

Noticing that it was making my head hurt, I eased off from sucking more oxygen out. As I did, Zephyr began moving, backing up slowly and heading around the back of the house closest to the approaching scouts.

I waited, keeping the barrier moving, but I was pretty sure we were going to be discovered if I didn't do something else soon. Sen readied her small dart gun and Roth came closer, preparing to use the water he stored inside himself. I tried not to panic as Zephyr continued to hurry away from me and around, no doubt to sneak up behind the scout group.

"Those two still haven't come back out. What do you think they're doing?" a voice said, growing louder as the speaker came closer.

"No idea, but something isn't right here. They probably went to investigate. Same as us," a woman replied.

"It's like something is up with the air. I feel... sort of breathless."

"You're just out of shape," a third voice said, but they hissed as they stumbled too.

I fought a laugh at how clueless they were to the danger they were in. It was almost as if they had no idea a threat was out here. They were beginning to grow suspicious, however, and they would soon come close enough to see around the corner and notice us.

Before I could act or decide how to best attack them, Zephyr made a move. He stepped out from behind the house and shook the earth underneath them. Three of them wobbled. Sen shot the other one with her dart gun, and I fired too, opening a small hole in the barrier briefly to allow the projectiles through.

My dart went wide, but I managed to grab it with my mind and bring it back on target. The earth elemental in the group was out cold before any of them could react.

I pulled the barrier to a smaller size and increased my effort to pull the air out and keep the sound in. The front water elemental ran at us, trying to pull in water, but the water froze around the edge of the cold barrier I'd made, frosting it over and beginning to obscure the view. At the same time, the elf ran into it and stopped.

It was a strange sensation, desperately trying to hold onto cold air that was growing colder and into more of a barrier. The elf seemed to stick in it, pushing through and making it hard for me to keep it in place. At the same time, I could see their skin getting iced up and the pain on their face.

Another of the elves reached out and pulled them back.

"Are you trying to kill yourself?" she said.

I grinned as I shot another one of them, opening the barrier once more to let the projectile through. As I did, I noticed the air try to rush in through the gap. I struggled to stop it, doing so much at once that my mind wasn't keeping up. At the same time, I noticed Zephyr growing more plants.

A fire started at my feet, making me jump back. Roth was soon there, dousing it with water, but it reminded me that these elves were still a threat.

I dropped the barrier and shot the rest as swiftly as I

could, Roth jumping in the way of a water blast that would have swept me off my feet.

Within a minute, the elves were out cold, and Zephyr was using the earth and plants to move them and hide them. I used the air to move them farther out of sight, then we made sure no other scouts were going to come near the truck.

It wasn't ideal. They'd know where we must have been when the scouts didn't report back, but it bought us some time to get moving and hide somewhere else while the sun finished sinking and the night grew darker.

It was time to sneak into a cult.

## CHAPTER TWENTY-FIVE

The stars were out by the time we felt as if it was dark enough to go any farther. I was sitting on Zephyr's back and watching the sky change. We'd had to deal with several more scout parties that had come our way and moved on each time. The scouts were growing warier, but each time, we'd managed to deal with them.

"I think we're good to go," Minsheng said a moment later, his voice coming from behind me.

I turned to face the edge of the mountain. We were close to the route that led down to the sea again, but I wasn't sure it was going to be a good route this time. If I'd been running the mountain, I'd have had the elves close the entire thing off, including the back staircase, but I was hoping that wasn't the case.

If it was closed, we were going to have to make a new plan in a hurry. Or do a lot of tunneling.

Thankfully we had a lot of earth tablets with us, and it was a strong enough element for us that we'd put a lot into them above the others. With any luck, it would be enough to get us into the mountain.

Of course, sneaking was only going to get us so far anyway. At some point, we would need to interact with the elves inside the mountain to get the answers we needed and the tablets they had back. It was time to get the job done.

I slid off Zephyr's back to let him take human form again. Although he could fit into the tunnels, it was going to be far more useful against so many elves for him to be able to control the elements. We were likely to need that. It also meant there were two of us who could control air and keep the group quiet and two of us who could control the earth.

Zephyr in dragon form doubled our power in using the elements. We were going to need that power.

We soon broke through the wall to the caves yet again, the wall something we'd broken through twice before. As soon as we were inside, I could hear waves crashing to our right, making it clear what direction we needed to go.

I took Zephyr's hand and we led the way, the dragon the best of us at seeing in low light. So everyone else could see enough not to stumble, Newton set the tiny tip of his tail alight. It was a different shade from normal in his attempt to make it less obvious, a dull blue that changed the hue of the world.

I was grateful that I had so many amazing people around me. On a dangerous mission like this, they had volunteered to go into the darkness with me. They were the family I could rely on.

Zephyr's fingers tightened as we got deeper, and we felt

the problem ahead. The tunnel had been blocked off as we'd feared.

*We should use an earth tablet and break through,* Zephyr said. *I'm sure that we can get through.*

*We have to either way,* I replied.

As I reached into the bag of tablets we had, I hesitated, not sure I wanted to use a whole one yet. Wouldn't it be better to use the tablets in an emergency?

I had no idea, but I handed Zephyr one anyway. I then grabbed another, but I didn't use it right away. I made it work, using my power as well as draining the tablet a little.

Slowly we worked our way forward, making a tunnel narrower than the original had been until we broke through to another section. While we were still widening the area so everyone could get through the gap, I felt my mind brush against the control of another elf. I stopped and reached for Zephyr's hand.

*Another elf,* I said.

*Close?* he replied.

*The cult elves can't usually control that far out, so possibly. I don't know, though. I pulled back, and I'm not sure we should try to attract their attention.*

*Maybe not, but I think that air elf used to know where we were by the merest of brushes. I felt him more than once. I think there's a good chance the earth elf was monitoring this tunnel for a reason.*

*Shitsticks.*

It meant one thing for sure. We needed to find that elf and fast.

I reached out with my mind again, feeling for the signs of control from another elf and trying to work out exactly where it was coming from. I was worried when I felt around the area where I'd last noticed it and couldn't feel it anymore. Had they run off to tell someone?

I kept pushing farther, however, and within seconds I was feeling them again. This time I plunged deeper, looking for the source. It would need to be somewhere that wasn't just rock and earth. Somewhere inside the mountain, so I pushed in that direction.

The elf's control grew stronger as I got closer to them, making it more obvious I was looking in the right place. As soon as I reached them, I told Zephyr which direction to tunnel in, but he ignored me.

Instead, Zephyr went up the tunnel several feet and began using his tablet to push through the side wall, tunneling in faster than I thought I was capable of. I tried not to get too jealous and instead focused on the elf I could feel, taking control of the air around her and making it harder for her to move. Thankfully she didn't try at first, her mind probing toward mine, like she wanted a mental battle.

I took the advantage and built a barrier around her that would hold her in place or freeze her if she tried to go through it and waited for Zephyr to tunnel to her. At the same time, I danced my mind around hers and gently challenged her control as if I was considering trying to push through it so I could come toward her.

Behind me, the others fanned out, none of them daring to interfere or get too close while Zephyr and I were doing something strange and inexplicable. Part of me wanted to say something; I wanted to include them since they understood what was going through my head a lot of the time. It wasn't wise, however. We needed silence right now.

At some point, the mountain elves would be aware of us. Until then, if they thought it was just me and my mythicals, great. The less the elf in front of me figured out about Zephyr and what he was capable of, the better, especially since he was tunneling closer.

When the elf realized she could feel someone else coming into the space she controlled and I wasn't sparring for the area with her, she diverted her attention to the rock nearest Zephyr and tried to hold it tight.

Helping Zephyr, I reached for it with my mind and took control of the tunnel on my side. I hoped to scare the woman into thinking she was being attacked from multiple different places and make her focus her attention on me. It worked; her abilities were either drained, or she was trying to conserve her ability in case she needed it for something else.

When Zephyr managed to get through to her, he grabbed her and pulled her into the tunnel with us as I dropped the barrier around her. I rushed to his side, impressed that she'd fought him to the end. There was no getting away from a dragon, however, not even when he was in human form. Minsheng shot her with darts when she tried to yell.

With the elf knocked out, tied up, and left in an enclosed space she had little choice but to use her powers to get out of, we went on our way. In our defense, we left her a small hole so she could breathe while she got herself untied and free, but given that we'd drained her, it would be hours before she could free herself. We'd be long gone by then.

Hoping that was the last eventful task, I walked alongside Zephyr until we found the hidden steps that led to the upper levels of the mountain. The route was still intact, and it brought back memories that made me shudder. I didn't like being in these tunnels. The abandoned stairwell was strange and cold.

We climbed despite my emotions, and I noticed that they'd made an effort to change and restructure the space. It was subtle things: slight twists in passages, protrusions in the walls which made it look as if it had been blocked. Of course, I knew the place well, and I had walked the stairs often enough to feel the differences and not be fooled.

After getting to the level of the research labs and once more using our earth abilities to get through the now-thicker wall, we paused.

It had taken at least an hour to get to this point, and we'd been on the way to the mountain during the latter part of the day. There was no one waiting for us or trying to find us. Wondering what they were up to had me on edge, but I wasn't going to complain about the clear route ahead.

Within seconds, our group of non-elementals slotted into the middle of my elves and Zephyr and me, everyone making sure they had a weapon out or was ready to defend us. It was time to get some answers.

It didn't take me long to realize that this very floor was one I'd been on with Zephyr the very first time we were there. We soon found the lab we'd hidden in as we made our way away from the elevator shaft and deeper into the floor. The gnome who had led me to Zephyr's egg had been working on this floor and thought the noise we'd made had been Chris. Anything either of them was working on was on a floor that I was interested in.

This time I wasn't trying to get out but in, however, and we weren't looking for a person so much as answers from anyone on the floor. If we saw Chris, we weren't going to be very happy about it, and he'd probably get more than a little anger from Minsheng.

That said, I expected my Shishou to want to find Chris, but he'd said nothing about our traitor recently. Minsheng seemed intent on following me and my mythicals and watching our backs.

We made our way down several corridors, Erlan and Minsheng conferring outside the labs now and then to work out if they might hold useful information at a glance inside. We passed several like this and were about to check out a fifth when there was the noise of footsteps around the next bend in the hallway. Everyone ducked into the nearest room except for Zephyr and me.

The two of us grabbed control of the air to form a barrier again, then I reached out to detect what or who might be coming. Before I could get much farther in my task, a gnome came around the corner.

I lifted my dart gun and pointed it at him. It was the gnome from the restaurant when I'd been nothing but a waitress. The gnome who had started it all. He stopped moving and stared at us, his mouth falling open.

No one moved, despite me expecting him to run or yell.

"Several years ago, you were helpful enough to guide me to Zephyr. Want to be that useful again?" I asked.

"I get the feeling that isn't a request," he replied, his eyes flicking to the gun I was aiming at him.

"Not really."

He smirked but didn't move yet.

"You've really come a long way since the day we met."

"And it feels as if you've fallen a long way. But I'm not here to reminisce. I want as much information on me, your experiments, and Zephyr and our parents as you have. It's this cult's fault that we don't have those things in our life. We want to know why and what you did. We want to know everything you do about us and our bond."

The gnome sighed and nodded.

"It's understandable you'd want answers. And for what it's worth, I think you can handle them and wanted you to have them in the first place. But others thought it would stop Zephyr from bonding with you, and you were the only one that could empower him the way you have." The man looked at us with a smile on his face.

"I don't care who decided what. Just take me where I need to go." The gnome took another look at the weapon in my hand and the bag of tablets I carried and nodded.

"All right, you and everyone with you and hiding around the corner can all come this way. I'll show you what you're looking for." I lifted an eyebrow at him knowing I wasn't alone as he glanced toward the lab, and then I called for everyone to join us.

We followed him back the way he'd come until we reached a door that had several locks and a sign in a language I didn't recognize.

"It says that only those with good knowledge of the Henera are allowed beyond that door," Minsheng explained before I could ask.

I paused again, not sure I liked where this was going but determined to see it through and find out what I could.

The gnome unlocked the door, scanning parts of his body and then doing something fancy with different buttons and locks. I was impressed with the combination, although I reached out with my mind and worked out how to use the elements I controlled to get the door open. It was almost as if someone had designed it so it needed all the elements to open it.

Of course, fire was fairly easy to replicate and the gnome did that last, lighting a match and holding it up to something that appeared to be sensitive.

As he did, there was an audible click, and the door swung inward. He motioned for us to go in and smiled. Before I could stop the others, Erlan went in, his hand reaching for a data stick in the side pocket of his pants.

I quickly followed, noticing that it was a pretty small room, but there were strange devices in there, including a baby incubator and many other maternity-based machines. Looking around made it clear that I had been here at some point previously in my life.

When I spotted a machine that kept eggs warm and was big enough to house Zephyr's dragon egg, I felt better. We'd probably been in the room together for a while.

Erlan soon sat down at the computer and started hacking into it.

"Now... Where are the rest of the tablets?" I asked as I

reached into my bag and pulled out another one. This one was an air one, and I saw his eyes widen.

"You've worked out how to use them already?" His voice matched his expression, but I frowned and made it clear I wasn't interested in his questions.

"They've taken the rest up to the portal," he said. "Most of them were full and ready for battle. And the rest were handed out to different elves who could fill them swiftly."

I studied him as he spoke, and I was pretty sure he was telling the truth. Although I didn't like the gnome, I could respect that.

"I'll stay here with Erlan," Ronan said. "We'll get the answers you seek and get back out of here."

"Roth and Sen will also stay," I replied, knowing that the pegasus was more than willing to lend himself to my cause but that this wasn't a good time to take him into the heart of the mountain when they couldn't be silent enough.

"I'll watch their six and keep this gnome from interfering," Daisy added. "You go get the last of those tablets and find that guy and make him regret ever messing with you."

I grinned as I motioned for Ascan, Emily, Minsheng, and Zephyr to come with me.

"Make sure this lab is never used to hurt anyone again when you're done," I said before walking out.

## CHAPTER TWENTY-SIX

The familiar tug in my stomach grew as I left Sen and Roth behind. I would have felt worse had I not been focused on trying to find the air elf who had led me on this chase and get him to hand over every tablet that they needed to open the portals. We had to stop this once and for all.

It felt strange to be striding along beside Zephyr but right in its way. We didn't get very far before we met more elves and gnomes, seeming to be coming our way deliberately.

I blasted them off their feet with an air blast from my new gloves before anyone could react. Minsheng and Ascan used dart guns to take the gnomes out before they could get up and Zephyr strode forward, bracing himself against a water blast to grab a tablet from one of the closest elves.

*Water*, he said as he held it out to Emily.

I nodded but made a mental note to keep track of how many tablets were passed where. Ideally, we wanted them evenly divided, although Zephyr and I both had some.

Although we dealt with the group of elves and gnomes effectively and swiftly, all of them out cold or restrained, the noise and commotion we had made would be sure to bring more people. No sooner had we gone around the next corner, trying to get to the staircase to climb higher, than the sound of rushing feet came from toward the elevator.

Sneaking was no longer an option. There was no way to get to the stairwell before more people discovered us, and I didn't want to leave the others in the lab with loads of elves bearing down on them. We were going to be fighting our way up the mountain from here.

*We can do this. One elf at a time. One dart or gas grenade at a time.* As Zephyr spoke, he pulled one of the small grenades with his paralyzing gas inside and pulled the pin before hurling it around the corner and guiding it toward the incoming group.

I raised an eyebrow at the preemptive strike, having no idea how many were around the corner and, worried it was an aggressive move, even for us. But then I reminded myself what we were up against and how they had frequently been aggressive and that it was simply Zephyr's gas weapon. It would wear off, and they would be unharmed.

Striding toward the corner, I reached forward with my mind, finding the reach and control of so many elves it was almost overwhelming. This was going to be one big battle, and there weren't many on our side of the fight.

We had the advantage of being in an enclosed space, however, and I was far more powerful than any single elf in the mountain. On top of that, I had the tablets, and my whole team of elementals, such as it was, had at least one.

I tried not to worry about what I was facing as I helped take control of the air and earth ahead and battled the elves trying to do the same. I pushed the elves back with several air blasts from the strange finger gloves, noticing we'd managed to knock several out or paralyze them.

As I advanced and threw up a barrier to block some of the worst of the attacks coming hurling at us, I worked out how to find the advantage.

The entire corridor was full of elves throwing around elemental magic for the purpose of subduing me. I wanted to get past them to find the tablets and the person with the answers. I pushed forward, hurling more air blasts and knocking elves back as I kept control of the bubble around me.

Zephyr came with me, using the earth to trap elves by limbs and the air to move his breath weapon until what had come out of the grenade was nothing but tattered wisps in the air.

I tried not to worry about what was going on around me as I took out as many of the elves around me as swiftly as possible, checking back now and then to make sure Emily, Ascan, and Minsheng were coping okay.

There was less water here for Emily to do anything with, but she'd been taking shooting lessons from Daisy and her mother, and she could handle herself incredibly well. The projectiles from the dart guns moved fast enough that few of the cult elves could defend against it, especially when I was in control of the air.

The elves were mostly focused on Zephyr and me,

which made our allies the ideal backup, but I was aware we were traveling through the pack of cult elves without knocking them all out, some of them getting free again and trying to attack from behind.

I frowned as more elves appeared ahead and we slowed, caught in the middle. Zephyr and I were working as hard and fast as we could, but we didn't have enough darts for all these elves, nor grenades of paralyzing gas.

*It's too narrow down here for me to take dragon form*, Zephyr said before I could finish thinking it. *I can only do so once we get to the portal level.*

He had a point, but before I could begin to think about how to get us moving through again and dealing with this many elementals at once beyond blocking their attempts at attacks, I heard a familiar voice.

"I wondered when we would see you here again, Henera," the male air elf I'd chased here said.

I glared in the direction it had come from as the battle stopped, the cult turning to look too. As the air elf came forward, they parted. He had at least two tablets on him since the pockets on his jacket bulged with them.

Preparing to be hit, I put up a barrier in front of me and the others, but I didn't strike yet.

"I want the tablets. All of them," I said. "They're not going to be used to open that portal."

"No. They can help, for sure, but on their own, they don't make the difference. They harness power, and it's true that most elves seem more powerful wielding them, but they're still limited by an elf's range. By their concentration levels. And by the imagination. Of course, Cherisse has been training many elves. The tablets could help them open the portals, but it would still be a huge risk and well, you saw what happened when an elf tried to do something these tablets weren't designed for the last time."

The air elemental paused, studying me. I did the same. He was confident and sure that he had the upper hand, but I had the others getting the answers I needed. Did that mean I didn't need him?

"Who are you?" I asked, stopping short of asking him if he was my father.

"You could say I was in charge of the Henera program. In charge of making you...this...a reality."

I frowned.

"I just want to find my parents."

"That's something you really should let go of."

"You won't help me find them?" I asked.

"I can't help you find your biological parents, but we can all choose adults in our lives who move into parental roles. You could find many of those here."

"Like you?"

"Perhaps. In time. Stop fighting us now. Come with me, and let me show you what you could achieve here."

I shook my head, not hesitating. I would not turn my back on my Shishou or my friends. Slowly I lifted my hands again, my eyes locked on the strange air elemental.

"I'm taking the tablets. Are you going to make this easy and hand them over, or are you going to insist I have to fight you to take them?"

"I can't let you do something so foolish. You're misguided."

"Am I? Everyone says I am Henera, the one who is supposed to protect all elves and this planet. I know that's not something I'll be able to do alone. Right now, those tablets in the wrong hands are a threat, and that means I have to act. Hand them over, or would you like me to risk destroying them as I come to claim them?"

The calm look on the air elemental's face changed, becoming almost beast-like as he snarled.

"You can't have them," he said, but it was too late.

I wasn't going to stick around and listen to him justify the cult any longer. This wasn't okay, and I needed to make it clear I wasn't playing his game.

Taking control of the air and stepping forward, I blasted out in a circle, pushing everyone back as I strode toward the air elemental. He grinned as he reached out, exerting his control over the air around him and fighting mine. At the same time, he reached into his jacket pockets, and I knew he was connecting with the tablets he held.

I reached for one of the air tablets I carried as I felt him trying to form a barrier around me. Surprised by the aggressive move, I fought his control and blasted more elves at the same time.

Zephyr, Minsheng, Ascan, and Emily opened fire too. Zephyr continued to use the walls and the ground to restrain elves so the others could shoot them.

Although I regularly blocked attacks meant for me and the others, I focused on the air elemental and the barriers he was trying to create. He'd decided what he was going to do ahead of time.

It had put me at a disadvantage, but I fought against him anyway. I was the stronger elf, and I had to last the longest.

The quickest way to end the fight was to get the tablets from him.

*Fight as many as you can,* I told Zephyr while I grabbed control of the barrier and tore it apart again.

I felt warmer, and I took another step forward. Water came from nowhere, soaking me and pushing me back until Emily stepped forward. We fought for control before pushing it back and turning the stream around.

I helped her guide it as I blasted another elf who was trying to do something I didn't like the look of, then turned to the smug air elemental. We hit him with the water Emily and I had successfully taken control of a moment before, making him step back. At the same time, his concentration faltered, and I grabbed his barriers and decimated them again.

I could see the frown growing deeper on the air elemental's face as Emily hosed down the guy some more and Zephyr shook the ground under his feet a little.

More elves attacked us, but I had enough barriers up that almost none of the attacks were getting through. In the tight space, only so many could attempt to hurl an element at us.

We were gaining the upper hand bit by bit as more elves were sedated. I could feel the tension, however, as a fresh wave of elves came from the elevator direction. At the same time, I noticed that my head was starting to ache. I wasn't going to be able to fling elements around like this forever, either.

This wasn't going well enough.

*I've got to get those tablets,* I said to Zephyr. *Only way this battle is going to end in our favor.*

*I agree. Use the air to make yourself faster after pretending to try to stick him in a barrier again. He inches forward every time you try to box him as if he's pulling away from the cold.*

Zephyr's words gave me focus once more as I set about pulling the air around and manipulating it until I was trying to box the air elemental in again. At the same time, I had to dodge a fireball as it came hurtling through the air and hit Zephyr.

I gasped, but I felt no pain.

*Fireproof, even in human form, remember?* Zephyr said.

*None of the rest of us are*, I replied, my concern for him giving way to concern for the others.

*We'll make sure they can't hurt us. Most of us are drenched anyway.*

He had a point, but I didn't have time to worry about it anymore. I needed to get this fight over and done with. With the barrier forming and the air elemental wrestling me for control, I was drained, so I reached for the air tablet again. It was also getting low, and was trying to encourage me to feed it.

With one last push, I let him break the barrier I'd created at the same time as I powered myself forward, using the air around me to make myself faster. I grabbed the air elemental's wrist and my muscles took over, remembering a move I'd practiced in the dojo a thousand times. Quickly I flipped him over as I took the air tablet out of his hand and pulled away again.

I soon found myself on the other side of him, surrounded by cult elves, but I didn't hesitate to act and used the air tablet I had gained to push them away from me as well as sending the air elemental flying again. This time he saw the plan in advance and he blocked me with his mind. I tried to circumvent him and push back, but only the elves nearest me were affected by my attack.

With the extra tablet, I had more raw power I could put through me and control the air with, but before I could move or do anything, the air elemental laughed and then grabbed Ascan, the nearest elf from my party.

"I thought I recognized you," the older elf said, one of his hands grabbing Ascan's cheek and holding him still. "You're one of ours."

"Not anymore," Ascan said, trying to struggle out of his grip.

"You and your Shishou. What was his name? You've been working with us for several years. Letting us know what's going on with Henera and her team."

I gaped as I stopped, not sure what to do. The fight came to a halt around us again, everyone listening. No one had expected this.

"I did for a few months. Then I met the Henera and realized you were the deluded cult and she was just trying to protect everyone on this planet. I stopped giving Jinto information. Minsheng and the others never fully trusted him."

"Do you have any idea what you cost us?"

"Only what you deserved." Ascan spat at the air elemental's feet.

This triggered everyone's rage, and I was almost blasted off my feet by yet another funnel of water so cold it stung every part of me. I gasped and formed a barrier. Minsheng pushed his way over to Ascan, and Zephyr got in the way of another fireball so it wouldn't hit the vulnerable, helpless elf.

More elves came around the corner, their power fresh as they joined the battle. Before I could do anything but hold up under the barrage of attacks from the newer and fresher elves, the elemental swung Ascan into the wall, using the air to make him move faster.

"Enough!" he yelled, then there was a sickening crunch. Ascan went as limp as a rag doll, and Emily screamed. I rushed forward as the air elemental let go and Ascan fell to the floor, his lifeless eyes staring up at us.

I couldn't move, the shock of him being dead making the battle fade into the background. Around me, water, rocks, and fire exploded on the barrier still held by my mind, but I didn't look away.

Emily rushed to Ascan's side, forgetting the nearby danger as sobs wrenched her body.

"No," she said as she shook him, the water sloshing over the floor around them, strangely fitting for the two water elves. Minsheng shot at more elves, and Zephyr blasted air at the elemental in charge as he went to grab Emily next and haul her to her feet.

Seeing the young elf in danger and realizing I couldn't do anything to help Ascan or Emily if I was frozen to the spot, I hurried forward, blasting the elemental off his feet as I did. He growled and rushed at me, using the air to make himself fast as I often did. At the same time, he fought hard for control of the barrier around me.

With the tablet power he was drawing from and the freshness he was experiencing from not fighting most of the battle, I couldn't hold up any longer. My barrier disintegrated, I was being pelted from every angle, and the elemental was coming closer. Zephyr rushed to my side, his arms going around me as another barrier appeared.

The elemental sneered and then yelled something in a language I didn't understand. Almost as if they were one, the cult fell back toward the elevator, some wanting me to let them pass. I didn't let anyone go anywhere, my mind pursuing the leader of the group as he fled.

Not fast enough or strong enough currently, I had to let him go and everyone else along with him. It was only temporary. I turned back to face the chaos of the room.

Ascan was dead, and it was my fault.

## CHAPTER TWENTY-SEVEN

Emily's sobs slowly quieted as I tried to comfort her. I couldn't look at the body she cradled in her arms. She'd been rocking him for a while now, his body no longer housing his mind or the quiet, fun-loving elf that we'd rescued over a year earlier.

Minsheng had his hand on Emily's shoulder, and Zephyr was close by.

I tried not to feel it, not wanting to let it get the better of me, but my mind replayed the moment over and over again. It was as if Ascan's life had been nothing. Had meant nothing. He'd been a way to get everyone's attention and end the battle.

Despite my best attempt to remain neutral and somber, rage rose inside me, giving me the strength to keep on that I'd not thought possible. I was going to make sure Ascan's death wasn't in vain.

"Stay here with him," I told Emily, my words coming out cold and clear.

She nodded, glancing at me with a gaze clouded and

distorted from the tears she cried. At that moment I vowed to avenge him. To make the elves here pay for his life.

Minsheng stepped closer to me before looking at the hallway that led to the others and then to the hallway to the elevator. More elves were appearing, either sent by the air elemental or coming to find us of their volition. It was time to get back into the fight.

"You don't have to join me," I said, knowing that Minsheng was hurting too. He'd found out that another organization member had been betraying what they stood for.

"No, I'm coming with you. Let us get Emily and Ascan to the others and safer," he said as he helped her to her feet and shot another elf trying to hurl fireballs.

Emily blasted water at the fire without properly looking, which was a good idea. She wasn't in a good state to fight.

"I'll hold them here and wait for you," I said, my voice sounding like it wasn't my own.

I turned to the nearest elves, trying to decide what to do with them. The compassion and the desire I'd felt earlier not to hurt any of them, thinking them misguided and irritating more than anything else felt very different. I cared less about their well-being and safety and more about getting them out of my way.

I wanted to find a way to get those tablets and the air elemental and make him pay for what he'd done. Enough was enough.

Fighting alongside Zephyr and using more of the darts we carried, we put down more elves, and blasted others with air or trapped them in rock.

I noticed another tablet a skilled earth elemental was carrying and focused on her, blasting a rock she hurled out of the air and hitting her with air until she was pinned down. At the same time, I spun up the air around Zephyr and me, shielding us with a makeshift tornado.

Walking forward within it, I grabbed the tablet off the earth elf and then smacked her with it as hard as I could. She flopped over, out cold.

Zephyr stared at me a moment, his mouth open. I stared back, not sure what to say or think. It was as if the only thing I could feel was numb anger and a drive to get this whole task finished as soon as we could.

A moment later, he gave me a slow nod, setting his jaw and helping me spin the air around us. Together we walked forward, pushing back the elves no matter how many more turned up and hurled the elements in our way.

More than once, we had someone try to launch fire at us, but the spinning air sucked it up, and it burned within the whirl of debris before being doused with water or fading to nothing. We kept pushing forward, but it wasn't until I heard Minsheng shout from behind us that I realized how far we'd progressed.

We stopped, letting the controlled tornado die, to see him rush from the end of the long hallway. We were near the elevator, and there were few elves between us and the door now.

Minsheng looked at the carnage, many elves groaning, injured or caught in rocks. Many more were slumped, out cold.

"You two are a lot more powerful than I realized."

"We are with the rune-covered stones to back us up," Zephyr replied. "They really make it easy to keep going."

"Be careful. I'll watch your back." Our Shishou nodded and raised his gun again. I noticed his pockets bulged with ammo, and there was another pistol holstered to his thigh.

Within seconds, we were focused on our task once more. The last few elves backed out of the way, their hands in the air as we strode toward the elevator. I felt panic and fear rising in me as I stared into the small box. It heralded my first venture into the mountain when I'd been brought here and separated from almost everyone.

I didn't ever want to feel as alone as that again. Zephyr had been so far from me for so long. Then I'd had to let Sen go to help get our friends there to rescue us. The memories of that always made me feel the same fear I had enduring the long nights, barely able to sleep but also exhausted. Trying to find a way out but trapped.

Somehow the time we'd spent in the dark didn't impact me as much now. Possibly because I'd had Zephyr there holding my hand the entire time. Zephyr reached for my hand now, and together, we strode into the elevator. Minsheng quickly slipped into it with us, and we sent it up to the portal floor.

I was sure it would stop along the way, trapping us. Or stop on another floor, where more elves would be ready to attack us, but the floors kept passing us by until we were on the portal floor.

Prepared to defend ourselves, Minsheng behind and Zephyr out in front, we let the door slide open. A fireball came at us, hitting the only one of us who could handle it. I quickly blasted the air out and away from us, taking the heat and the danger along with it.

Zephyr rushed out as I used the gloves to send another jet of air to either side of him and help push everyone back. Unable to see, I followed the human-form dragon and began spinning up the air.

As soon as I could move to the side and Minsheng could tuck in behind us, I started looking for signs of the air elemental. He wasn't far away, standing near the back of a large group of elves. They were curled in a moon shape around the elevator shaft, focused entirely on us.

"Are you going to hide at the back of the group like a coward?" I asked as Zephyr and I continued to advance, nothing hitting us despite water, fire, air, and rocks coming our way.

I heard a laugh, but there was no direct response. A moment later, I felt the attack as he formed a barrier around us to take control of more of the air. I fought back, pushing hard, feeling the steel in his mind and certain he was using another air tablet. I reached into the bag on my shoulder and found another fragment.

Although we'd picked up a few along the way, I'd been pushing the air far more than any other element, knowing I controlled it most effectively but could make use of the others if I needed to.

With the other hand, I grabbed a small water tablet, and I started pulling the water from the nearby vicinity and using it to sweep the combatants back. At the same time, I kept the air around us controlled, fighting any mind that tried to stop me.

I could feel the constant barrage, but even in the mountain, with marked elements and where they had the most practice, I was skilled enough and boosted by the tablet, so none of them could challenge me and win.

Despite my confidence, I proceeded with caution, aware that I was holding the fort so Zephyr and Minsheng could attack. I didn't care for now. We were making progress, and this entire mountain of elves couldn't stop us. Not anymore.

The elves here were stronger, and most of the attacks Zephyr and Minsheng launched were deflected or diffused, but I noticed darts hitting here and there, and some were starting to struggle with the rocks Zephyr was wrapping around limbs. I kept the air whirling around us, blasting air and water at other elves, but my eyes never left the face of the air elemental ahead of us.

I could feel him as he tried to find a way to gain control of the air nearby. At each turn I resisted, but it was draining me, and I couldn't keep it up. We needed to find a way forward. These elves could easily exhaust us and the tablets we carried.

*He's sucking the air out*, Zephyr said.

*From all of the elves too?* I asked, not sure I believed what my dragon was telling me.

*Yes. He's holding a barrier around this entire area. I can feel things changing and the slight movement of air as it's sucked out.*

I blinked as I kept up my attacks, plus defended against the massive onslaught coming our way. It was too intense for me to begin figuring out where the barriers were.

*Keep us safe. I'll break it*, Zephyr added.

Although I wanted to argue, he was right. Taking over Zephyr's job, I began using the very rock of the mountain to pin down the elves. At the same time, I walked forward, powering the air around to keep the three of us protected and safe.

I could feel the power draining from both me and the tablet, but I kept my eyes fixed on the air elemental Zephyr was trying to challenge. I could feel the fight between the pair of them as they wrestled back and forth, the control of the air letting me know where Zephyr was attacking.

A part of me wanted to help, but a large rock almost came through the barrier and hit me, making me refocus on the elves attacking us. I wished we'd had more elves and soldiers with us, but that they'd gotten us here and given so much for our cause.

Blocking another water blast, I spun it around and sent it back, knocking three more elves off their feet as Minsheng hit another elf with a second dart and he lost consciousness.

Finally, the group seemed to waver, and I was starting to feel the air around also changing and my body panting harder and harder. I took more control of the air, keeping a larger portion of air steady and away from the elves to try to stop the oxygen draining from the section Minsheng, Zephyr, and I were in.

I didn't know how much it would help, but I had to try to keep us going while we broke through these forces.

Feeling the pounding in my head as we got closer to the portal area and the air elemental, I struggled. I noticed I wasn't the only one, but the commanding elemental stopped our adversaries from pulling back or running. As they pushed harder than ever on my mind, it made it almost impossible for me to find a way through. We needed to find an advantage and we needed it now.

*Got it*, Zephyr yelled. I noticed the air elemental as he staggered back, having succumbed to Zephyr's assault. I grinned as I helped guide one of Minsheng's darts back on target and another elf left the battle for sedated oblivion.

I fired more shots myself, using my mind to guide each one and take out the stronger elves I'd identified. By the time my gun was empty and the air was easier to breathe again, there were seven more elves out cold, and the strength of force hitting us was noticeably less.

Zephyr stepped back as if he'd had his mind attacked a moment later.

This time I reached out for the air and the barrier or signs of it, dropping my gun and taking another step forward. It took me a moment to feel it, but then I worked out where the restricted areas were.

I didn't hesitate to attack the elf, pushing at his control and giving it everything I could. He gave, and once again, I felt as if we were getting the upper hand.

This time there was no immediate retaliation, and the elves drew a collective breath and retreated.

Frowning, we strode after the elves, me and Minsheng and Zephyr, trying to work out what was going on. Minsheng didn't waste any opportunity to take out more elves, and Zephyr pinned them to the ground. I blocked attacks and doused another flame with water.

Within minutes the portal came into view, and I could see the way it had changed. The cave had been opened up to the surface, and light was streaming into the site. Standing on this edge of the pillar range were Cherisse and several other elves I recognized. Each of them held a tablet of their elements.

I didn't need any of the elves to explain what was going on. We'd been held up and challenged so that the elves could try to open the portal unhindered.

Before anyone could suggest it was a bad idea or good, I powered into the air.

*Look after Minsheng*, I said to Zephyr as I dropped the barrier and flew forward.

"Cherisse, stop this madness," I said at the top of my lungs as I continued to fly closer.

I felt elves trying to grab control and stop me from flying completely, but I resisted and landed on the other side of them. Cherisse glanced my way before carrying on.

Growling, I knocked four of them out of the pillar range and toward me, having to fight the pillars for air control to hit them with it. It worked, but an air elemental I recognized from the air battle the day I'd escaped the mountain used the trick I did to keep upright.

I strode closer, using water to blast one of their tablets over to me, and picked it up. It was another water rune-covered tablet, and I was pretty sure it was so loaded with magic that it was going to be spectacular. Cherisse got to her feet, the tablet she had been holding in my hands.

Somewhere behind me, I heard Zephyr yell and felt a blast of air get through the bodies toward me. I could only hope he wasn't getting into too much trouble and that he was keeping Minsheng safe.

I was torn between stopping the elves in front of me and protecting my friends and the others I cared about. Ascan was dead, and the pain hit me once again.

"Is that all you've got to fight with, chosen one?" Cherisse asked, spitting as she gave me a strange honorific.

The jibe made me see red. I flew at her, using the water around her to drown her. The air elemental with the tablet rose into the air, pushing ahead of me and taking the tablet he held farther away.

*Careful, Aella,* Zephyr said. *They seem pleased that they've gotten you away from us. They've switched their strategy into just keeping us contained and not trying to hit us so much.*

*Can you break through?* I asked, not slowing. I was going to get these tablets. I had to stop them from being able to open the portals.

*I'll try. Minsheng is almost out of ammo, and most of these tablets are dead.*

*Then I'll get these ones, and we'll get out.*

Working harder, I fixed my eyes on the three left that I didn't have. The earth and water elf had gathered together on the ground to one side, and they would be more difficult to get. It made sense for me to get the air one next.

I was pretty sure the air elemental ahead of me knew this too. He flew higher, slowly positioning over the pillars and the bubble of controlled elements. This made me hesitate. It wasn't a safe place to be flying over.

Before I could decide how to flush them out, a familiar air elf appeared at my side, the one I'd knocked out the day I'd escaped from the mountain. We'd used his limp body to make a point. Clearly remembering me, he blasted me with air as he went to join the air elf I faced. I noticed they had a tablet each and were beginning to use them. This had gone from hard to almost impossible.

## CHAPTER TWENTY-EIGHT

I faced the two air elementals, powerful magic users wielding tablets. One of them was the strongest air elemental the mountain had, and he had been about to attempt to break a pillar and open the portal. The other, an older elf, acted like he was a father figure or an instigator in my life. I needed to stop them.

Hoping I had the advantage despite them both holding rune-covered air devices, I powered toward them, hitting them with air as I did. If I could get one of them to make a mistake and get one of the stones, I could get the others, and we could leave.

Trying not to get hit back, I darted around the space above the portal and the pillars that protected it. It wasn't ideal, and I was playing with danger, but so were the elves with me. The younger elf repeatedly glanced at the barrier beneath me, making it clear that he was wary of it.

Knowing he was the easier target although he might have more energy reserves, I focused on him, pushing him around, making him react to the air I was blasting around.

With the gloves I wore, it was easier than ever to fly and hit, using less energy for a blast that was still effective and could quickly send them reeling.

In the background, I could feel Zephyr coming closer bit by bit, the commotion of battle sounding everywhere and echoing around the dome-like cavern area that surrounded the portal.

"Simon, get down from there and come help!" I heard Cherisse yell from somewhere down and to one side.

The older elf I battled looked her way, hesitating. It gave me a name, and by the frown and anger that flicked across his face, Simon didn't like taking orders.

While he was distracted, I hit him with another blast of air to get him to drop the tablet or wobble long enough I could fly by and snatch it.

He reacted far faster than I'd have thought possible, however, and although he was hit, he righted himself and continued to bombard me. I was momentarily off-balance, the tablet I carried slipping from my grasp and flying down into the forcefield below. It broke, pieces going flying as the pillars did their work.

I saw the younger air elf gulp and clutch his tablet tighter. This had gotten a whole level harder again.

Now using nothing but my energy reserves and aware they were low, I darted to the side as the elementals tried to knock me out of the sky. As I dodged, I reached toward the air holding up the younger adversary and took control of it.

Yelping, he plummeted.

Simon didn't move to help him as I expected, however, hitting me from behind with another blast of air that almost knocked me so off-balance I spun. Once more, the gloves helped as I rebalanced myself and turned to face him.

He studied me as he came closer, but I didn't say anything or let him distract me too much. I needed to keep an eye on the other elf, noticing he slipped into the force-field, screeching in pain before he snatched control and got himself back into the air above. This time I felt Simon also trying to take control of the air from me, no doubt hoping to try the same trick on me.

If there had been no tablets involved, I was sure I could hold up under such a barrage, but I wasn't so confident now. This was going to be tough.

*I might need some help*, I told Zephyr as I dodged another attack, flying higher and trying to blast Simon away from me. As I put more distance between us, I felt the pressure on my control lessen. At the same time, the younger air elf got into the air, and his confidence came back swiftly as I backed up and appeared to be doing nothing but fleeing.

Keeping distance between Simon and me didn't mean doing so between me and the younger elf, however. I flew in his direction, once again challenging him, making him defend himself, and trying to knock the tablet from his hands.

I was draining myself fast, but I was on my own, feeling Zephyr stuck, surrounded by elves and taxed.

*I've managed to get an earth tablet*, he said. *I think it was one of the main elves about to break the pillars.*

*That just leaves the air ones here and the fire one*, I replied, knowing I had to make a bold move if I wanted to get this over and done with. I rushed the air elemental, taking control of the air as I reached him, using the last of my energy to do so, but grabbing the tablet he held at the same time. It was still full enough that I could draw on it to blast him back.

He toppled and didn't seem to be able to right himself. I did my best to blast him again, not to hurt him, but to make sure he didn't land in the forcefield when he had no tablet either. At the same time, Simon came at me again, my mind sensing the movement in the element I controlled before I could see it.

I dodged to the side, letting the blast go right past me, and it hit the younger elf again. There was a loud crunch as he hit the rock wall, leg first, something breaking and forcing the limb to bend unnaturally.

There was a yelp, and then he fell. I cushioned him with my mind and placed him down before focusing on Simon.

One down.

One to go.

Our eyes met again, and neither of us did anything but hover above the forcefield dome. I was exhausted, out of any power but the tablet in my hand, but I wasn't about to show that to the man in front of me.

He'd started all this so many years ago. Orchestrated so much. Clearly, he'd had a hand in my life in ways I hadn't realized at the time, and he'd killed a young elf who could have had a beautiful future simply because they dared to defy him.

For the first time in my life, I didn't want to hold back and didn't want to show any mercy. This elf deserved none.

"Stop this foolishness, Henera," Simon said as we

moved, powering to the sides, responding to each other like boxers sizing each other up. "Your destiny is to see the portals opened and to protect our people. The blood of all four greats runs in your veins. You should be standing with us."

"I won't stand with murderers who don't value all life as much as those with them," I replied, anger making my words come out through almost gritted teeth. At the same time, I tried to blast him out of the air hard, wanting him to feel the pain of breaking a limb on a rock wall. The lack of concern he'd had for the younger air elemental made the desire stronger.

For several minutes, we flew around each other, mostly dodging and weaving around, never coming too close, but never being far from each other either. I was aware the tablet I held was draining as I flew and attacked, my mind using the power to defend against his attempts to snatch control and blast me off-balance.

Zephyr had gotten closer again, the tug on my stomach less, but he still wasn't beside me or close enough that I felt as if I could glance in his direction. This was going to be on me.

I dodged yet again and noticed Simon had overbalanced, pushing too hard. I seized the moment and battered his mind for control. At first, I thought he'd keep me out, but it was as if something broke within him a moment later. I sent him flying, moving nearer as the man tumbled, blasting him toward the wall again and again.

While I was still too far away to do anything about it, the tablet he held fell. It hit the forcefield and shattered, unable to withstand the pillars when there was no elf to protect them. I could have sworn, knowing the one I carried was almost depleted. I had to end this battle, and I had to end it now.

As Simon tried to right himself, I kept control of the area ahead of me and blasted him with jets from my hands, closing the distance and intending to fight hand to hand in the air if I had to.

For the first time, I saw panic in his eyes, his concentration taken up in keeping himself upright. I kept coming, focused on this last thing, making him regret what he'd done to Ascan. Making him understand how much pain he had caused Zephyr and me.

I hit him with air again and again until I was right in front of him.

My fist connected with his face, rocking his head back as blood spurted out of his nose. I punched again, this time to the stomach. My body knew the moves automatically, having trained to perform martial arts for so long that in the strange situation, flying through the air, my muscles took over.

Simon tried to get away from me, but I spun and grabbed him, holding him in place as I pummeled him. Trying to defend himself, I could see him speeding up his movements with the air element as I was doing, learning from me. We fought on, nothing in my world but him.

I felt him sag, his body defeated, but I didn't stop.

*Enough, Aella. Don't lower yourself to murder. Land him somewhere safe, and come down yourself. It's done.*

Zephyr's words snapped me out of my anger, and I pulled the next punch back. As I did, Simon's eyes went wide, his face showing his surprise at not being hammered yet again.

I blasted him back instead, feeling the fight go out of him. His powers were gone, so I blasted him again, pushing him away from the forcefield and reangling my air blasts to power myself forward.

Before I could safely land away from the forcefield, a blur of movement caught my attention. I looked left in time to see a ball of angry young air elf come barreling toward me, blasting air at me and trying to hit me with his fists.

I tried to dodge, but I hadn't noticed in time. Reeling backward, I was hit in the side, blocking one of the punches but not the other.

*Aella!* I heard Zephyr yelling as the tablet I carried ran out of power.

At the same time, the angry elf stole the control, giving me nothing to work with. Still spinning, there was little I could do but call for Zephyr's help in my mind.

I felt him rushing toward me, but I was right over the portal and the pillars around it. I smashed into it, pain flaring in my body the second I did. I did everything I could to take control of my body before I felt Zephyr and another doing the same, keeping the pillars from tearing me apart as I fell.

Although I didn't hit the ground as hard as I ought to have done, I did land with a bump that knocked the stuffing out of me. I couldn't move, the sensations in my body overwhelming and so sudden it was all I could do to fight them. Zephyr ran toward me, but he stopped, just out of range.

I could hear yelling and feel what was left of my power draining, but I couldn't seem to get to my feet. This close to the portal, I could feel it. Feel the bond with something on the other side. It reached out to me, grabbing hold, and then *he* was there again. Whatever evil lay on the other side.

*Get up, Aella, Get out of there. I can't protect you for long.* Zephyr's words were desperate, panicking, but it was as if he called to me from the other side of a fog. No matter what I tried to do, my body seemed not to want to respond.

I managed to get one arm under me. And then the other, but the pain grew, something working its way along the bonds I felt. Something muting Zephyr.

Before I could stop him, Zephyr stepped into the forcefield.

*I'm sorry, Aella. I can't let you die. We'll face whatever comes, I promise.*

No sooner had Zephyr finished saying this than a loud bang filled the cave along with a bright flash of light. One of the pillars was gone, entirely exploded. Another exploded, and then another. Slowly, I got to my feet, the sensations in my body lessening, the strength I had left enough for me to start fighting whatever was attacking through the portal.

A moment later, I saw a fire elf move closer to Zephyr's side. Erlan stood beside Zephyr, his face stern and his jaw gritted. He was staring straight at me and gave me a nod a moment before he tore his gaze away and looked at the final pillar.

I could see Zephyr speaking, but I was starting to feel

dizzy and sick, the pain in my head so great I couldn't stand. I was struggling to keep going, the power in me fading. The evil on the other side of the portal continued to pull at me as if it wanted to get to Zephyr, Sen, and Roth through me. I fought it, trying to crawl away from the portal as my eyes fixed on a fragment of rune-covered stone. It was glowing red hot, the fire pillar no doubt trying to set it alight, but for now, it was unbroken.

Hoping it wouldn't break me to grab it, I reached for it, slamming my hand down on it. The pain was immediate and intense, but I drew power from it, pushing the elf trying to control my bonds back. A moment later, another pillar exploded, and everything that had overwhelmed me was gone.

I let go of the tablet, my hand throbbing in agony as Zephyr appeared at my side. His arms wrapped around me as I leaned into him.

*It's okay. It's over*, he said as he picked me up and carried me away.

Erlan appeared nearby, then Sen bounded onto my stomach. I was also aware of Roth, and Minsheng's bruised face appeared next.

"It's time for us to go," Zephyr's deep booming voice said next. "You got what you wanted. We're leaving, even if I have to return to dragon form and tear this mountain apart from the inside."

I tilted my head, wincing as pain shot through it, then noticed Cherisse standing there with elves on either side of her. She looked at Zephyr, ignoring everyone else, including me.

Without a word, she moved to one side, and Zephyr led

everyone out of the mountain. We went via the laboratories, finding the few who had stayed with our fallen friend. Then Ascan was borne, floating in the air by Zephyr, his body covered in a sheet someone must have found.

It was only when we were at the bottom of the back stairwell that I remembered I should have also looked for the belt. I tried to move again, but Zephyr shook his head and held me against him.

*Today isn't the right time. I have no doubt this won't be the last we see of these elves.*

I sighed. Zephyr was right. The portal could now be opened. There were no pillars in the way, and there were plenty of powerful elves on the mountain who could band together to get the portal open.

That said, I wasn't sure anyone in their right mind would want to. Not when they felt what was waiting on the other side. Something evil was waiting. And there was a chance it would soon have free access to Earth.

## EPILOGUE

Finally recovered from everything that had happened but feeling a strange weight in my heart, I sat beside Zephyr. He was in dragon form, and we were perched on a hill not far from the Mexican mountain where we had been the previous day.

So far, there had been nothing to indicate if the portal had been opened or not. The various governments of the world had been informed about it. Several of them were still in denial, as they had been at the beginning. Others were trying to strong-arm Mexico into making a tactical move and seizing the portal. They had increased the guard around the site, but that was the only obvious sign that they had responded in any way.

I had slept for a long time, curled up against Zephyr. Sen and Roth were nearby. We'd arranged for Ascan's body to be taken to the Sanctuary. He hadn't lived there, but we felt that was fitting. It was the closest thing we had to a gathering of our kind that had a safe place to bury anyone.

Not everyone had stayed in Mexico with us, Daisy

taking a group back to the warehouse, including Emily. But I had Minsheng, my mythicals, and Ronan with me.

All of us wanted answers, our eyes fixed on the mountain. This was going to be where the action was if there was anything to be seen.

I had no idea for sure that we would see anything, but I hoped we would and the only book that Minsheng had on the subject implied there was a large bright light when a portal was reopened.

No one knew how accurate that was or if something like that would be visible. It was what we waited for now, however.

Now I'd woken up and chowed down on a whole load of pizza, I was ready to go again. I could attack, even if I felt like I was doing so through a mental fog.

Minutes after I thought this, a light appeared on the horizon, coming from the side of the mountain lion's den. It rose into the air like a beacon, then it was gone.

A moment later, there was noise and commotion as if someone was partying.

It was quiet after that, and I got to my feet.

"That was a little anticlimactic," Minsheng said. "I was expecting them to start fighting with whatever lies on the other side. See some troops flying up out of the mountain, or have them come to try to find us and beg us to shut it again."

"We don't know for sure that they aren't," I pointed out, saying the first thing since I'd woken up.

"Do you think they knew what was lurking on the other side?"

"We warned them often enough."

There was nothing to say in response. We *had* warned them. If this backfired, it would be their fault. I shuddered as I thought about the monster who had connected with me on more than one occasion.

If they hadn't realized what was going on, they were in for a shock. If I was wrong, I would apologize and put it right, but that was unlikely.

Something evil lurked on the other side of those portals. Twisted.

*It's okay*, Zephyr said. *We'll face it the same way we have everything so far: together.*

FIRE BOUND

The story continues with *Fire Bound*, book 10 in the Dragon of Shadow and Air series.

Claim your copy today!

ACKNOWLEDGMENTS

I have so many things to be thankful for sometimes that I find it hard to know what to begin with and who deserves it most, but I know none of these books would be possible without LMBPN and all the amazing people in the company who get my book from first draft to finalised and in the hands of my wonderful readers. I am constantly blown away by how amazing everyone in the company is and how much they care.

And my wonderful readers. I read every message you send me and every comment and discord ping. I love you all and wouldn't have the career of my dreams without all of you either. You're amazing and make this author's dreams come true on a regular basis. I hope I can fuel all of your dreams with my words and stories.

To Bryan, for being with me in the late night moments where my whole world feels like it crashed down around me and I can't find the next step. You have an amazing capacity to shine just the right amount of light and take my hand to find the way back out of the dark.

## ACKNOWLEDGMENTS

To my two beautiful children, who give me a reason to get up each day and carry on, even if it's far earlier than I'd like and I'm sure you must have decided to start the day before it's humanly possible.

And always to God, for not letting go, even when I'm running in the wrong direction.

## ABOUT THE AUTHOR

Jess was born in the quaint village of Woodbridge in the UK, has spent some of her childhood in the States and now resides near the beautiful Roman city of Bath. She lives with her husband, Phil, her two tiny humans (one boy and one girl) and her very dapsy cat, Pleaides.

During her still relatively short life Jess has displayed an innate curiosity for learning new things and has therefore studied many subjects, from maths and the sciences, to history and drama. Jess now works full time as a writer and mummy, incorporating many of the subjects she has an interest in within her plots and characters.

When she's not busy with work and keeping her tiny humans alive she can often be found with friends, playing with miniature characters, dice and pieces of paper covered in funny stats and notes about fictional adventures her figures have been on.

You can find out more about the author and her upcoming projects by joining her on facebook, by watching her live D&D streams, or emailing her via books@jessmountifield.co.uk. Jess loves hearing from a happy fan so please do get in touch!

Jess is also opening up her discord for fans to come chat about what she's up to, and see a few sneak peaks of future work. There's also a chance to become one of her beta readers. If you'd like to check that out you can do so here.

CONNECT WITH JESS

**Connect with Jess Mountifield**

Mailing list sign up
Facebook group.
Discord group
Actual play D&D stream: Twitch or Youtube
Email address: contact me here.

BOOKS BY JESS MOUNTIFIELD

**Already published**

**Urban Fantasy**

**Dragon of Shadow and Air:**

Air Bound

Shadow Sworn

Dragon Souled

Earth Bound

Night Sworn

Dryad Souled

Water Bound

Day Sworn

Pegasus Souled

**Fantasy**

**Tales of Ethanar:**

Wandering to Belong (Tale 1)

Innocent Hearts (Tale 2 & 3)

For Such a Time as This (Tale 4)

A Fire's Sacrifice (Tale 5)

**Winter Series:**

The Hope of Winter (Tale 6.05)

The Fire of Winter (Tale 6.1)

**Guild of the Eternal Flame:**

Wayfarer's Sanctuary

Protector's Secret

Healer's Oath

**Other Fantasy:**

The Initiate (under Holly Lujah)

**Writing with Dawn Chapman:**

Jessica's Challenge (#5 in the Puatera Online series)

Dahlia's Shadow (#6 in the Puatera Online series)

Lila's Revenge (#7 in the Puatera Online series)

**Sci-Fi:**

**Fringe Colonies:**

Alliance

Haven

Rebellion

Rebirth

Reclamation

**Star Trail:**

Hunted

**Sherdan series:**

Sherdan's Prophecy

Sherdan's Legacy

Sherdan's Country

Sherdan's Road (A short story in the anthology 'The End of the Road')

The Slave Who'd Never Been Kissed (A short in the charity anthology 'Imaginings')

New Beginnings

Santa's Little Space Pirate

**In the multi-author Adamanta series:**

Episode 1 – Adamanta

Episode 3 – Excelsior

Episode 8 – Phoenix

Episode 13 – New Contacts

Episode 17 – Sacrifice

**Other:**

Clues, Claws and Christmas

**Non-Fic:**

How to Write Lots, and Get Sh*t Done: the Art of Not Being a Flake

Find purchase links here

**Coming soon:**

**Urban Fantasy:**

**Dragon of Shadow and Air:**

Fire Bound

Light Sworn

Phoenix Souled

**Fantasy**

**(Tales of Ethanar):**

The Pursuit of Winter (#2 in the Winter series, Tale 6.2)

**Books under Amelia Price**

**Mycroft Holmes Adventures**:

The Hundred Year Wait

The Unexpected Coincidence

The Invisible Amateur

The Female Charm

The Reluctant Knight

The Ambitious Orphan

The Unconventional Honeymoon Gift

The Family Reunion

The Immortal Problem

**Coming soon:**

The Unremarkable Assistant

OTHER BOOKS FROM LMBPN PUBLISHING

**Sign up for the LMBPN** email list to be notified of new releases and special deals!

**https://lmbpn.com/email/**

For a complete list of books by LMBPN please visit:

**https://lmbpn.com/books-by-lmbpn-publishing/**

www.ingramcontent.com/pod-product-compliance
Lightning Source LLC
LaVergne TN
LVHW041621060526
838200LV00040B/1378